NAN A. TALESE

Doubleday

New York   London   Toronto   Sydney   Auckland

*

Brodeck

Brodeck

A NOVEL

✳

PHILIPPE CLAUDEL

Translated from the French
by John Cullen

Copyright © 2007 by Éditions Stock
English translation copyright © 2009 by John Cullen

All Rights Reserved

Published in the United States by Nan A. Talese/Doubleday, a division of Random House, Inc., New York.
www.nanatalese.com

Originally published in France as *Le rapport de Brodeck* by Éditions Stock, Paris, in 2007. Copyright © Éditions Stock, 2007. This edition published by arrangement with Éditions Stock.

DOUBLEDAY and the DD colophon are registered trademarks of Random House, Inc.

Book design by Donna Sinisgalli

Library of Congress Cataloging-in-Publication Data
Claudel, Philippe, 1962–
  [Rapport de Brodeck. English]
  Brodeck : a novel / Philippe Claudel ; translated from the French by John Cullen.
    p. cm.
  I. Cullen, John. II. Title.
  PQ2663.L31148R3713 2009
  843'.92—dc22

                                                    2008038252

ISBN 978-0-385-52724-8

PRINTED IN THE UNITED STATES OF AMERICA

10 9 8 7 6 5 4 3 2 1

First Edition in the United States of America

For all those
who think they're nothing

*

For my wife and my daughter,
without whom I wouldn't be much

I'm nothing, I know it, but my nothing comprises a little bit of everything.

—Victor Hugo, *The Rhine*

Brodeck

*

I'm Brodeck and I had nothing to do with it.

I insist on that. I want everyone to know.

I had no part in it, and once I learned what had happened, I would have preferred never to mention it again, I would have liked to bind my memory fast and keep it that way, as subdued and still as a weasel in an iron trap.

But the others forced me. "You know how to write," they said. "You've been to the University." I replied that my studies hadn't amounted to much—I hadn't even finished my courses and didn't remember much about them. They didn't want to hear it. "You know how to write, you know about words and how to use them, you know how they can say things. That's what we need. We can't do it ourselves. We'd get into a muddle, but you, you'll say it right, and people will believe you. Besides, you've got the typewriter."

It's very old, the typewriter. Several of its keys are broken, and I have nothing to repair it with. It's capricious. It's worn out. Sometimes, for no apparent reason, it jams, as though suddenly balking. But I said nothing about any of that, because I had no desire to end up like the *Anderer*.

Don't ask me his name—no one ever knew it. Very quickly, people coined some expressions in dialect and started applying them to him: *Vollaugä*, literally "Full Eyes" (because his bulged a bit); *De Murmelnër*, "the Whisperer" (because he spoke very little, and always in a small voice that sounded like a breath); *Mondlich*, "Moony" (because he seemed to be among us but not of us); *Gekamdörhin*, "Came from over There."

To me, however, he was always *De Anderer*, "the Other." Maybe I thought of him that way because not only had he arrived out of nowhere but he was also different, and being different was a condition I was quite familiar with, sometimes, I must admit, I had the feeling that—in a way—he was me.

As for his real name, none of us ever asked him what it was, except the mayor, perhaps, and then only once, and in any case I don't believe he received an answer. Now we'll never know. It's too late, and no doubt better that way. The truth can gash you so deeply that you can't live with the wounds any longer, and for most of us, what we want to do is live. As painlessly as possible. It's only human. I'm certain you'd be like us if you'd known the war and what it did here, and above all what followed the war, what those weeks and months were like, particularly the last of them, the period when that fellow arrived in our village and settled here, just like that, from one day to the next. Why our village? There are dozens and dozens of villages in the foothills of the mountains, lying amid forests like eggs in nests, and many of those villages are a lot like this one. Why did he choose precisely *our* village, so far from everything, so utterly remote?

When they informed me that they wanted me to write the Report, we were all at Schloss's inn. It was about three months ago, right after . . . right after . . . I don't know what to call it. The event? The drama? The incident? Or maybe the *Ereigniës*.

Ereigniës is a curious word, full of mists and ghosts; it means, more or less, "the thing that happened." Maybe the best way to say that is with a word taken from the local dialect, which is a language without being one, and which is perfectly wedded to the skin, the breath, and the souls of those who live here. *Ereigniës*, a word to describe the indescribable. Yes, I shall call it the *Ereigniës*.

So the *Ereigniës* had just taken place. With the exception of two or three ancient villagers who had stayed home, close to their stoves, as well as Father Peiper, who was no doubt sleeping off his liquor somewhere in his little church, all the men were at the inn, which is like a great cave, rather dark, and suffused with tobacco fumes and smoke from the hearth; and the men, all of them, were dazed and stunned by what had just happened, yet at the same time—how shall I say it?—relieved, because clearly, one way or the other, it had been necessary to resolve the situation. You see, they could bear it no longer.

Each was folded into his own silence, so to speak, even though there were nearly forty of them, pressed together like withies in a bundle, choking, inhaling the others' odors: their breath, their feet, the acrid reek of their sweat and their damp clothes, old wool and broadcloth impregnated with dust, with the forest, with manure, with straw, with wine and beer, especially wine. Not that everybody was sloshed; no, it would be too easy to use drunkenness as an excuse. Saying that would just be a way of diluting the horror. Too simple. Much too simple. I'm going to try not to simplify what's very difficult and complex. I'm going to try. I don't promise that I'll succeed.

Please understand me. I repeat: I could have remained silent, but they asked me to tell the story, and when they made the request, most of them had their fists clenched or their hands in their pockets, where I imagined them grasping the handles of their knives, the very knives which had just . . .

I mustn't go too fast, but it's hard not to because now I keep sensing things behind my back—movements, and noises, and staring eyes. For some days, I've been wondering if I'm not changing, bit by bit, into quarry, into a tracked animal with the whole hunt, led by a pack of snuffling dogs, at its heels. I feel watched, tailed, surveilled, as if from now on there will always be someone just over my shoulder, alert to my smallest gestures and reading my thoughts.

I will come back to what was done with the knives. I will perforce come back to that. But what I wanted to say was that to refuse a request made under such conditions, in that special mood when everyone's head is still full of savagery and bloody images, is impossible and even quite dangerous. And so, however reluctantly, I agreed. I simply found myself in the inn at the wrong time, that is, some few minutes after the *Ereigniës,* in one of those moments of bewilderment characterized by vacillation and indecision, when people will seize upon the first person who comes through the door, either to make a savior of him or to cut him to pieces.

Schloss's inn is the biggest of the six taverns in our village, which also boasts a post office, a notions shop, a hardware store, a butcher shop, a grocery store, a tripe-and-offal shop, a school, and a branch of a legal office based in S. Over this last place, which is as filthy as a stable, preside the senile lorgnettes of Siegfried Knopf, who's called an attorney even though he's only a clerk. In addition, there's Jenkins's little office; he served as our policeman, but he died in the war. I remember when Jenkins left. He was the first to go. Ordinarily he never smiled, but that day he shook everyone's hand, laughing as though he were on his way to his own wedding. Nobody recognized him. When he turned the corner at Möberschein's sawmill, he waved broadly and threw his helmet into the air in a joyful farewell. He was never seen again. He has never been replaced. The shutters in his office are closed, its threshold now covered by a small growth of moss. The door is locked. I don't know who has the key, and I've never tried to find out. I've learned not to ask too many questions. I've also learned to take on the color of the walls and the color of the dust in the street. It's not very difficult. I look like nothing at all.

Widow Bernhart pulls down the metal shutter of her grocery store at sunset; after that, the only place where you can buy a few provisions is Schloss's inn. It's also the most popular of the taverns. It has two public rooms. The one at the front is the larger of the two; its walls are blackened wood, its floor is covered with sawdust, and you practically fall into it when you enter because you have to go down two steep steps carved into the very sandstone and hollowed out in the middle by the soles of the thousands of drinkers who have trod there. And then there's the smaller room in the back, which I've never seen. It's separated from the first room by an elegant larch-wood door with an engraved date: 1812. The little room is reserved for a small group of men who meet there once a week, every Tuesday evening; they drink and smoke either tobacco from their fields in porcelain pipes with carved stems or bad cigars from who knows where. They've even given themselves a name: *De Erweckens'Bruderschaf,* which means something like "the Brotherhood of the Awakening." A peculiar name for a peculiar association. No one knows exactly when it was created or what its purpose is or how you get into it or who its members are—the big farmers, no doubt, maybe Lawyer Knopf, Schloss himself, and definitely the mayor, Hans Orschwir, who owns the most property in these parts. Likewise unknown is what they get up to or what they say to one another when they meet. Some say that room is where essential decisions are taken, strange pacts sealed, and promises made. Others suspect that the brothers dedicate themselves to nothing more complex than the consumption of brandy and the playing of checkers and cards, accompanied by much smoking and jocularity. A few people claim to have heard music coming from under the door. Maybe Diodemus the teacher knew the truth; he rummaged everywhere, in people's papers and in their heads, and he had a great thirst to know things inside and out. But the poor man, alas, is no longer here to speak of what he knew.

I almost never go to Schloss's inn because, I must confess, Dieter Schloss makes me uneasy, with his darting mole's eyes, his bald pink cranium, his eternally sweaty forehead, his brown teeth that smell like dirty bandages. And then there's another reason, namely that ever since I came back from the war, I don't seek out human company. I've grown accustomed to my solitude.

The evening when the *Ereigniës* took place, old Fedorine had sent me to the inn to get a bit of butter because we'd run out and she wanted to make some little shortbreads. Ordinarily, she's the one who fetches provisions, but on that baleful evening my Poupchette was lying in bed with a bad fever, and Fedorine was at her side, telling her the story of "Bilissi and the Poor Tailor," while Amelia, my wife, hovered nearby, ever so softly humming the melody of her song.

I've thought a great deal about that butter since then, about the few ounces of butter we didn't have in the pantry. You can never be too aware of how much the course of your life may depend on insignificant things—a little butter, a path you leave to take another path, a shadow you follow or flee, a blackbird you choose to kill with a bit of lead or decide to spare.

Poupchette's beautiful eyes shone too brightly as she listened to the old woman's voice, the same voice I'd listened to in days gone by, coming from the same mouth—a younger version of the same mouth, but already missing a few teeth. Poupchette looked at me with her eyes like little black marbles, burning with fever. Her cheeks were the color of cranberries. She smiled, stretched out her hands to me, and clapped them together, quacking like a duckling. "Daddy, come back Daddy, come back!"

I left the house with the music of my child's voice in my ears, mingled with Fedorine's murmuring: "Bilissi saw three knights, their armor bleached by time, standing before the doorstep of his thatched cottage. Each of them carried a red spear and a silver shield. Neither their faces nor even their eyes could be seen. Things are often thus, when it's far too late."

Night had dropped its cape over the village as a carter flings his cloak over the remains of his campfire. The houses, their roofs covered with long pinewood tiles, exhaled puffs of slow blue smoke and made me think of the rough backs of fossilized animals. The cold was beginning to settle in, a meager cold as yet, but we'd lost the habit of it because the last days of September had been as hot as so many baking ovens. I remember looking at the sky and seeing all those stars, crowded against one another like scared fledglings looking for company, and thinking that soon we would plunge, all of a sudden, into winter. Where we live, winter seems as long as many centuries skewered on a giant sword, and while the cold weather lasts, the immensity of the valley around us, smothered in forests, evokes an odd kind of prison gate.

When I entered the inn, almost all the men of the village were there. Their eyes were so somber and their immobility so stony that I immediately guessed what had happened. Orschwir closed the door behind me and stepped to my side, trembling a little. He fixed his big blue eyes on mine, as if he were seeing me for the first time.

My stomach started churning. I thought it was going to eat

my heart. Then I asked, in a very weak voice—staring at the ceiling, wanting to pierce it with my gaze, trying to imagine the *Anderer's* room, trying to imagine him, the *Anderer,* with his sideburns, his thin mustache, his sparse curly hair rising in tufts from his temples, and his big round head, the head of an overgrown, good-natured boy—I said, "Tell me you haven't . . . you didn't . . . ?" It was barely a question. It was more like a groan that escaped from me without asking permission.

Orschwir took me by the shoulders with both hands, each of them as broad as a mule's hoof. His face was even more purple than usual, and a droplet of sweat, tiny and glistening like a rock crystal, slid very slowly down the bridge of his pockmarked nose. He was still trembling, and since he was holding me like that, he made me tremble, too. "Brodeck . . . Brodeck . . ." That was all he managed to say. Then he stepped backward and melted into the crowd. Everyone's eyes were on me.

I felt like a tiny weak tadpole in the spring, lost in a great puddle of water. I was too stunned for my brain to work properly, and, oddly enough, I thought about the butter I'd come to buy. I turned to Dieter Schloss, who was standing behind the bar, and I said, "I'm just here to buy some butter, a little butter, that's all . . ." He shrugged his narrow shoulders and adjusted the flannel belt he wore around his pear-shaped belly, and I believe it was at that very moment that Wilhem Vurtenhau, a rabbit-headed peasant who owns all the land between the Steinühe forest and the Haneck plateau, took a few steps forward and said, "You can have all the butter you want, Brodeck, but you're going to tell the story. You're going to be the scribe." I rolled my eyes. I wondered where Vurtenhau could possibly have come up with that word "scribe." He's so stupid, I'm sure he's never opened a book in his life, and besides, he said the word wrong; in his mouth, the *b* became a *p*.

Telling stories is a profession, but it's not mine. I write only brief notices on the state of the flora and fauna, on the trees, the seasons, and the available game, on the water level of the Staubi River, on the snowfalls and the rainfalls. My work is of little importance to my administration, which in any case is very far away, a journey of many days, and which could not care less about what I write. I'm not sure my reports are still reaching their destination, or, if they are, whether anyone reads them.

The mails have been quite unreliable since the war, and I think it will be a long time before the postal service functions smoothly again. I hardly ever receive money anymore. I have the impression that I've been forgotten, or that they think I'm dead, or indeed that they no longer need me.

Alfred Wurtzwiller, the postmaster, makes the trip to the city of S. and back on foot once every fifteen days—he's the only one who can go, because he alone has the *Genähmigung,* the "authorization"—and sometimes he gives me to understand that he's brought back a money order for me and doles out a few banknotes. I ask him for explanations. He makes big gestures I can't interpret. Sounds ground up like meat come out of his mouth, which is creased by a large harelip, and I can't understand the sounds, either. He bashes a receipt three times with a big rubber stamp; I take up the crumpled, illegible document and the little money that comes with it. That's what we live on.

"We're not asking you for a novel." The speaker was Rudi Gott, the blacksmith. Despite his ugliness—long ago, a horse's hoof crushed his nose and shattered his left cheekbone—he's married to a beautiful woman called Gerde who's forever posing outside the forge, as if in eternal expectation of the painter destined to do her portrait. "You'll just tell what happened, that's all. The way you do in your reports." Gott was clutching a big hammer in his right hand. His naked shoulders burst out of his leather apron. He was standing near the hearth. The fire burned his face, and the steel head of the tool he held gleamed like a well-peened scythe blade.

"All right," I said, "I'll tell the story—that is, I'll try. I promise you I'm going to try. I'll write in the first person, I'll say 'I' the way I do in my reports, because I don't know how to tell a story any other way, but I warn you, that's going to mean everyone. Everyone, you understand me? I'll say 'I' but it'll be like saying the whole village and all the hamlets around it, in other words, all of us. All right?"

There was a hubbub, a noise like a draft animal relaxing in its harness and grunting a little, and then they said, "Agreed, do it like that, but be careful. Don't change anything. You must tell the whole story. You must really say everything, so that the authority who reads the Report will understand and forgive."

I don't know who'll read it, I thought. Maybe he'll understand, but forgiveness is another matter entirely. I didn't dare advance this point of view openly, but I thought it in the deepest part of myself. When I said yes, a sound filled the inn, the sound of relief, and fists were unclenched. Hands were removed from pockets. It was as though a crowd of statues had become men again. As for me, I was breathing very hard. I had come within inches of something. I preferred not to know what.

This was at the beginning of last fall. The war had been over for a year. Mauve autumn crocuses were blooming on the slopes, and often in the morning, on the granite crests of the Prinzhornï, which border our valley to the east, the first snows left a fresh, dazzling white powder, soon to melt away in the hours of full sunlight. It was just three months, almost to the day, since the *Anderer* arrived in our village, with his big trunks, his embroidered clothes, his mystery, his bay horse, and his donkey. "His name is Mister Socrates," he said, pointing to the donkey, "and this is Miss Julie. Please say hello, Miss Julie." And the pretty mare bowed her head twice, whereupon the three women who were present stepped back and crossed themselves. I can still hear his small voice when he introduced his beasts to us as though they were humans, and we were all dumbfounded.

Schloss brought out glasses, goblets, bowls, cups, and wine for everybody. I was required to drink, too. As if to seal a vow. I thought with terror about the *Anderer*'s face, about the room he lived in, a room I was somewhat familiar with, having entered it at his invitation three times to exchange a few mysterious words while drinking some strange black tea, the likes of which I had never drunk before. He had several books with obscure titles, some of them in languages which aren't written the way ours is; they must sound like sliding scree and clinking coins. Some of the books had tooled, gilt bindings, while others looked like piles of bound rags. There was also a china tea service, which he kept in a studded leather case, a chess set made of bone and ebony, a cane with a cut-crystal pommel, and a quantity of other things stored in his trunks. He always had a big smile on his face, a smile that often substituted for words, which he tended to use sparingly. He had beautiful jade green eyes, very round and slightly bulging, which made his look even more penetrating. He spoke very little. Most of all, he listened.

I thought about what those men had just done. I had known them all for years. They weren't monsters; they were peasants, craftsmen, farmworkers, foresters, minor government officials; in short, men like you and me. I put down my glass. I took the butter Dieter Schloss handed me, a thick slab wrapped in crystal paper that made a sound like turtledove's wings. I left the inn and ran all the way home.

Never in my life have I run so fast.

Never.

III

When I got back to the house, Poupchette had fallen asleep and Fedorine was dozing beside the child's bed, her mouth slightly open, exposing her three remaining teeth. Amelia had stopped humming. She raised her eyes to me and smiled. I couldn't say anything to her. I quickly climbed the stairs to our room and dove into the sheets as one dives into oblivion. I seemed to fall for a long time.

That night I slept only a little, and very badly. I kept circling and circling around the *Kazerskwir*. The *Kazerskwir*—that was because of the war: I spent nearly two long years far from our village. I was taken away like thousands of other people because we had names, faces, or beliefs different from those of others. I was confined in a distant place from which all humanity had vanished, and where there remained only conscienceless beasts which had taken on the appearance of men.

Those were two years of total darkness. I feel that time as a void in my life, very black and very deep, and therefore I call it the *Kazerskwir,* the crater. Often, at night, I still venture out onto its rim.

Old Fedorine seldom leaves the kitchen. It's her own private realm. She spends the nighttime hours in her chair. She doesn't sleep. She declares that she's past the age of sleeping. I've never known exactly how old she is. She herself says she doesn't remember, and in any case, she says, not knowing didn't prevent her from being born and won't prevent her from dying. She also says she doesn't sleep because she doesn't want death to take her by surprise; when it comes, she wants to look it in the face. She closes her eyes and hums a tune, she mends stories and memories, she weaves tapestries of threadbare dreams, with her hands resting on her knees in front of her, and in her hands, her dry hands, marked with knotty veins and creases straight as knife blades, you can read her life.

I've described to Fedorine the years I spent far from our world. When I returned, it was she who took care of me; Amelia was still too weak. Fedorine looked after me the way she'd done when I was little. All the movements came back to her. She fed my broken mouth with a spoon, bandaged my wounds, slowly but surely put the flesh back on my bare bones, watched over me when my fever mounted too high, when I shivered as though plunged into a trough of ice and raved in delirium. Weeks passed like that. She never asked me anything. She waited for the words to come out of their own accord. And then she listened for a long time.

She knows everything. Or almost everything.

She knows about the black void that returns to my dreams again and again. About my unmoving promenades around the rim of the *Kazerskwir.* I often tell myself that she must make similar excursions on her own, that she too must have some great absences which haunt her and pursue her. We all do.

I don't know if Fedorine was ever young. I've always seen her twisted and bent, covered with brown spots like a medlar long forgotten in the pantry. Even when I was a small child and she took me in, she already looked like a battered old witch. Her milkless breasts hung down under her gray smock. She came from afar, far back in time and far away in the geography of the world. She had escaped from the rotten belly of Europe.

This was a long time ago, at the beginning of another war: I stood in front of a ruined house from which a little smoke was rising. Was it perhaps my father's house, my mother's? I must have had a family. I was a full four years old, and I was alone. I was playing with a hoop half consumed by the fire. Fedorine passed by, pulling her cart. She saw me and stopped. She dug in her bag, brought out a beautiful, gleaming red apple, and handed it to me. I devoured the fruit like a starveling. Fedorine spoke to me, using words I didn't understand, asked me questions I couldn't answer, and touched my forehead and my hair.

I followed the old woman with the apples as if she were a piper. She lifted me into the cart and wedged me among some sacks, three saucepans, and a bundle of hay. There was also a rabbit with pretty brown eyes and tawny fur; its stomach was soft and very warm. I remember that it let me stroke it. I also remember that Fedorine stopped on a bend in the road (broom was growing along its borders) and, in my language, asked me my name. She told me hers—"Fedorine"—and pointed down below us at what remained of my village. "Take a good look, little Brodeck. That's where you come from, but you'll never go back there because soon there will be nothing left of it. Open your eyes wide!"

So I looked as hard as I could. I saw the dead animals with their swollen bellies, the barns open to the four winds, the crumbled walls. There were also a great many puppets lying in the streets, some with their arms crossed, others rolled up into balls.

Although they were big puppets, at that distance they seemed tiny. And then I stared at the sun, and it poured burning gold into my eyes and made the tableau of my village disappear.

I tossed and turned in the bed. I was certain that Amelia wasn't sleeping any more than I was. When I closed my eyes, I saw the *Anderer*'s face, his pond-colored irises, his full amaranth-tinged cheeks, his sparse frizzy hair. I smelled his violet scent.

Amelia moved. I felt her warm breath against my cheek and lips. I opened my eyes. Her lids were closed. She seemed utterly tranquil. She's so beautiful that I often wonder what it was I did to make her take an interest in me one day. It was because of her that I didn't founder back then. When I was in the prison camp, it was her I thought about every minute.

The men who guarded us and beat us were always telling us that we were nothing but droppings, lower than rat shit. We didn't have the right to look them in the face. We had to keep our heads bowed and take the blows without a word. Every evening, they poured soup into the tin bowls used by their guard dogs, mastiffs with coats the color of honey and curled-up lips and eyes that drooled reddish tears. We had to go down on all fours, like the dogs, and eat our food without using anything but our mouths, like the dogs.

Most of my fellow prisoners refused to do it. They're dead. As for me, I ate like the dogs, on all fours and using only my mouth. And I'm alive.

Sometimes, when the guards were drunk or had nothing to do, they amused themselves by putting a collar and a leash on me. I had to crawl around like that, on all fours, wearing a collar attached to a leash. I had to strut and turn round in circles and bark and dangle my tongue and lick their boots. The guards stopped calling me "Brodeck" and started calling me "Brodeck the Dog" and then laughing their heads off. Most of those who were imprisoned with me refused to act the dog, and they died, either of starvation or from the repeated blows the guards dealt them.

Some of the other prisoners never spoke to me except to say, "You're worse than the guards, Brodeck! You're an animal, you're shit!" Like the guards, they kept telling me I was no longer a man. They're dead. They're all dead. Me, I'm alive. Maybe they had no reason to survive. Maybe they had no love lodged deep in their hearts or back home in their village. Yes, maybe they had no reason to go on living.

Eventually the guards took to tying me to a post near the mastiffs' kennels at night. I slept on the ground, lying in the dust amid the smells of fur and dogs' breath and urine. Above me was the sky. Not far away were the watchtowers and the sentinels, and beyond them was the country; the fields we could see by day, the wheat rippling with fantastic insolence in the wind, the clumped stands of birch, and the sound of the great river and its silvery water were all quite near.

But in fact I was very far from that place. I wasn't leashed to a post. I wasn't wearing a leather collar. I wasn't lying half naked near sleeping dogs. I was in our house, in our bed, pressed against Amelia's warm body and no longer couched in the dust. I was warm, and I could feel her heart beating against mine. I heard her voice, speaking to me the words of love she was so good at finding in the darkness of our room. For all that, I came back.

Brodeck the Dog came home alive and found his Amelia waiting for him.

───────

IV

*T*he morning after the *Ereigniës,* I got up very early. I shaved, dressed, and left the house without a sound. Poupchette and Amelia were still sleeping, while Fedorine was in her chair, dozing and talking a little. She spoke words without coherence or logic in a strange babble drawn from several languages.

Daylight was just beginning to bleach the sky, and the whole village was still bound up in sleep. Very softly, I closed the door behind me. The grass in front of the house was drenched with whitish, almost milky dew, which quivered and dripped on the edges of the clover leaves. It was cold. The peaks of the Prinzhornï looked higher and sharper than usual. I knew that this was a portent of bad weather, and I told myself that before long snow would begin to fall on the village, enveloping it and isolating it even more.

"*Zehr mogenhilch,* Brodeck!"

I jumped as though caught in some shameful act. I knew that I had done nothing wrong, that I had nothing to feel guilty about, but I nevertheless leapt like a kid called to order by the goatherd's switch. I hadn't recognized the voice, even though it belonged to Göbbler, our neighbor.

He was sitting on the stone bench built against the wall of his house, leaning forward and steadying himself on the stick he held with both hands. I'd never seen him sit on that bench before, except perhaps once or twice on one of the rare summer nights when the air is stifling and oppressive and there are no cool breezes to refresh the village.

Göbbler's a man past sixty, with a rough-hewn face; he never smiles and seldom speaks. A milky veil is slowly covering his eyes, and he can't see farther than five meters. The war brought him back to the village, although people say he occupied a position in some administration in S. for years before his return; but no one knows exactly which administration that was, and I don't think anyone has ever asked him. Now he lives on his pension and his henhouse. Moreover, he's come to resemble his roosters a little. His eyes move in the same way, and the skin hanging down below his neck has ruddy patches like wattles. His wife, who's much younger than he, is called Boulla. She's fat and fond of talking; she smells of grain and onion. They say that a great heat burns between her legs, and that it would take many buckets of water to extinguish it. She seeks men as others look for reasons to exist.

"Yes, indeed, up very early!" Göbbler repeats. "So where are you going?"

It was the first time he'd ever asked me a question. I hesitated. I got fuddled. Words stumbled in my mouth and collided with one another, like stones in a mountain torrent. With the tip of his stick, Göbbler pushed back a snail that was calmly moving toward him and then turned it over. It was a little snail with a yellow-and-black shell and a fine, delicately marked body, full of innocent grace. Caught by surprise, the creature took a few moments to withdraw its body and its fragile horns into its shell, whereupon Göbbler raised his stick and brought it down on the little mollusk, which exploded like a walnut. Then, without taking his eyes off the debris of the snail's shell and body, now reduced to a slimy, beige pulp, he murmured, "Be careful, Brodeck. Be careful. There's been trouble enough already."

He turned his eyes toward me and smiled, drawing back his lips. It was the first time I'd ever seen him really smile, and I got my first glimpse of his teeth. They were gray and pointy, very pointy, as though he'd spent many an evening filing them down. I made no reply. I almost shrugged my shoulders, but I stopped myself. A great shudder ran up and down my back. I pulled my cap down to my ears, pressed the flaps against my temples, and moved away without looking at him again. There was a little sweat on my forehead. One of his cocks crowed, followed by all the others. Their shrieks struck my head like a series of blows. Gusts of wind from the depths of the valley swirled around me, laden with odors of beechnuts, of peat bogs, of heather and wet rock.

On Püppensaltz Street, our main street, old *Ohnmeist* was going from door to door. *Ohnmeist's* a dog, but of a very unusual kind. He gets his name from the fact that he has no master and has never wanted one. He avoids other dogs and children, makes do with very little, and goes around begging for food under kitchen windows. He accompanies whomever he fancies to the fields and sleeps under the stars, and when it's too cold, he scratches on the doors of barns; people are glad to give him a little hay to lie on and some soup to eat. He's a big, gangling beast, brown with reddish spots, about the size of a griffon but with a pointer's short, dense fur. No doubt his blood is a mixture of many strains, but it would be a clever man who could say which ones they were. As he ambled over to sniff me, I remembered how, whenever he crossed the *Anderer's* path, *Ohnmeist* would give two or three little yelps of joy and wag his tail in all directions. Then the *Anderer* would stop, remove his gloves—beautiful gloves of fine, soft leather—and stroke the animal's head. It was very strange to see the two of them like that, the dog placid and happy, quietly accepting the *Anderer*'s caresses, when ordinarily none of us could get close to the beast, much less touch him, and the *Anderer*, patting the big fellow with his bare hand and looking at him as if he were a human. That morning, *Ohnmeist*'s eyes were both bright and shifty. He walked beside me for a while, occasionally uttering a brief, melancholy groan. He kept his head low, as if it were suddenly too heavy for him, too filled with distressing thoughts. He left me near the Urbï fountain and disappeared down the narrow street that leads to the river.

I had my own idea, which I'd mulled over at length during the course of my agitated night: I had to speak to Orschwir, the mayor. I had to see him, and he had to tell me what it was that he and the others expected from me. I was almost at the point of doubting my reason. I wondered if I'd understood Göbbler's words correctly, or if perhaps I'd dreamed him sitting there on his bench, or if the scene at the inn the previous night—that clamp of bodies tightening around me, that vise of faces, that request, and that promise—if all that weren't made of the same stuff that composed some of my stranger dreams.

Orschwir's house is the only one that truly has the forest at its back. It's also the biggest house in our village. It gives an impression of affluence and power, but in fact it's only a farmhouse, a big farmhouse, old, prosperous, paunchy, with immense roofs and walls whose granite and sandstone form an irregular checkerboard, and yet people think of the place as something of a manor house, a château. What's more, I'm sure Orschwir's pleased to think of himself, if only occasionally, as lord of the manor. He's not a bad man, although he's as ugly as an entire barbarian regiment. People say it was his ugliness, strangely enough, which assured his conquests in former days, when he was young and went to all the dances. People talk a good deal, and so often with nothing to say. One thing that's sure is that Orschwir wound up marrying the richest girl in the region, Ilde Popenheimer, whose father owned five sawmills and three water mills. In addition to her inheritance, she gave her husband two sons, each the spitting image of his father.

The resemblance didn't matter much. I speak in the past tense because, in any event, they're both dead. They died right at the beginning of the war. Their names are carved on the monument the village put up between the church and the cemetery. The statue depicts a woman, swathed in great veils and kneeling on the ground; it's hard to say whether she's praying or meditating revenge. The inscribed names include GÜNTER AND GEHRART ORSCHWIR, AGED TWENTY-ONE AND NINETEEN YEARS. My name was on the monument as well, but after I returned, Baerensbourg, the road mender, erased it. The job caused him a great deal of difficulty—it's always a very delicate undertaking to remove what is written in stone. I can still manage to read my first name on the monument. This makes me smile, but the thing gives Amelia the creeps. She doesn't like to pass it.

According to a persistent whisper, Orschwir owes his position as mayor to the deaths of his sons; their sacrifice, however, was anything but heroic. They killed themselves at their lookout post while playing with a grenade like a pair of children. After all, that's what they were, big children still, who thought the war would suddenly make men of them. The explosion could be heard in the village. It was our first explosion. Everyone ran to the little sentry box, which had been built to overlook the road to the border. The post stood right in the middle of the Schönbehe pasture and atop its highest elevation, a hill sheltered by a great brown-red boulder covered with lichen the color of jade. Nothing much was left, either of the box or of the boys. One had died pressing both hands against his belly, trying to hold in his guts; the other's head, blown clean off by the blast, stared at us fixedly. We buried them two days later, wrapped in sheets of white linen and lying in the oaken coffins which Fixheim, the carpenter, had fashioned with great care. Those two were our first war dead. Father Peiper, who in those days still drank only water, pronounced a sermon on the themes of chance and deliverance. Few of us understood it, but the congregation very much liked the words he chose, most of them rare or very old, and the way he sent them rolling among the pillars, the vaults, the clouds of incense, the soft light of the candles, and the stained-glass windows of our little church.

I entered the farmyard, still deserted at this hour. It's an immense yard, a little country all by itself, bordered by handsome piles of manure. The entrance is a large postern made of hand-turned wood, painted bright red, and carved with a motif of chestnut leaves; in their midst is the motto BÖDEN UND HERZ GELIECHT, which means, more or less, "Belly and heart united."

I've often pondered the meaning of that phrase. Someone told me the inscription had been added in Orschwir's grandfather's day, and on his orders. When I say "someone," I mean Diodemus, the teacher, who spoke to me about the Orschwir motto. Diodemus was my elder by several years, but we got along like two old comrades. If he had the time, he liked to accompany me while I went around collecting information for my reports, and it was a pleasure to chat with him. He was an uncommon man, who often—not always, but often—showed good sense, who knew many things, doubtless many more than he admitted to knowing, and who had perfect command of reading, writing, and arithmetic. This last quality, in fact, was the reason why the previous mayor appointed him as the teacher, even though Diodemus wasn't from the village and came from another village to the south of ours, about a four-day hike away.

It's been three weeks since Diodemus died, in circumstances so strange and so poorly defined that his death made me even more alert to all the little signs I was noticing around me. Fear began to brew gently in my brain. The day after he died, I started writing this account alongside the Report the others had already assigned me to do. I'm writing the two of them at the same time.

Diodemus spent most of his free hours in the village archives. Sometimes I saw a light in his window very late at night. He lived alone, above the school, in a tiny, uncomfortable, dusty apartment. Books, documents, and the records of olden times were his only furniture. "What I'd like to do is to understand," he confided to me one day. "We never understand anything, or if we do, not much. Men live, in a way, as the blind do, and generally, that's enough for them. I'd go so far as to say that it's what they're looking for: to avoid headaches and dizzy spells, to fill their stomachs, to sleep, to lie between their wives' thighs when their blood runs too hot, to make war because they're told to do so, and then to die without knowing what awaits them afterward, but hoping that something's awaiting them, all the same. Ever since I was a child, I've loved questions, and I've loved the paths you must follow to find the answers. Sometimes, of course, I end up knowing nothing but the path itself, but that's not so bad; at least I've made some progress."

Maybe that was the cause of his death: Diodemus wanted to understand everything, and he tried to give words and explanations to what is inexplicable and should always remain unexplored. On the day I'm referring to, I couldn't think of anything to say to him; I think I smiled. Smiling costs nothing.

But there was another time, on a spring afternoon, when we talked about Orschwir, about his postern and the phrase carved on it. This was before the war. Poupchette was not yet born. Diodemus and I had been sitting on the short grass in one of Bourenkopf's stubble fields, which lie on the way to the valley of the Doura and, beyond it, to the border. Before going back down to the village, we rested for a while near a wayside cross that represented Jesus with an unusual face, the face of a Negro or a Mughal. It was the end of the day. From where we sat, we could see the whole village and cup it in one hand. Its houses looked like the little houses in children's toys. A fine sunset was gilding the roofs, which were already glistening from the recent rain. Plumes of smoke rose from every dwelling, and in the distance, the slow, sluggish smoke clouds mingled with the shimmering air, blurring the horizon and making it appear almost alive.

Diodemus took some pieces of paper out of his pocket and read me the last pages of the novel he was writing. Novels were his obsession; he wrote at least one a year, on whatever crumpled writing material came to hand, including strips of wrapping paper and the backs of labels. He kept his manuscripts to himself and never showed them to anybody. I was the only one to whom he occasionally read passages from his work. He read them to me, but he expected nothing in return. He never asked my opinion about the passages he read or the subjects they treated. So much the better, because I wouldn't have been able to say anything. The stories were always more or less the same: complicated tales written in tortuous interminable sentences which evoked conspiracies, treasures buried in deep holes, and young women held as prisoners. I loved Diodemus. I was also very fond of his voice. Its music made me feel drowsy and warm. I would look out at the landscape and listen to the melody. Those were wonderful moments.

I never knew Diodemus's age. Sometimes I thought he looked quite old. On other occasions, I persuaded myself that he was only a few years my senior. He had a noble face. His profile looked like the head on an ancient Greek or Roman coin, and his curly jet-black hair, which lightly brushed the tops of his shoulders, made me think of certain heroes of the distant past who lie asleep in fairy tales and tragedies and epics, and whom a magic charm sometimes suffices to awaken or destroy. Or, perhaps better than a hero, one of those shepherds of Antiquity, who (as is well known) are more often than not gods in disguise, come among men to seduce them, to guide them, or to bring them to ruin.

"*Böden und Herz geliecht,*" Diodemus concluded, chewing on a blade of grass as the evening gradually fell on our shoulders. "Funny motto. I wonder where the old fellow came across that. In his head, or in a book? You find some really bizarre things in books sometimes."

V

Orschwir was sitting at one end of his kitchen table, a
table four meters long, carved in a single piece from the bole of
an oak tree several hundred years old—one of those trees that
stand like lords in the heart of the Tannäringen forest. A young
serving girl stood beside him. I didn't know her. She couldn't have
been more than sixteen, with a pretty, round face, like the face of
the Virgin in certain very old paintings. Despite her rosy cheeks,
she was pale, and so in a way resembled a peony. She moved so
little that she might have been taken for a dressmaker's man-
nequin or an unusually large doll. Later, I learned that she was
blind. This seemed strange, for her eyes, although somewhat
fixed, appeared to see everything around her, and she moved about
easily, never bumping into furniture or walls or other people. She
was a distant cousin whom Orschwir had taken in; she'd come
originally from the Nehsaxen region, but her parents were dead,
their house destroyed, and their lands confiscated. The villagers
called her *Die Keinauge,* "the No-Eyed Girl."

Orschwir dismissed her with a whistle, and she went away
soundlessly. Then, gesturing, he bade me approach and sit down.
In the morning, he looked less ugly than usual, as if sleep had
tightened his skin and softened his imperfections. He was still

in his undershorts. Around his waist, a leather belt awaited the trousers it was destined to hold up. He'd thrown a goatskin jacket over his shoulders, and his cap of otter fur was already on his head. On the table before him was a gently steaming plate of eggs and bacon. Orschwir ate slowly, occasionally pausing to cut himself a slice of brown bread.

He poured me a glass of wine, looked at me without the least sign of surprise, and simply said, "So how are things?" Then, without waiting for a reply, he directed his attention to the last rasher of bacon, a thick chunk whose fat, rendered almost translucent by the cooking, dripped onto his plate like melted wax from a candle. He carefully carved the bacon into small, even-sized pieces. I watched him, or rather I watched his knife, which that morning he was using to feed himself, as naturally as you please, and which the previous evening had no doubt been thrust several times into the *Anderer*'s body.

It's always been difficult for me to speak and express my innermost thoughts in person. I prefer to write. When I sit down and write, words grow very docile, they come and feed out of my hand like little birds, and I can do almost what I want with them; whereas when I try to marshal them in the open air, they fly away from me. And the war did nothing to improve things; it made me even more silent. In the camp, I saw how words could be used and what could be required of them. Before then, before the camp, I used to read books, especially books of poetry. During the time of my studies in the Capital, Professor Nösel instilled this taste in me, and I had retained it as a pleasant habit. I never forgot to stick a volume of poems in my pocket when I set out to gather information for my reports, and often, surrounded by the great spectacle of the towering mountains, the shouldering forests, and the checkerboard pastures, while the sky above seemed to look on, contented with its own infinite expanse, I would read verses aloud. The ones I liked and read again aroused in me a kind of agreeable buzzing, like an echo of some confused thoughts which lay in the deepest part of myself, but which I was incapable of expressing.

When I returned from the camp, I put all my books of poetry in the stove and burned them. I watched the flames as they consumed everything, first words, then sentences, then whole pages. The smoke that rose from the burning poems was neither better nor nobler nor more charming than any other smoke. There was nothing special about it. I later learned that Nösel had been arrested during the first raids, like a number of professors and others whose occupation it was to study the world and explain it. He died shortly afterward in a camp similar to mine, a camp little different from hundreds of other camps which had sprung up all over the place on the other side of the border like poisonous flowers. Poetry had been of no use to him in the matter of his survival. Perhaps it had even hastened his demise. The thousands of verses, in Latin, Greek, and other languages, which he kept locked in his memory like the greatest of treasures, had availed him nothing. I felt certain that he, unlike me, had refused to act the dog. Yes, that was it. Poetry knows nothing of dogs. It ignores them.

Orschwir mopped his plate with a piece of bread. "Brodeck, Brodeck, I can see you haven't had much sleep," he began, speaking softly, in a tone of muffled reproach. "I, on the other hand— well, it's been a long time since I've slept so well, quite some time indeed. Before, I couldn't so much as close my eyes, but last night

I felt like I was six or seven years old again. I laid my head on the pillow, and three seconds later I was asleep . . ."

By this time, the sun had fully risen, and its white light entered the kitchen in oblique rays, which struck the scarlet flagstones of the floor. Farm sounds could be heard: animals, servants, creaking axles, unidentifiable thwacks, and snatches of conversation.

"I want to see the body." I spoke the words without realizing what I was doing. They came almost of their own accord, and I let them pass. Orschwir looked surprised and upset. His face changed in an instant. He froze, like a shellfish when you douse it with a few drops of vinegar, and quite suddenly, his features regained all their ugliness. He lifted his cap, scratched the crown of his head, stood up, turned his back to me, walked over to one of the windows, and planted himself in front of it.

"What good would that do, Brodeck? Didn't you see your fill of corpses during the war? And what does one dead man look like, if not another dead man? You must tell the story, in sequence, one event after another. You mustn't forget anything, but you mustn't add useless details, either. They'll make you veer off your course, and you'll run the risk of confusing or even irritating your readers. Because you will be read, Brodeck, don't forget that; you will be read by people who occupy important positions in S. Yes indeed, you will be read, even though I have a feeling you don't believe it . . ."

Orschwir turned around and looked me up and down. "I respect you, Brodeck, but it's my duty to put you on your guard. It's my duty as mayor, and as . . . Please don't leave the path, I beg you, and don't go looking for what has never existed—or what doesn't exist anymore."

He drew up his great carcass to its full height, yawned, and stretched his huge arms toward the ceiling. "Come with me," he said. "I want to show you something."

He was a good head taller than I was. We left the kitchen and entered a long corridor which wound its way through the entire house. I had the feeling we'd never get out of that corridor; it made my head spin and filled me with dread. I knew Orschwir's house was big, but I would never have imagined it to be so labyrinthine.

It was an ancient structure, frequently remodeled, and it bore witness to a time unconcerned with alignment or logic. Diodemus told me that the oldest walls of the house dated back more than four centuries. According to an act he'd found in the archives, the Emperor stopped there in the fall of 1567, on his way to the marches of Carinthia and an encounter with the Grand Turk. I walked behind Orschwir, who stepped out smartly, displacing a quantity of air. I felt as though I were being pulled along in his wake, drawn by his scent, a combination of leather, night, fried bacon, beard, and unwashed skin. We met no one. Sometimes we went up a few steps or down two or three others. I would be hard put to say how long we walked—a few minutes, a few hours—because that corridor erased all the reference points of space and time. Finally Orschwir stopped in front of a large door covered with weathered green copper and square nails. He opened the door, and the milky light behind it dazzled me. I had to stand still for a moment with my eyes closed before I could open them to the light again. And see.

We were about to step out into the area behind the house. I had never gotten a look at this part of Orschwir's property except from very far away, while hiking up in the mountains. I knew that the sheds and outhouses back here sheltered the mayor's entire fortune, and before him his father's fortune, and that of his father's father. A pink, noisy fortune, which spent its time wallowing in mud. A squealing fortune, which produced a diabolical racket all day long.

Orschwir's gold was swine. For several generations, his family had lived on and grown rich from hog fat. They had the largest pig farm for fifty kilometers around. Every morning, vehicles left the property—carrying either freshly killed corpses or panic-stricken, squealing animals bound for slaughter—and drove to the villages, the markets, and the butcher shops in the surrounding region. These daily rounds constituted a well-ordered ballet which not even the war had managed to disrupt. People eat in wartime, too. At least some of them.

For three months after the war began, there was a long moment of stupefied calm when everyone gazed eastward and cocked an ear for the sound of marching boots, a specialty of the still-invisible *Fratergekeime*. (That's the word in our dialect for those who came here to spread death and ashes, for the men who made me become an animal, men very much like us. Having gone to university in their Capital, I happened to know them well. We associated with some of them, since they often visited our village, brought here by business and trade fairs, and spoke a language which is the twin sister of ours and which we understand with little difficulty.) When the calm ended and our border posts were suddenly swept aside like paper flowers scattered by a child's breath, Orschwir was not even slightly worried: He kept on raising, selling, and eating his pigs. His door remained immaculate; no obscenities were painted on it. Although the conquerors marching in triumph through our streets bore at least a little responsibility for the idiotic deaths of his two sons, he had no qualms about selling them the fattest of his hogs in exchange for the pieces of silver they pulled out of their pockets in handfuls, having no doubt stolen them somewhere along the way.

In the first pen that Orschwir showed me, dozens of piglets a few weeks old were playing on fresh straw. They chased one another, collided with one another, and poked one another with their snouts, all the while emitting little cries of joy. Orschwir tossed them three shovelfuls of grain, which they rushed to devour.

In the next pen, eight-month-old hogs were walking around, jostling and challenging one another. You could feel their strange, gratuitous violence and aggressiveness, which nothing in evidence justified or explained. They were already large, thick beasts, with drooping ears and brutish faces. An acrid stench assailed my nostrils. The straw the animals sprawled on was filthy with their excrement. Their grunts caromed off the wooden walls and struck my temples. I wanted to get out of there as quickly as possible.

Farther on, in the last pen, pale, immense, long-loined adult hogs were dozing. They looked like so many small boats. They all lay on their sides, panting through open snouts, and wallowing in black mud as thick as molasses. Some of them watched us with great weariness. One might have thought them giants changed into beasts, creatures condemned to a fearful metamorphosis.

"The ages of life," Orschwir murmured. I'd nearly forgotten his presence, and the sound of his voice made me jump. "First you saw innocence, then stupid aggression, and now, here, wisdom." He paused for a while and then began speaking again, slowly and very softly. "But sometimes, Brodeck, wisdom's not what we think it is. The creatures you see before you are savage beasts.

Truly savage, however much they look like beached whales; brutes with no heart and no mind. With no memory, either. Nothing counts but their belly, their belly; they think of one thing and one thing only, all the time: keeping that belly full."

He stopped talking and looked at me with an enigmatic smile that contrasted sharply with the heavy features of his dirty face. Bread crumbs adorned his mustache, and his lips still glistened a little with bacon fat.

"They're capable of eating their own brothers, their own flesh. It wouldn't bother them at all—to them, it's all the same. They chew it up, they swallow it down, they shit it out, and then they start all over again, indefinitely. They're never sated. And everything tastes good to them. Because they eat everything, Brodeck, without question. Everything. Do you understand what I'm telling you? They leave nothing behind, no trace, no proof. Nothing. And they don't think, Brodeck, not them. They know nothing of remorse. They live. The past is unknown to them. They've got the right idea, don't you think?"

VI

I'm trying to return to those moments, to get as close to them as I can, but what I'd really like to do is to forget them and run away, run far away, on light feet and with a brand-new brain.

I have the feeling that I'm the wrong size for my life. I mean, I feel that my life is spilling over everywhere, that it was never cut to fit a man like me, that it's full of too many things, too many events, too many torments, too many flaws. Is it my fault, perhaps? Is it because I don't know how to be a man? Because I don't know how to sort things, how to take what I need and leave the rest? Or maybe it's the fault of the century I live in, which is like a great crater; the excesses of every day flow into it, and it's filled with everything that cuts and flays and crushes and chops. My head—sometimes I think my head's on the point of exploding, like a shell crammed with gunpowder.

That famous day, the day after the *Ereigniës,* wasn't so long ago, and yet, in spite of everything, it's slipping through my fingers. I remember only certain scenes and certain words, very exact and very clear, like bright lights against a deep black background. And I also remember my fear, my fear above all, which I've worn like a garment ever since. I can't cast it off; in spite of my efforts, it's grown tighter and tighter, as if it shrank a little more every week. The strangest thing is that back in the camp, after I became Brodeck the Dog, I wasn't afraid anymore. Fear no longer existed for me there; I had moved well beyond it. For fear still belongs to life. Like hyenas circling carrion, fear cannot do without life. That's what nourishes and sustains it. But I—I was out on life's margins. I was already halfway across the river.

After I left Orschwir's farm, I believe I wandered the streets. It was still quite early. My memory focused on the image of the pigs, lying on their sides and looking at me with their glaucous eyes. I tried to banish that vision, but it was tenacious. It planted roots I'll never be able to destroy. Those animals, their enormous faces, their swollen bellies, and their eyes, their pale eyes, examining me. And their stench, too. Good God . . . My thoughts joined hands and did a dance together inside my skull. Everything—the hogs, the *Anderer*'s calm trusting face—spun in a saraband, with no music but the solo violin of Orschwir's appalling serenity.

I found myself in front of Mother Pitz's café, which stands against a wall of the old washhouse. I had no doubt headed there because I wanted to be certain I wouldn't meet anyone, or at least not any man. Only old women frequented the café. You could see them there at any hour, but especially toward evening, drinking cups of herbal tea or little glasses of marc mixed with geneva and a bit of sugar. We call such drinks *Liebleiche,* "charmers."

To tell the truth, that café isn't altogether a café. It's part of a house, a room adjoining the kitchen. There are three little tables covered with embroidered tablecloths, a couple of chairs around each table, a narrow chimney that draws badly, some green plants in glazed ceramic pots, and on the wall, a severely faded photograph of a young man, who smiles at the camera and smoothes his mustache with two fingers. Mother Pitz is over seventy-five years old. She's bent in half, as though folded at a right angle. When kids pass her in the street, they call her *Die Fleckarei*—"the Bracket." The young man in the photograph is her husband, Augustus Pitz, who died half a century ago.

I must be the only male villager who occasionally sets foot in Mother Pitz's place. Sometimes she helps me, and that's why I go there. She knows all the plants that grow on the plateau, even the rarest ones, and when I can't find them in my books, I go and ask her, and we spend a few hours talking about flowers and grasses, about footpaths and undergrowth, about pastures grazed by sheep, goats, and cows, and also by the hungry wind, which never stops; about all the places where she can't go anymore and hasn't seen for a long time.

"My wings have been clipped, Brodeck," she says. "My life was really up there, with the flocks in the high stubble. Down here I suffocate. The air's too low. Down here it's like being a worm, you creep along the surface of the earth and eat dust, but up there . . ."

She has the finest dried-plant collection I have ever seen: an entire armoire, filled to bursting with large books between whose dark-brown cardboard covers she's pressed examples of flowers and plants from the mountain for years and years. She's recorded below each specimen the place where it was collected, the day, the appearance of the sky, the scent of the plant, its exact color and its orientation, all in her careful handwriting, and occasionally she's added a brief commentary that has nothing to do with the specimen in question.

That day, when I pushed open her door and the little bells jangled, she asked me at once, "So, Brodeck, you've come to see the Great Book of Dead Things again?" To be more precise, since she spoke in dialect, she called her herbarium *De Buch vo Stiller un Stillie,* which sounds softer and less tragic.

I closed the door as though someone were following me. I'm sure I was making a ghastly face and acting like a conspirator. I went and sat at the table deep in the corner of the room, the one that looks as though it wants to disappear. I asked Mother Pitz for something very strong and very hot, because I was shivering like an old wooden ratchet in the Easter wind. Although the fully risen sun was now reigning over the sky uncontested, I was freezing.

Mother Pitz returned quickly, carrying a steaming cup, and with a gesture bade me drink. I obeyed her like a child, closing my eyes and letting the liquid invade me. My blood grew warmer, followed by my hands and my head. I loosened my jacket collar a little, and then my shirt collar, too. Mother Pitz watched me. The walls moved gently, like poplar leaves, and so did the chairs, approaching the walls as though wanting to ask them to dance. "What's wrong with you, Brodeck?" she asked me. "Have you seen the devil?"

She was holding my two hands in her own, and her face was quite close to mine. She had big green eyes, very beautiful, with flecks of gold all round the edges of her irises. I remember thinking that eyes have no age, and that when you die, you still have the eyes you had as a child, eyes that opened upon the world one day and haven't ever let it go.

She gave me a little shake and repeated her question.

What did she know, and what could I tell her? The previous night, only men had been present at Schloss's inn, and it was with those men that I had come to an agreement. After I returned home, I had said nothing to my women, and in the early hours of the following morning, which was not yet over, I had left the house before they awakened. The others, all the others, hadn't they done the same with their wives, their sisters, their mothers, their children?

She kept gently pressing my hands, as if she were trying to squeeze the truth out of them. I spoke the words in my mind: "Nothing's wrong, nothing at all, Mother Pitz. Everything's normal. Last night, the men of the village killed the *Anderer*. The killing took place at Schloss's inn, very simply, like a game of cards or a verbal agreement. It had been building up for a long time. Me, I arrived right after it happened, I'd gone there to buy some butter, and I had nothing to do with the slaughter. I've simply been charged with writing the Report on it. I'm supposed to explain what went on from the time he arrived in the village and why they had no choice but to kill him. That's all."

Those words never passed my lips. They remained inside. I tried to let them out, but they didn't want to leave. The old woman stood up, went to the kitchen, and returned with a small pink enamel saucepan. She poured the rest of the brew into my cup and motioned to me to drink it. I drank. The walls started swaying once more. I was very hot. Mother Pitz went away again. When she came back the next time, she was carrying one of the large books that contained her dried plant collection. The label on the cover read *Blüte vo Maï un Heilkraüte vo June*, which can be translated as "May Flowers and June Simples." She placed the book on the table in front of me, sat down beside me, and opened the book. "Whatever you've got, Brodeck, have a look at my little *Stillies* and they'll take your mind off of it."

Then, as if he had been summoned by those words, I was aware of the *Anderer* standing behind me and adjusting the gold-rimmed eyeglasses, as I'd often seen him do, on his kind, round, overgrown child's face; he smiled at me before bowing his big head, adorned with frizzy sideburns, to contemplate the desiccated leaves and lifeless petals in Mother Pitz's book.

I've already noted that he spoke but little. Very little. Sometimes, when I looked at him, the figure of a saint crossed my mind. Saintliness is very odd. When people encounter it, they often take it for something else, something completely unlike it: indifference, mockery, scheming, coldness, insolence, perhaps even contempt. But they're mistaken, and that makes them furious. They commit an awful crime. This is doubtless the reason why most saints end up as martyrs.

---

have to tell the story of the *Anderer's* arrival among us, but I'm afraid: afraid of waking ghosts, and afraid of the others. The men of the village, I mean, who are no longer with me the way they used to be. Yesterday, for example, Fritz Aschenbach, whom I've known for more than twenty years, failed to return my greeting when we met on the slope of the Jornetz. He was coming down from cutting firewood; I was going up to see whether I might still be able to find some chanterelles. For a moment, his silence dumbfounded me. I stopped, turned around, and said to his back, "What's this, Fritz, you don't tell me hello?" But he didn't even slow down or turn his head. He contented himself with spitting copiously to one side; that was his sole reaction. Maybe he was so lost in his thoughts that he didn't see or hear me—but thoughts of what? Thoughts about what?

I'm not crazy. I'm not going crazy. Nevertheless, there's Diodemus's death to consider, too. (Another death! And a strange death indeed, as I shall soon describe.) Since my time in the camp, I know the wolves outnumber the lambs.

De Anderer arrived late in the afternoon of May 13, which will be a year ago next spring. A gentle, blond-tinged year. Evening came on tiptoe, as if unwilling to bother anyone. In the fields surrounding the village, and in the high pastures, as far as the eye could see, was a vast ocean of white and yellow. The green grass practically disappeared under a dandelion carpet. The wind swayed the flowers or brushed them or bent them, according to its whim, while above them bands of clouds hastened westward and vanished into the Prätze gap. A few patches of snow on the stubble fields still held out against the early-spring warmth, which was slowly lapping them up, reducing them from one day to the next, and would soon change them into clear, cold pools.

It was around five o'clock, perhaps five-thirty, when Gunther Beckenfür, who was busy mending the roof of his shepherd's hut, looked up and saw, heading his way on the road that comes from the border—a road on which nothing has been seen since the end of the war, on which no one travels anymore, and on which it would have occurred to no one to travel—a strange crew.

"Coming on like a real slow train, they were." That's Beckenfür talking, answering my question. I write down every word he says in a notebook, literally every word. We're at his house. He has served me a glass of beer. I'm writing. He's chewing on the cigarette he has just rolled for himself, half tobacco and half lichen, which fills the room with a stench of burned horn. His old father's sitting in a corner; his mother's been dead for a good while. The old man talks to himself. The words rumble and gurgle in his mouth, where no more than two or three teeth remain, and he shakes his fragile starling's head continuously, like one of the moving cherubs in a church. Snow has started falling outside—the first snow, the one that delights children, the one whose whiteness blinds. We can see the flakes drifting close to the window, like thousands of curious eyes turned on us, and then, as though frightened, rushing away in great clouds toward the street.

"They were barely moving, like the fellow was hauling a

load of granite boundary stones all by himself. I stopped working and took a long look, just to see if I was dreaming. But no, I wasn't dreaming, I definitely saw something, even though I wasn't sure yet what it was. At first I thought it might be stray animals, and then I thought it was people who'd lost their way or vendors of some kind, because now I could see that there was something a little human about whatever it was. I remember shivering, a real shiver, and not from cold, but from remembering the war, the war and the road it came on, that shitty goddamned road that brought the people here nothing but bad luck and trouble, and there he was, a creature in the shape of a man, with his two beasts which I couldn't tell what they were, there he was, coming toward the village on that very same road. He could only have come from over there, from the *Fratergekeime,* those shit-assed sons of infected old whores . . . Do you remember what they did to Cathor, those sick bastards?"

I nodded. Cathor was the pottery mender. He was also Beckenfür's brother-in-law. After the *Fratergekeime* arrived in the village, he tried to play games with them, and he lost. Perhaps I'll tell about him later.

"I was so fascinated I put down my roofing stones and my tools. I rubbed my eyes and squinted, trying to see as far as I could. It was a vision out of the past. I was flabbergasted. He looked like a fairground entertainer, with his fancy old-style clothes and a pair of circus animals for mounts. Like something from a variety show or a puppet theater."

Where we live, the horses were slaughtered and eaten a long time ago. And after the war, no one ever gave serious thought to getting new ones. The people of the village didn't want horses anymore. We preferred donkeys and mules. Real, beastly beasts, with nothing human about them and nothing to remind us of the past. And if someone was arriving on horseback, that necessarily meant that he had come from very far away and that he knew nothing about our region, or about what had happened here, or about our misfortunes.

It wasn't so much that riding a horse looked old-fashioned; after the war, we all seemed to go back in time. All the misery that the war had sown sprouted up like seeds in an auspicious spring. Farm implements from days gone by—including rickety buggies and patched-up carts—were brought out of barns and mended one way or another with whatever had not been destroyed or stolen. People still work their fields with plowshares forged more than a century ago. Haymaking is manual labor. Everyone's taken a few steps backward, as if human history has given man a violent kick in the ass and now we have to start over again almost from scratch.

The apparition was moving at a slow trot, looking (according to Beckenfür) left and right, stroking his mount's neck, and often speaking to the beast (Beckenfür could see his lips moving). The second animal, tied to the horse, was an old but still robust donkey with upright pasterns. It stepped surely, showing no sign of weakness and never swerving, even though it had three large and extremely heavy-looking trunks lashed to its back, as well as various sacks dangling down on either side, like strings of onions hung up in a kitchen.

"Finally, though it took a while, he got close to where I was standing. I thought he looked like some sort of genie, or maybe the *Teufeleuzeit* my father used to tell me about when I was a little boy and he wanted to scare the crap out of me. It lived in burrows all over the valley, among the foxes and the moles, and fed on lost children and fledglings. Anyway, the new arrival was wearing a strange, melon-shaped hat that looked as though it had been planed. He took it off and greeted me with great ceremony. Then he started dismounting from his horse, a pretty mare with a clean, shiny coat. An elegant, graceful animal, she was. He let himself slide down the side of her belly, very slowly, breathing hard and rubbing his own paunch, which was big and round. When he got his feet on the ground, he dusted off his operetta outfit, namely a kind of frock coat made of cloth and velvet, covered with crimson braids and other froufrous. He had a balloon for a face, with tight skin and red, red cheeks. The donkey groaned a little. The horse answered and shook her head, and that's when the odd fellow smiled and said, 'What magnificent country you live in, sir. Yes, truly magnificent country . . .'

"I figured he was pulling my leg. His animals hadn't moved—they were like their master, too polite. Right under their noses there was a lot of fine grass, but they didn't so much as give it a nudge. Other beasts would have had no problem grazing away, but they contented themselves with looking at each other and occasionally exchanging a few words, animal words. Then he pulled out a fancy little watch on a chain and seemed surprised at the time, which made his smile even broader. He nodded in the direction of the village and said, 'I must arrive before nightfall . . .'

"He didn't say the name of our village. He just moved his head in that direction. And then he didn't even wait for a reply. He knew very well where he was going. He knew! And really, that's the strangest part of the whole thing, the fact that he wasn't some hiker who got lost in the mountains, he was actually *trying* to get to our village. He came here on purpose!"

Beckenfür fell silent and drained his fifth glass of beer. Then he stared dully at the tabletop, whose nicks and scratches formed mysterious patterns. Outside the window, the snow was now falling steadily and straight down. At this rate, it could be piled up a meter high on the roofs and in the streets by morning. And then we, who were already on the margins of the world, would be still more completely cut off from it. That's often a terrible thing: For some people, isolation can lead only to fantastic ruminations, to a brain full of convoluted, unsound constructions. And when it comes to that game, I know many players who manage to perform some peculiar feats of mental architecture on snowy winter evenings.

VIII

The fact remains that the *Anderer* made a couple of calm remarks on that fateful spring day, smiling all the while, then got back on his horse, abandoned Gunther Beckenfür without another word, and continued on to the village. Beckenfür stood there for a long time, watching him go until he disappeared behind the Kölnke rocks.

But before he reached the village, he must necessarily have stopped somewhere. I've worked out the times, and there's a gap between the moment when Beckenfür lost the *Anderer* from sight and the instant when he passed through the village gate, at dusk, under the eyes of the eldest Dörfer boy, who was hanging about, reluctant to go home because his father was roaring drunk again and threatening to disembowel him. It's a gap that not even the indolent gait of the *Anderer*'s horse can sufficiently explain. Upon reflection, I think he stopped near the river, by the Baptisterbrücke, at the place where the road makes a curious winding turn in a field of grass as tender as a child's cheek. I can't see where else he might have gone. The view is very beautiful in that spot, and if someone doesn't know our region, that's the place where he can feel it like a piece of fabric, for from there he can see the roofs of the village, he can hear its sounds, and above all, he can be amazed by the river.

The Staubi isn't a watercourse that fits the landscape it's in. One would expect to find here a sluggish, meandering stream, overflowing and spreading out into the meadows and bogging down among the golden-headed buttercups; one would expect slow-moving algae, as soft as wet hair. Instead we have an impetuous, romping torrent, which hisses, cries, collides, churns up gravel, and wears down the rocks showing through its surface as it hurls water and foam into the air. The Staubi's a true, untamed mountain savage, clear and sharp as crystal; you can see the gray flashes of trout in its depths. Summer and winter, its water is cold enough to chill the inside of your skull, and occasionally, during the war, creatures other than fish were found floating in the river, blue creatures, some of them still looking a bit astonished, others with their eyes well closed, as if they'd been put to sleep by surprise and tucked into lovely liquid sheets.

From my conversations with him, I'm certain that the *Anderer* took the time to observe our river. Staubi—it's a funny name. It means nothing, not even in our dialect. No one knows where it came from. Diodemus himself, in all the pages that he read and rummaged through, failed to find its origin or its meaning. They're strange, names are. Sometimes you know nothing about them, and yet you're always saying them. Basically, they're like people: I mean like the ones whose paths you cross for years but never know, until one day, before your eyes, they reveal themselves to be what you would never have imagined them capable of being.

I don't know what the *Anderer* must have thought when he saw our roofs and our chimneys for the first time. He had arrived. His journey was over. He had reached his goal, which was our village and nowhere else. Beckenfür was the first to realize that, and later we all felt as he did. There was no mistake. Without any doubt, the *Anderer* came here of his own free will and deliberate choice, having prepared his adventure and brought along everything he would need. His coming was the result of no sudden impulse or passing fancy.

His calculations must have included even the hour of his arrival. An oblique hour, during which the light exalts things—the mountains that watch over our narrow valley, the forests, the pastures, the walls and gables, the hedgerows, the voices—and makes them more beautiful and more majestic. Not an hour of full daylight, yet sufficiently bright to give every event a unique sheen and the arrival of a stranger a distinct impact, in a village of four hundred souls already quite busy imagining things, even in ordinary times. And conversely, an hour which by the mere fact of its ongoing attachment to the dying day arouses curiosity, but not yet fear. Fear comes later, when the windows are down and the shutters closed, when the last log has slipped beneath the ashes, and when silence extends its realm over the inmost depths of every house.

I'm cold. My fingertips are like stones, hard and smooth. I'm in the shed behind my house, surrounded by abandoned planks, pots, seeds, balls of string, chairs in need of reseating—a great clutter of more or less decrepit things. This is where life's dross is piled up. And I'm here, too. I've come here of my own accord. I need to isolate myself so that I can try to put this terrible story into some semblance of order.

We've been in this house for nearly ten years. We left our cabin to come here after I'd managed to buy the place with the money saved from my salary and from the sale of Amelia's embroidery. When I signed my name to the act of sale, Lawyer Knopf vigorously shook both my hands. "Now you've really got a home

of your own, Brodeck. Never forget: a house is like a country."
Then he brought out some glasses and we drank a toast, he and
I, because the seller refused the drink the notary held out to him.
Rudolf Sachs was his name; he wore a monocle and white gloves
and had made a special trip from S. He looked down on us from
a great height, as if he lived on a white cloud and we wallowed in
liquid manure. The house had belonged to one of his great-
uncles, whom, as it happened, Sachs had never known.

The cabin had been given to us when we—Fedorine, her
cart, and I—first arrived in the village, more than thirty years
ago. We came from the ends of the earth. Our journey had lasted
for weeks, like an interminable dream. We'd traversed frontiers,
rivers, open country, mountain passes, towns, bridges, languages,
peoples, forests, and fields. I sat in the cart like a little sovereign,
leaning against the bundles and stroking the belly of the rabbit,
which never took its velvet eyes off me. Every day, Fedorine fed
me with bread, apples, and bacon, which she drew out of big blue
canvas sacks, and also with words; she slipped them into my ear,
and I had to let them out again through my mouth.

And then, one day, we arrived in the village which was to
become our village. Fedorine stopped the cart in front of the
church and told me to get out and stretch my legs. Back in those
days, people weren't yet afraid of strangers, even when they were
the poorest of the poor. The villagers gathered around us. Women
brought us food and drink. I remember the faces of the men who
insisted on pulling the cart and leading us to the cabin, declaring
that Fedorine had done enough. Then there was Father Peiper,
who was still young and full of energy, who still believed what he
said, and also the mayor, Sibelius Craspach, a former medical officer in the imperial army, now an old man with impressive white

mustachios and a beribboned ponytail. They settled us in the cabin and made it clear that we could stay there one night or several years. The main room contained a large black stove, a pine-wood bed, a wardrobe, a table, and three chairs; there was also a smaller, empty room. The wooden walls were the color of honey, soft and warm, and the cabin itself was warm as well. Sometimes at night, we could hear the murmur of the wind in the high branches of the nearby fir trees and the creaking of the wood caressed by the warm breath of the stove. I'd fall asleep thinking about squirrels and badgers and thrushes. It was Paradise.

Here, in the shed, I'm alone. It's no place for women, whether young or old. In the evening, the candles cast their fantastic shadows all around. The wooden beams play a dry music. I have the feeling that I'm very far away. I feel, perhaps mistakenly, that nothing can disturb or reach me here, that I'm safe from everyone and from all harm, completely safe, even though I'm in the heart of the village, surrounded by the others, and they're aware of everything about me, every deed I do, every breath I take.

I've placed the typewriter on Diodemus's table. After his death, Orschwir had everything Diodemus owned—his clothes, his few pieces of furniture, his novels—thrown away and burned, under the pretext that it was imperative to make a clean sweep in order to welcome the new teacher properly. Johann Lülli, a local boy, has replaced Diodemus as teacher. He's got one leg shorter than the other and a pretty wife who has borne him three children, the youngest of them still in swaddling clothes. Lülli isn't very knowledgeable, but he isn't an idiot, either. Before succeeding to his current position, he did the accounts for the mayor's office, and now he draws letters and numbers on a blackboard and makes children stammer out their lessons. He was present on the night of the *Ereigniës*. Among all those heads that were looking at me, I saw his red mane and his broad, square shoulders, which always look as though he forgot to remove the hanger when he put on his coat.

I didn't really need Diodemus's table, but I wanted to keep something of his, something he'd touched and used. His table's like him. Two handsome panels of polished walnut glued edge to edge and set on four simple legs, without airs or ornaments. A big drawer locked with a key, but I don't have the key. Nor have I been curious enough to break into the drawer to see if there's anything in it. When I shake the table a little, I hear no sound coming from inside. The drawer is clearly empty.

’m facing the back wall of the shed. The typewriter's on the table in front of me. It's very cold. My fingers are not alone in resembling stones; my nose, too, is as hard as a rock. I can't feel it anymore.

When I raise my eyes from my page, searching for words, I confront the wall, and then I tell myself that maybe I shouldn't have put the table against it. It has too much personality. It's too present. It speaks to me of the camp. I encountered a wall there much like this one.

When we arrived at the camp, the first stop for all of us was the *Büxte*—the "box." That's what the guards called the place, which was a little stone room, about a meter and a half by a meter and a half. Once inside it, you could neither stand up nor lie down.

They drove us out of the railway cars with clubs and a great deal of yelling. Then we had to run to the camp. Three kilometers of bad road, amid shouts and barking dogs, which sometimes bit as well. Those prisoners who fell were finished off at once, bludgeoned by the guards. We were weak; for six days, we had eaten nothing and drunk very little. Our bodies were stiff and numb. Our legs could hardly carry us.

The person toiling along at my side was a student, Moshe

Kelmar. We'd traveled to the camp in the same suffocating, crowded boxcar, talking for six days while the big metal vise we were in advanced at a snail's pace through countryside we couldn't even see, while our throats became as dry as straw at the end of August, and while the great mass of humanity around us moaned and wept. There was no air and no room. There were people of all ages in the car—old folks, little girls, young men and women. Very close to us, there was a young mother and her child of a few months. A very young mother and her tiny child. I shall remember them all my life.

Kelmar spoke Fedorine's language, the ancient tongue she had deposited in me, and it came back to my lips quite suddenly and without effort. He knew a great number of books, as well as the names of many flowers; although he'd always lived in the Capital, far from our village and far from the mountains, he even knew the valley periwinkle, which is a sort of legendary flower in our region. He'd never set foot in mountain country, a fact that troubled him exceedingly. He had a young woman's fingers, fine blond hair, and a delicate face. He was wearing a shirt that had been white, a shirt made of fine linen with an embroidered front, the kind you'd wear to a dance or a romantic rendezvous.

I asked him for news of the Capital, which I knew from my younger days, when I was a student. Back then, people from our province had to cross the border to go to the University. Even though it was located in the *Fratergekeime*'s capital city, our region had been connected to their country for so many years under the empire that we still felt at home there. Kelmar talked to me about the cafés where students went to drink hot wine and eat cinnamon cakes sprinkled with sesame seeds; about the Elsi Promenade, a walk around a pretty lake where in the summer you could invite girls to go boating and in the winter you could skate; about the main library on Glockenspiel Street, with its thousands of books in gilt bindings; and about the Stüpe canteen, where a fat woman named Fra Gelicke assumed the role of our mother, filling our plates with heaping servings of ragout and our bowls with sausage soup. But when I asked him about some of my very favorite places, Kelmar usually replied that he hadn't seen them for at least three years, ever since the day when he and all those designated as *Fremdër* were confined to the old part of the Capital, which had been transformed into a ghetto.

Inside the ghetto, however, there was a place he frequented and about which he talked at length, a place so dear to me that the simple fact of evoking it again today makes my heart beat faster and brings a smile to my soul: the minuscule Stüpispiel Theater, with its tiny stage and its mere four rows of seats. The shows put on there were doubtless the worst in the city, but tickets cost almost nothing, and on cold days in November and December, the little room was as warm and pleasant as a hayrick.

One evening, I went there with a comrade of mine named Ulli Rätte, a fellow student and a lover of the good life, whose constant laughter sounded like a cascade of copper pieces and who was crazy about an apprentice actress. This girl, a roundish brunette, was playing a minor role in a pointless farce. I had nearly dozed off when a young woman took a seat two places away from me. Her unseasonably light clothing showed that her chief reason for coming to the theater was the same as mine. She shivered a little. She resembled a small bird—a fragile, lively willow tit. Her pale pink lips were slightly parted in a smile. She breathed on her small hands, turned in my direction, and gazed at me. An old mountain song says that when love knocks at the door, everything else disappears and the door is all that remains. And so our eyes spoke for more than an hour, and we left the theater like a pair of robots; it took the cold outside to wrench us out of our dream. A bit of snow fell on our shoulders. I dared to ask her to tell me her name. She gave it to me, and it was the most precious of gifts. In the course of the night, I kept murmuring that name, saying it over and over again, as if repeating it endlessly were going to make its owner appear before me, the angel with the hazel eyes: "Amelia, Amelia, Amelia . . ."

Kelmar and I got out of the freight car at the same time. Like the others, we began to run, protecting our heads with our hands. The guards yelled. Some of them even managed to laugh as they yelled. You might have thought it was just a big comedy, but people were groaning and there was an odor of blood. Kelmar and I grew breathless. We were very hungry and very thirsty. Our legs were unsteady, our joints full of rust. We ran as best we could. The road went on and on. The morning began to drop its pale light on the fields around us, even though the sun had yet to appear in the sky. We passed a big, twisted oak, part of whose foliage had been scorched by lightning. It was shortly after that when Kelmar stopped running. All of a sudden.

"I won't go any farther, Brodeck," he said.

I told him he was crazy. The guards were going to catch up with us, I said, and then they would fall on him and kill him.

"I won't go any farther," he repeated. "I can't go on living with that . . . with what we did."

I tried to grab him by the sleeve and pull him along willynilly. He didn't budge. I pulled harder. A piece of his shirt remained in my hand. The guards, far off, had by now noticed something. They stopped talking and looked in our direction.

"Come on, come on, quick!" I begged him.

Kelmar calmly sat down in the middle of the dusty road. He said again, "I won't go any farther," very softly, very calmly, like someone speaking aloud a serious decision which he has pondered for a long time in the silence of his thoughts.

The guards started walking toward us, faster and faster, and then they began to shout.

"Kelmar," I murmured. "Kelmar, come on, get up, I beg you!"

He looked at me and smiled. "You'll think of me when you get back to your country, Brodeck. When you see the valley periwinkle, you'll think about the student Moshe Kelmar. And then you'll tell our story. All of it. You'll tell about the freight car, and about this morning. You'll tell the story for me, and you'll tell it for everyone else . . ."

The small of my back was suddenly aflame. A second truncheon blow cut my shoulder. Two guards were upon us, shouting and striking. Kelmar closed his eyes. A guard shoved me, bellowing at me to get moving. Another blow from his club split my lips. Blood ran into my mouth. I started to run again, weeping as I ran, not because of the pain but because I was thinking of Kelmar, who had made his choice. The shouting receded into the distance behind me. I turned around. The two guards were savaging him as he lay on the ground. His body rocked from right to left, like a poor puppet attacked by wicked boys intent on the fun of breaking its every joint. And some hideous shortcut in my mind brought me to the evening of *Pürische Nacht,* the Night of Purification.

I have never found the valley periwinkle in our mountains; I have, however, seen it in a book, a precious book. It's a low-growing flower, with deep-blue petals that appear to be fused shut, never really willing to open. But maybe it no longer grows anywhere. Maybe Nature decided to withdraw it permanently from the big catalogue and deprive humans of its beauty because they didn't deserve it anymore.

At the end of the road and the end of my run was the entrance to the camp: a large gate of handsomely worked wrought iron, like the entrance to a leisure park or a pleasure garden. There were two sentry boxes, one on either side, painted pink and bright green; the guards inside them stood stiff and straight, and above the gate was a large, gleaming hook, like a butcher's hook for suspending entire carcasses of beef. A man was hanging from the hook—his hands tied behind his back, a rope around his neck, his eyes wide open and bulging from their sockets, his tongue thick, swollen, protruding between his lips—a poor fellow who resembled us like a brother. His skinny chest bore a placard, on which someone had written in their language, the language of the *Fratergekeime* (which in the old days was the double of our dialect, its twin sister), ICH BIN NICHTS, "I am nothing." The wind made his body sway a little. Not far away, three crows watched and waited, craving his eyes like sweetmeats.

Every day a man was hanged like that at the entrance to the camp. When we got up in the morning, each of us thought that perhaps today it would be his turn. The guards rousted us out of the huts where we slept in heaps on the bare ground and lined us up outside. We stood and waited like that for a long time, whatever the weather; we waited for them to choose one of us as that day's victim. Sometimes the choice was made in three seconds. On other occasions they rolled dice or played cards, with us as the stakes. And we had to stand there, close to them, and wait, unmoving, in perfect ranks. Their games went on and on, and in the end, the winner had the privilege of making his choice. He walked though our ranks. We held our breath. Everyone tried to make himself as insignificant as possible. The guard took his time. Eventually, he stopped in front of a prisoner, touched him with the end of his stick, and simply said, *"Du."* The rest of us, all the rest of us, felt a mad joy welling up in the depths of our hearts, an ugly happiness that would endure only until the following day, until the new ceremony, but which allowed us to hold on, to keep holding on.

The *"Du"* walked off with the guards, who escorted him to the gate. They made him climb a stepladder to the hook. They made him detach the previous day's hanged man, carry him down on his back, dig a grave for him, and bury him in it. Then the guards made the new victim put on the placard with the words ICH BIN NICHTS, looped the rope around his neck, made him climb to the top of the ladder, and waited for the arrival of the *Zeilenesseniss.*

Die Zeilenesseniss was the camp commandant's wife. She was young and moreover inhumanly beautiful, with a beauty composed of excessive blondness and excessive whiteness. She often went walking inside the camp, and we were ordered under pain of death never to meet her eyes.

The *Zeilenesseniss* never missed the morning hanging. She approached the gate slowly, fresh-faced, her cheeks still ruddy from pure water, soap, and cream. Sometimes the wind carried her scent to us, a scent of wisteria, and ever since then, I can't smell the fragrance of wisteria without retching and weeping. She wore clean clothes. She was impeccably dressed and coiffed, and as for us, standing a few meters away from her—eaten by the vermin in the rags we wore, which no longer had either shape or color, our bodies filthy and stinking, our skulls shaved and scabby, our bones threatening to poke through every square inch of our skin—we belonged to a different world from hers.

She never came alone. She always carried an infant in her arms, a baby boy a few months old swathed in gay clothes. She gently rocked the child, whispering in his ear or humming the melody of some nursery song. I remember one of them: *"Welt, Welt von licht / Manns hanger auf all recht / Welt, Welt von licht / Ô mein kinder so wet stillecht"*—"World, world of light / Man's hand on everything / World, world of light / Be still, my child, my king."

The baby was always calm when they arrived. He never cried. If he was asleep, she would awaken him with small, patient, infinitely tender gestures, and only when he opened his eyes at last, waved his little arms, wiggled his little thighs, and yawned at the sky would she signal to the guards, with a simple movement of her chin, that the ceremony could start. One of them would give the stepladder a mighty kick and the body of the *"Du"* would drop, his fall quickly ended by the rope. The *Zeilenesseniss* watched him for a few minutes, and as she did so a smile came to her lips. She missed nothing and observed everything: the jumps and jolts, the throaty noises, the outthrust, kicking feet, vainly searching for the ground, the expulsive sound of the bowels emptying them-selves, and the final immobility, the great silence. At this point, sometimes the child cried a little, I daresay not so much from fright as from hunger and the desire to be suckled, but in any case his mother planted a long kiss on his forehead and calmly left the scene. The three crows took up their positions. I don't know whether or not they were the same three every day. They all looked alike. So did the guards, but they didn't peck out our eyes;

they contented themselves with our lives. Like her. Like the commandant's wife. The one we privately called the *Zeilenesseniss. Die Zeilenesseniss:* "the Woman Who Eats Souls."

In the aftermath, I've often thought about that child, her child. Did he die like her? Is he still alive? If he's alive, he must be about my little Poupchette's age. How has he turned out, that little one, who for months was nourished each morning on the warm milk from his mother's breasts and the spectacle of hundreds of men hanged before his eyes? What does he dream about? What words does he use? Does he still smile? Has he gone mad? Has he forgotten everything, or does his young mind return to the juddering movements of bodies nearing death, to the strangled groans, to the tears running down hollow gray cheeks? To the birds' harsh cries?

During my first days in the camp, when I was in the *Büxte,* I talked to Kelmar constantly, as if he were alive at my side. The *Büxte* was a windowless dungeon cell. The scant light of day came in under the big, iron-bound oaken door. If I opened my eyes, I saw the wall. If I closed my eyes, I saw Kelmar, and behind him, farther off, much farther off, Amelia, her sweet, narrow shoulders, and farther still, Fedorine, weeping and gently shaking her head.

I don't know how long I remained in the *Büxte* with those three faces and that wall. A long time, no doubt. Weeks, perhaps months. But be that as it may, over there, in the camp, days, weeks, and months meant nothing. Time didn't count.

Time didn't exist anymore.

—————

I'm still in the shed. I'm having trouble calming down. About half an hour ago, I thought I heard a funny sound coming from near the door, a sound like scraping. I stopped typing and listened closely. Nothing. I held my breath for a long time. No more sound. However, I was sure I'd heard something, and it wasn't my imagination, because the sound started again a little later, only now it wasn't near the door, it was along the wall. The sound moved slowly, very slowly, as if it were crawling. I blew out the candle, spun the page out of the typewriter, and stuffed what I'd written inside my shirt. Then I curled up in a corner behind some tools, near an old crate filled with cabbages and turnips. The sound hadn't stopped. It was still moving, slowly but steadily, sliding along the walls of the shed.

This went on for a long time. Sometimes the sound stopped for a while and then started again. It moved around the perimeter of the shed, always advancing at the same slow pace. As I listened to it turning around me, I felt that I was caught in an invisible vise, and that an equally invisible hand was closing on me, slowly but surely.

The sound traveled along each of the four walls, making a complete circuit around the shed and returning to the door. In the most absolute silence, I watched the metal door handle pivot downward. I thought about all the tales that Fedorine knows by heart, stories in which objects speak, châteaux cross mountains and plains in a single night, queens sleep for a thousand years, trees change into noble lords, roots spring from the earth and strangle people, and springs have the power to heal festering wounds and soothe overwhelming grief.

The door opened, just barely, in the unbroken silence. I tried to shrink deeper into the corner, to envelop myself in darkness. I could see nothing. And I couldn't hear my heart anymore. It was as if it had stopped beating, as if it too were waiting for something to happen. A hand took hold of the door and opened it wide. The moon stuck its face between two clouds. Göbbler's body and bumpkinish head were outlined in the doorway. I was reminded of the silhouettes that street vendors in the Capital used to cut out; they worked in the big Albergeplatz market, scissoring smoke-blackened paper into the shapes of gnomes or monsters.

A gust of wind rushed through the open doorway, carrying the scent of frozen snow. Göbbler stood unmoving, searching the shadows. I didn't budge. I knew that he couldn't see me where I was, nor for that matter could I see him, but I smelled his odor, an odor of henhouse and damp fowl.

"Not gone to bed yet, Brodeck? You won't answer me? But I know you're there. I saw the light under your door, and I heard the typewriter . . ."

In the darkness, his voice took on some odd intonations. "I'm watching you, Brodeck," he said. "Be careful!"

The door closed again, and Göbbler's silhouette disappeared. For several seconds, I could hear his retreating footsteps. I imagined his heavy greased-leather boots and their muddy soles leaving dirty brown marks on the thin layer of snow.

I stayed in my corner, unmoving, for a good while. I breathed as little as I could and told my heart to calm down. I spoke to it as one speaks to an animal.

Outside, the wind began to blow harder. The shed started shaking. I was cold. All of a sudden, my fear gave way to anger. What did that chicken merchant want with me? And what was he up to, anyway? Did *I* watch *his* movements, or spy on his fat wife? Had he barged into my house without knocking just to make a few veiled threats? By what right? The fact that he'd joined the others in their awful deed didn't make him a judge! The one real innocent among them all was me! It was me! The only one! The only one . . .

The only one.

Yes, I was the only one.

As I said those words to myself, I suddenly heard how dangerous they sounded; to be innocent in the midst of the guilty was, after all, the same as being guilty in the midst of the innocent. Then it occurred to me to wonder why, on that famous night—the night of the *Ereigniës*—all the men of the village were in Schloss's inn at the same time; all the men except me. I had never thought about that before. I'd never thought about it because until then I'd told myself, quite naïvely, that I was lucky not to have been there, and I'd let it go at that. But they couldn't all have just happened to decide, at the same time, to go over to the inn for a glass of wine or a mug of beer. If they were all there, it must have been because they had an appointment. An appointment from which I had been excluded. Why? *Why?*

Another cold shiver ran over me. I was still in the dark: in the dark inside the shed, and in the dark about my question. And all at once the memory of the first day started bouncing around in my head like a saw in wood too green to cut. The day of my return from the camp, at the end of my long march, when I finally entered the streets of our village.

The faces of all those I encountered that day appeared before my mind's eye: first, at the gate, the two Glacker girls—the older one, with a head like a garden dormouse, and her younger sister, whose eyes are buried in fat; then, in the narrow street that leads to the pressing sheds, Gott the blacksmith, his arms covered with red fur; in front of her café at the corner of Unteral Lane, old lady Fülltach; near the Bieder fountain, Ketzenwir, hauling on a rope attached to a sick cow; at the entrance to the covered market, holding his belly in his hands and talking to Prossa the forester, Otto Mielk, who when he saw my ghostly self opened his mouth so wide that his crooked little cigar dropped from his lips; and then all the others, some of whom emerged from their walls as though from their graves and formed a circle around me, surrounding me without speaking all the way to my house; and, especially, those who quickly withdrew into their own houses and shut their doors, as if I had come back carrying a full load of trouble or hate or vengeance, which I intended to scatter into the air like cold ashes.

I could paint them, those faces, if I had colors and brushes and the *Anderer*'s talent. Most of all, I'd want to paint their eyes, in which at the time I read only surprise. Now that I seem to know them better, I realize that they contained a great many things; they were like the ponds that summer leaves behind in the drained peat bogs in Trauerprinz glade, which harbor all manner of aggressive rot, tiny grinders ready to chew to bits anything that might hinder them from accomplishing their narrow destiny.

I had recently returned from the bowels of the earth. I was

lucky to get out of the *Kazerskwir* alive, to climb up out of that pit, and every step I took away from it had seemed like a resurrection. My body, however, was the body of a dead man. In the places I passed through on the long road back, children fled weeping at the sight of me, as if they had seen the devil, while men and women came out of their houses and approached me, turning in circles around me, almost touching me. Some gave me bread, a bit of cheese, a roasted potato, but others treated me like a wicked thing, throwing pebbles and spitting at me and calling me filthy names. None of that was anything compared to what I had left behind. I knew that I had come from too far away for them, and it wasn't a matter of mere kilometers. I came from a country which had no existence in their minds, a country which had never appeared on any map, a country no tale had ever evoked, a country which had sprung from the earth and flourished for a few months, but whose memory was destined to weigh heavily for centuries.

How I was able to walk so far, to trample all those paths under my bare feet, I couldn't say. Perhaps quite simply because, without knowing it, I was already dead. Yes, maybe I was dead like the others in the camp, like all the others, but I didn't know it, I didn't want to know it; and maybe by refusing I'd managed to elude the gatekeepers of the Underworld, the real Underworld, who had such a multitude arriving just then that they'd allowed me to turn back, telling themselves that, after all, I was bound to return sooner or later and take my place in the great cohort.

I walked and walked and walked. I walked to Amelia. I was heading for her. I was going home. I never stopped repeating to myself that I was going home to her. Her face was on the horizon, her sweetness, her laugh, her skin, her voice of velvet and gravel, and her accent, which gave each of her words a certain awkwardness; when she spoke, she was like a child who stumbles on a stone, nearly falls, regains its balance, and bursts out laughing. There was also her fragrance, a scent of infinite air, of moss and sun. I spoke to her as I walked. I told her I was coming home. Amelia. My Amelia.

To be fair, I must point out that not all those whom I met on my long road treated me like a stray dog or a plague-stricken beggar. There was also the old man.

One evening, I came to a small town on the other side of the border, in the land of the *Fratergekeime,* in their country, a place which had been strangely spared, and where all the houses were still standing, still intact: no holes, no yawning gaps, no collapsed roofs, no burned barns. The sturdy, well-preserved church overlooked the little cemetery spread out at its feet between some carefully tended vegetable gardens and an alley lined with lime trees. None of the shops had been pillaged in any way. The town hall was unharmed, and some pretty cows with brown coats and peaceful eyes were silently drinking from the troughs of the big fountains, while the boy in charge of the beasts, which were on their way to the milking shed, played with a red wooden top.

The old man was sitting on a bench set against the façade of one of the last houses on the way out of town. He seemed to be sleeping, his hands resting on a holly-wood cane and his pipe gone out. A felt hat covered up half of his face. I'd already passed him when I heard him call me. He had a slow voice, a voice very like a brotherly hand placed on a shoulder: "Come . . . come here . . ."

For a moment, I thought I'd dreamed his voice. Then he said, "Yes, I'm talking to you, young man!"

That was a funny thing for him to call me, "young man." I even felt an urge to smile. But I didn't know how to smile anymore. The muscles of my mouth, my lips, and my eyes had forgotten how to do it, and my broken teeth hurt.

I was no longer a young man. I had aged several centuries in the camp. I had exhausted the topic. But the longer we prisoners labored in our strange apprenticeship, the more our bodies melted away. I had left home as round as a ball, but in the camp I watched as my skin got closer and closer to my bones. In the end, we all looked the same. We'd become shadows, each of us indistinguishable from the rest. We could be mistaken for one another. A couple of us could be eliminated every day, because a couple of others could be added immediately, and no one could tell the difference. The camp was always occupied by the same silhouettes and the same bony faces. We weren't ourselves anymore. We didn't belong to ourselves anymore. We weren't men anymore. We were all of the same sort.

XI

The old man ushered me into his house, which smelled of cool stones and hay. He pointed to a handsome, polished sideboard and told me to drop my bundle there. To tell the truth, it didn't contain very much: two or three tattered rags I'd extracted one morning from the ashes of a barn, and a piece of blanket that still smelled like fire.

In the front room, which was very low-ceilinged and completely covered with fir paneling, a round table stood ready, as if I'd been expected. Two places had been laid, facing each other over a cotton tablecloth, and in a terra-cotta vase there was a bouquet of fragile, touching wildflowers, which moved at the least breath of air, spreading fragrances that were like memories of perfumes.

At that moment, with a mixture of sadness and joy, I remembered the student Kelmar, but the old man put a hand on my shoulder and, with a little movement of his chin, signed to me that I should sit. "You need a good meal and a good night's sleep," he said. "Before my servant left, she cooked a rabbit with herbs and a quince pie. They've been waiting just for you."

He went to the kitchen and came back with the rabbit, arranged on a green earthenware platter and garnished with carrots, red onions, and branches of thyme. I couldn't manage to move or say a word. The old man stepped to my side and served me copiously, then cut a thick slice of white bread for me and poured some limpid water into my glass. I wasn't completely sure whether I was sitting in that house or lost in one of the numerous pleasant dreams that used to visit me at night in the camp.

My host sat down across from me. "If you don't mind, I'm not going to join you—at my age, one eats very little. But do please start."

He was the first man in a long time who addressed me as if I were a man, too. Tears began to flow from my eyes. My first tears in a long time, as well. I clutched the seat of my chair with both hands, as if trying to keep from falling into the void. I opened my mouth and tried to say something, but I couldn't.

"Don't speak," he said. "I'm not asking any questions. I don't know exactly where you've come from, but I think I can guess."

I felt like a child. I made awkward, rash, incoherent gestures. He looked at me kindly. Forgetting my broken teeth, I fell upon the food the way I did in the camp when the guards threw me a cabbage stalk, a potato, or a bread crust. I consumed the whole rabbit, gobbled up the bread, licked my plate, devoured the pie. I still carried inside of me the fear that someone might steal my food if I ate it too slowly. My stomach felt full, as it had not done for months and months, and it hurt. I had the feeling that I was going to explode and die in that lovely house, under my host's benevolent gaze; die from having eaten too much after being nearly dead from hunger.

When I'd finished cleaning plate and platter with my tongue and picking up the scattered crumbs from the table with my fingertips, the old man showed me to my room. There a wooden tub filled with hot soapy water was waiting for me. My host un-dressed me, helped me step into the tub, sat me down, and bathed me. The water ran over my skin, which no longer had any color, my skin, which stank of filth and suffering, and the old fellow washed my body without repugnance and with a father's tender-ness.

The next day, I woke up in a high, mahogany bed between fresh, starched, embroidered sheets that smelled like wind. On all the walls of the room, there were engraved portraits of men wear-ing mustaches and jabots; a few of them were in military attire. They all looked at me without seeing me. The softness of the bed had made my whole body ache. Getting up was difficult. Look-ing through the window, I could see the well-kept fields border-ing the village; some of them were already sown, and in others, which were still being plowed, teams of oxen pulled harrows that gouged and aerated the soil. The earth in those fields was black and light, quite the opposite of ours, which is red and as sticky as glue. The sun was close to the horizon, its jagged line broken by poplars and birches. But what I took for dawn turned out to be dusk. I had slept all night and all day, sunk in a deep sleep with-out dreams or interruptions. I felt heavy, but at the same time re-lieved of a burden whose contents I couldn't have described with any precision.

Clean clothes had been laid out on a chair for me, along with some walking shoes of supple, strong leather, shoes meant to last forever. (I still wear them; they're on my feet as I write.) When I finished dressing, I saw a man in the mirror looking at me, a man whom I seemed to have known in another life.

My host was sitting outside on the bench in front of his house, as he'd been doing on the previous day. He was smoking a pipe, sending a pleasant smell of honey and ferns into the evening air. He invited me to sit at his side. I realized then that I hadn't yet spoken a single word to him. "I'm Brodeck," I said.

He took a stronger pull on his pipe. For an instant, his face disappeared in the fragrant smoke, and then he repeated, very softly, "Brodeck . . . Brodeck . . . I'm very glad you accepted my invitation. I suspect you still have a long journey ahead of you before you reach home."

I didn't know what to say to him. I'd lost the habit of words and the habit of thoughts.

The old man spoke again. "Don't be offended," he said, "but sometimes it's best not to go back where you came from. You remember what you left, but you never know what you're going to find there, especially when madness has raged in men for a long time. You're still young . . . Think about that."

He scratched a match on the stone bench and relit his pipe. By that time, the sun had definitively fallen to the other side of the world. All that remained of its light were reddish traces, spreading like scribbles of fire and licking along the borders of the fields. Above our heads, floods of ink were drowning the pale sky. A few bright stars already shone through the blackness, between the streaks of the last swifts and the first bats.

"Someone's waiting for me." It was all I could manage to say.

The old man slowly shook his head. I successfully repeated myself, but I didn't say who was waiting for me; I didn't say Amelia's name. I had kept it closed inside me for so long that I was afraid to let it go, afraid it might get lost out in the open.

I stayed in his house for four days, sleeping like a dormouse and eating like a lord. The old man looked upon me kindly as I ate and served me second helpings, though he himself never swallowed a thing. Sometimes he remained silent; sometimes he made conversation. It was a one-sided conversation, with him doing all the talking, but he seemed to enjoy his monologues, and as for me, I took a curious pleasure in letting myself be surrounded by his words. Thanks to them, I felt I was returning to the language, the language behind which there lay, prostrate, weak, and still sick, a humanity that needed only to heal.

Having regained some of my strength, I decided to leave one morning, very early, while the sun was rising and the smells of young grass and dew rose with it and invited themselves into the house. My hair, which was growing back in patches, gave me the look of a convalescent who'd survived a disease no physician could have identified with any precision. I still had a lemony complexion, and my eyes were sunk very deep in their sockets.

The previous evening, I'd told the old man that I was thinking about continuing on my way, and he was waiting for me on his threshold. He handed me a gray canvas sack with leather shoulder straps. It contained two large round loaves of bread, a slab of bacon, a sausage, and some clothes. "Take them," he said. "They're just your size. They belonged to my son, but he won't be coming back. It's probably better so."

The sack I'd just taken hold of suddenly seemed very heavy. The old man extended his hand to me. "Have a good journey, Brodeck."

For the first time, his voice shook. So did his hand, which I clasped: a dry, cold, spotted hand that crumpled in my palm. "Please," he said. "Forgive him . . . forgive them . . ." And his voice died, dwindling into a murmur.

XII

It's been at least five days since I left off writing this account. And then, a short while ago, when I took out the packet of pages I keep in a corner of the shed, some of them already had a bit of dirt and a yellow dust like pollen on them. I'm going to have to find a gentler hiding place.

The others suspect nothing. They're convinced that I'm busy putting together the Report they asked me to write; they think I'm entirely absorbed by my task. The fact that Göbbler found me in my shed very late the other evening has worked in my favor. When I met Orschwir, quite by chance, in the street the following morning, he put his hand on my shoulder and said, "It seems you're working hard, Brodeck. Keep it up." Then he went on his way. It was very early. And I paused to reflect: despite the early hour, Orschwir has already been informed that at midnight I was in my shed, tapping on the typewriter keys. My reflections were interrupted by his voice, which came to my ears again through the freezing dawn mist: "By the way, Brodeck, where are you going with that sack in this weather?" I stopped. Orschwir watched me steadily as he seized both sides of his fur cap and pulled it down a little lower on his head. When he pounded his hands together to warm himself, big streams of vapor surged out of his mouth and rose in the air.

"Am I obligated from now on to answer any question anybody asks me?"

Orschwir produced a small smile, but his smiles greatly resemble grimaces. Then he shook his head slowly, very slowly, as he had done when I went to see him on the day after the *Ereigniës*. "Brodeck, you wound me. It was a friendly question. Why do you feel you must be on your guard?"

My breath failed me, but I was able to shrug my shoulders, in a way I tried to make as natural as possible. Then I said, "I'm going to see what I can figure out about the foxes. I have to write up a small report on them, too."

While Orschwir weighed what I had said, he cast several glances at my sack, as if attempting to see what was inside it.

"The foxes? Ah, right . . . the foxes. Well, have a good day, Brodeck. Better not go too far from the village, though. And . . . keep me informed," he said. Then he turned his back to me and continued on his way.

Two weeks or so previously, several hunters and foresters had told me about the foxes. While beating the woods to flush game on one of the first hunts of the season or cutting wood in the forest or simply coming and going, many of them had found dead foxes: young and old, males and females. At first, each of those who came upon the fox carcasses thought they'd died of rabies, which appears regularly in our mountains, does a little killing, and disappears. But none of the dead animals that were found showed any of the characteristic signs of the disease: tongue covered with white froth, pronounced thinness, eyes rolled back, coat dull and matted. On the contrary, the dead foxes were superb specimens and seemed to have been well nourished and in full health. At my request, Brochiert, the butcher, opened up three of them. Their bellies were filled with berries, beechnuts, mice, birds, and green worms. The foxes' unmarked, unwounded bodies gave no indication of a struggle, so it appeared that they had not died violent deaths. And all the men who found the dead animals had been surprised at their position: lying on their side or on their back, with their forepaws extended as if they were about to take hold of something. Their eyes were closed, and they seemed to be sleeping peacefully.

When I first heard about this, I paid a visit to Ernst-Peter Limmat, who was the principal of the village school for two generations of pupils, including me. He's over eighty now and hardly ever leaves his house anymore, but time hasn't been able to dent or damage his brain. He spends most of his time sitting in a high-backed chair in front of his hearth, where a fragrant fire redolent of fir and hornbeam is always burning. He watches the flames, rereads the books in his library, smokes tobacco, and roasts chestnuts, which he then peels with his long, elegant fingers. When I visited him, he gave me a big handful of chestnuts, and after blowing on them, we ate them in small pieces, savoring their hot, oily flesh, while my drenched jacket dried by the fire.

Besides having taught hundreds of children to read and write, Ernst-Peter Limmat was without a doubt the greatest hunter and woodsman in our region. With his eyes closed, he could draw an accurate and detailed map of every forest, every boulder, every mountain crest, and every stream for many kilometers around.

In former days, when class was over, he would take a hike, greatly preferring the company of the tall firs, the birds, and the springs to the company of men. If school happened to be closed during hunting season, he'd sometimes disappear for days on end. We'd see him coming back, his eyes gleaming with pleasure and his game bag filled with grouse, pheasant, and fieldfare; occasionally he had a chamois slung across his shoulders, a beast he'd tracked all the way to the sheer rocks of the Hörni, where in the past more than one hunter had broken his bones.

The oddest thing about Limmat was that he never ate what he killed; he distributed his game among the neediest of the village. When I was little, it was thanks to him that Fedorine and I had meat to eat now and then. As for Limmat himself, he ate nothing but vegetables, clear broths, eggs, trout, and mushrooms; among these last, his decided preference was for the ones called "trumpets of death." One day he told me that this type was the monarch of mushrooms, and that its sinister look served merely to repel fools and discourage the ignorant. Trumpets of death always adorned the inside of his house, hanging down everywhere in long garlands, and as they dried they filled the place with a smell of licorice and manure. He'd never married. A servant named Mergrite lived with him, a woman very nearly his own age; in the old days, wicked tongues used to say she surely did more than wash his clothes and polish his furniture.

I told him about the fox mystery, about the discoveries of the numerous carcasses, about their peaceful appearance. He searched his memory in vain, unable to recall any precedents, but he promised to consult his books assiduously and report back to me should he discover any references to similar cases in regions other than ours or in other times. Then our conversation turned to the winter, which was approaching with rapid strides, and to the snow, which was encroaching on the village from higher ground, slowly but surely descending the slopes of the mountains and the sides of the valley, and would soon be arriving outside our doors.

Like all the other old men, Limmat had been absent from Schloss's inn on the night of the *Ereigniës,* and I wondered if he'd been informed of what had happened. I wasn't even sure whether he'd known or been told about the *Anderer's* presence in our village. I would certainly have liked to talk to him about the affair and get it off my chest.

"I'm delighted to see you haven't forgotten your old teacher, Brodeck," he said. "Indeed, I'm touched. Do you remember when you first came to school? I remember your arrival very well. You looked like a skinny dog, with eyes too big for the rest of you. And you spoke a gibberish only you and Fedorine understood. But you learned fast, Brodeck, very fast. Not just our language; the rest, too."

Mergrite came in, bringing two glasses of hot wine. It smelled of pepper, orange, cloves, and anise. She added two logs to the fire, sending showers of bright sparks into the darkness, and then disappeared.

"You weren't like the others, Brodeck," my old schoolteacher went on. "And I don't say that because you weren't from here, because you came from far away. You weren't like the others because you always looked beyond things . . . You always wanted to see what didn't exist."

He fell silent, cracked open a chestnut, slowly ate it, drank a mouthful of wine, and threw the pieces of nutshell into the fire. "I'm thinking about your foxes again. The fox is an odd animal, you know. We say foxes are sly, but in fact, they're a lot more than that. Man has always hated foxes, doubtless because they're a little too much like him. Foxes hunt for food, but they're also capable of killing just for the fun of it."

Limmat paused for a while and then began to speak again, in a pensive voice: "So many people have died these last years, in the war, as you know better than anyone in the village, alas. Maybe the foxes are only imitating us, who knows?"

I didn't dare tell my old teacher that I couldn't put that sort of thing in my account. The officials in the administration who read what I write—if what I write is read at all anymore—would understand nothing, and perhaps they'd think I'd gone mad and decide to do without my services altogether, in which case the paltry sums I receive so irregularly, the money my family lives on, would stop coming to me at all.

I stayed a little longer in his company. We spoke no more about foxes but about a beech tree which some woodcutters had recently felled—because it was sick—on the far side of the Bösenthal. According to them, the tree had to be more than four centuries old. Limmat reminded me that in other climates, on distant continents, there were trees that could live two thousand years. He'd already taught me that when I was a child, and at the time, I thought that God, if he existed, must be quite a strange character, who chooses to allow trees to live peacefully for centuries but makes man's life so brief and so hard.

After presenting me with two garlands of trumpets of death and walking me to his threshold, Ernst-Peter Limmat asked me for news of Fedorine, and then, more gently, more gravely, he inquired about Amelia and Poupchette.

The rain hadn't stopped, but now some heavy flakes of wet

snow were mingled with it. A little stream flowed down the middle of the street, making the sandstone cobbles gleam. The cold air smelled good, a combination of smoke and moss and undergrowth. I thrust the dried mushrooms into my jacket and went back home.

I asked Mother Pitz the same question about the foxes. Her memory isn't as good as the old teacher's, and she's surely not the expert he is on the subject of game animals and pests, but back in the days when she used to drive her beasts to and from the mountain pastures, she covered all the local roads, side paths, and stubble fields so thoroughly that I hoped she might be able to provide some sort of explanation. By tallying all the figures reported by my various sources, I'd arrived at a total of eighty foxes found dead—a considerable figure, if you think about it. Unfortunately, the old woman had no memory of ever having heard of such a phenomenon, and in the end I realized that she couldn't possibly care less about it. "I'll be glad if they all croak!" she declared. "Last year, they carried off my three hens and all their chicks. And then, they didn't even eat them! They just ripped them to shreds and disappeared. Your foxes are *Scheizznegetz'zohns,* 'sons of the damned.' They're not even worth the blade of the knife that slits their throats."

In order to speak to me, she'd interrupted a conversation with Frida Niegel, a magpie-eyed hunchback who always smells like a stable. She and Mother Pitz love to review all the widows and widowers in the village and the surrounding hamlets and imagine possible remarriages. They write the names on little pieces of cardboard, and for hours, like cardplayers, with mounting excitement they arrange and rearrange the deck into pairs, conjuring up wedding celebrations and mended destinies, all the while drinking little glasses of mulberry liqueur. I could see that I was disturbing their concentration.

In the end, I concluded that the only person who could possibly shed light on the matter was Marcus Stern, who lives alone in the middle of the forest, an hour's walk from the village. He was the person I was off to see on the morning when I ran into Orschwir.

XIII

The path that leads to Stern's cabin begins its steep climb almost as soon as you exit the village. You enter the woods, go around a few hairpin curves, and in no time at all you're looking down at the roofs. At the halfway point on the path, a rock shaped like a table invites the hiker to take a break. The rock is called the *Lingen,* from the dialect name of the little woodland sprites that are said to gather there and dance on it by moonlight, singing their songs, which sound like muffled laughter. Here and there on the broad rock, small cushions of milky green moss soften its hard surface, and heather provides bouquets of flowers. It's a fine place for lovers and dreamers. I remember seeing the *Anderer* there one day in high summer—on July 8, in fact (I make a note of everything)—around three o'clock in the afternoon, that is, in the very hottest part of the day, when the sun seemed to have stopped its course across the sky and was pouring its heat like molten lead on the world. I had gone there to pick some raspberries for my little Poupchette, who's crazy about them. I wanted to surprise her when she woke up from her afternoon nap.

The forest was alive and humming with busy bees and darting wasps, with frenzied flies and horseflies buzzing around in every direction, as if seized by a sudden madness. It was a great symphony, which seemed to arise out of the ground and emerge from the air. In the village, I hadn't come across a living soul.

Although brief, the climb unsteadied my legs and winded me. My shirt was already soaked through, covered with dust, and sticking to my skin. I stopped on the path to catch my breath, and that was when I noticed him: a few meters away from where I stood, his back turned to me, there was the *Anderer,* contemplating the roofs of the village from a position on the rock. He was sitting on his strange, portable seat, which had been an object of fascination for everyone the first time we saw him deploy it. It was a folding stool, big and sturdy enough to support his ample buttocks, but when collapsed and stashed away, it looked like a simple cane.

In that landscape, all greenery and bright yellow, his dark clothing, his eternal, impeccably ironed black cloth frock coat, cast a shadow that looked out of place. Drawing a little closer to him, I noticed that he was also wearing his ruffled shirt, his woolen waistcoat, and gaiters on his heavy, highly polished shoes, which reflected light like the shards of a mirror.

Some twigs cracked under my feet, and he turned in my direction and saw me. I looked, I have no doubt, like a thief, but he didn't seem startled. He smiled at me, raising his right hand and doffing an imaginary hat in a gesture of greeting. He had very pink cheeks, and the rest of his countenance—forehead, chin, nose—was covered with white lead. With the black curls on either side of his balding skull providing the final touch, he looked like an old actor. Great drops of perspiration ran down his face, which he mopped with a handkerchief whose embroidered monogram I couldn't read.

"May I assume that you have also come here to take the

measure of the world?" he asked me in his soft, mellifluous, mannered voice, gesturing at the countryside spread out before us. Then I noticed that an open notebook was lying across his perfectly round knees and that he was holding a graphite pencil in one hand. There were straight lines and curving lines and shadowed areas sketched on the notebook page. When he realized what I was looking at, he closed the book and put it in his pocket.

It was the first time I'd been alone with him since his arrival in the village, and also the first time he'd ever spoken to me. "Would you be so kind as to render me a service?" he asked, and since I made no reply and my face no doubt hardened a little, he went on, flashing the enigmatic smile that was never far from his lips. "Nothing to worry about. I simply hoped you might tell me the names of all these heights that enclose the valley. I fear that my maps may be inaccurate."

And accompanying his words with a sweep of his hand, he indicated the mountains outlined in the distance, shimmering in the torpor of that summer day. Parts of them almost blended into the sky, which seemed intent on dissolving them. I stepped over to him, knelt down to be on his level, and starting from the east, I began to give the names: "This one, the one closest to us, is the Hunterpitz, so called because its profile looks like a dog's head. Next you have the three Schnikelkopfs, then the Bronderpitz, and after that the ridge of the Hörni mountains, with its highest point, which is Hörni peak. Then there's the Doura pass, the crest of the Florias, and finally, due west, the peak of the Mausein, which is shaped like a man bent over and carrying a load on his back."

I stopped speaking. He finished writing the names in his notebook, which he had taken out of his pocket, but which he very quickly put away again. "I'm infinitely grateful to you," he said, warmly shaking my hand. A gleam of satisfaction brightened his big green eyes, as if I'd just presented him with a treasure. As I was about to leave him, he added, "I understand that you are interested in flowers and herbs. We are alike, the two of us. I am fond of landscapes, forms, portraits. Quite an innocent vice, aside from its other charms. I have brought with me some rather rare books that I believe you would find interesting. I should be delighted to show them to you, if one day you would honor me with a visit."

I nodded my head slightly but made no other response. I'd never heard him talk so much. I went away and left him on the rock.

"And you gave him all the names!?" Wilhem Vurtenhau raised his arms to heaven and glared at me. He'd just come into Gustav Röppel's hardware store, at the moment when I was relating my encounter with the *Anderer,* some hours after it had taken place. Gustav was a comrade of mine. We were bench mates in school, sitting side by side, and when we were working out problems, I'd often let him see the solutions in my exercise book; in exchange for this service, he'd give me nails, screws, or a bit of twine, things he'd managed to nick from the store, which at the time was owned and operated by his father. I just wrote that Gustav *was* a comrade, because now I'm not sure that's true anymore. He was with the others at the *Ereigniës.* He did what cannot be undone! And ever since, he hasn't spoken a single word to me, even though we've met every Sunday after Mass in front of the church, where Father Peiper, red-faced and wobbly on his feet, accompanies his flock before bestowing upon them the incomplete gestures that constitute his last blessing. I don't dare enter Gustav's hardware store, either. I'm too afraid that there's nothing left between us but a great void.

As I believe I've already mentioned, Vurtenhau is very rich and very stupid. He beat his fist on Röppel's counter, causing a box of thumbtacks to tumble down from its shelf. "Do you realize what you did, Brodeck?" he asked. "You gave him the names of all our mountains, and you say he wrote them down!"

Vurtenhau was beside himself. All the blood in his body seemed to have been pumped into his huge ears. In vain, I pointed out that the names of mountains are no secret, that everybody knows them or can find them in maps or books; my observations failed to calm him down. "You're not even considering what he might be up to, coming here out of the blue, nosing around everywhere the way he does, asking all his innocent questions, him with his fish face and his smooth manners!"

I tried to soothe Vurtenhau by repeating some of what the *Anderer* had said to me on the subject of forms and landscapes, but that only made him angrier. He stormed out of the hardware store, flinging over his shoulder one final remark which at the time seemed unimportant: "Don't forget, Brodeck, if anything happens, it'll be your fault!"

Only today do I realize the enormity of the menace his words contained. After he banged the door, Gustav and I looked at each other, shrugged our shoulders simultaneously, and burst into loud laughter, the way we used to do in the old days, in the time of our childhood.

XIV

It took me nearly two hours to reach Stern's cabin, whereas normally one good hour is enough. But no one had opened a trail, and as soon as I passed the upper limit of the broadleaf trees and entered the forest of tall firs, the fallen snow became so thick that I sank into it up to my knees. The forest was silent. I saw no animal and no bird. All I heard was the sound of the Staubi, about two hundred meters below me, where it rushes into a fairly sharp bend and crashes into some large rocks.

When I passed near the *Lingen,* I turned my eyes away and didn't stop moving. I even increased my pace, and the frigid air penetrated into my lungs so deeply that they hurt. I was too afraid of seeing the *Anderer's* ghost, in the same position as before, sitting on his little stool, surveying the landscape, or maybe stretching out his arms to me in supplication. But supplication for what?

Even had I been in the inn when the others all went mad that night, what could I have done on my own? The least word, the least gesture from me would have meant my life, and I would have suffered the same fate he did. That thought, too, filled me with terror: the knowledge that if I had been in the inn, I wouldn't have done anything to stop what happened, I would have made myself as small as possible, and I would have looked on impotently as the horrible scene unfolded. That act of cowardice, even though it had never actually taken place, filled me with disgust. At bottom, I was like the others, like all those who surrounded me and charged me with writing the Report, which they hoped would exonerate them.

Stern lives outside the world—I mean, outside our world. All the Sterns have lived the way he does, for as long as anyone can remember: staying in the midst of the forest and maintaining only distant relations with the village. But he's the last of the Sterns. He's alone. He's never taken a wife, and he has no children. His line will die out with him.

He lives by tanning animal skins. He comes down to the village twice every winter, and a little more often in fine weather. He sells his furs as well as various objects that he carves from the trunks and branches of fir trees. With the cash thus acquired, he buys some flour, a sack of potatoes, some dried peas, tobacco, sugar, and salt. And if he's got any money left over, he drinks it in fruit brandy and makes the climb back to his cabin dead drunk. He never gets lost. His feet know the way.

When I reached the cabin, I found him sitting on the threshold, busy with binding some dead branches together to make a broom. I greeted him. Always suspicious of visitors, he replied with a movement of his head but spoke no word. Then he got up and went inside, leaving the door open.

Many things, both animal and vegetable, were hung up to dry from the ceiling beams; the acrid, violent odors blended and clung to whoever was in the room. The fire in the hearth produced some stingy little flames and a great deal of smoke. Stern dipped a ladle into a kettle and filled two bowls with thick soup, a porridge of groats and chestnuts, which had no doubt been simmering since the early morning. Then he cut two thick slices of hard bread and filled two glasses with dark wine. We sat facing each other and ate in silence, surrounded by a stench, with its overtones of carrion, that many would have fled from. But as for me, I was familiar with stenches. That one didn't bother me. I had known worse.

In the camp, after my stay in the *Büxte* and before becoming Brodeck the Dog, for a few long months I was the *Scheizeman,* the "shit man." My task consisted of emptying out the latrines into which more than a thousand prisoners relieved their bowels several times a day. The latrines were large trenches a meter deep, two meters wide, and about four meters long. There were five of them, and my job was to muck them out thoroughly. To accomplish this task, I had only a few tools at my disposal: a big pan attached to a wooden handle, and two large tin buckets. I used the pan to fill the buckets, and then, under escort, I went back and forth to the river, into which I emptied their contents.

The pan, which only a few lengths of old string kept fastened to the handle, often came loose and fell into the latrine. When that happened, I had to jump down, plunge my hands into the mass of ordure, and feel around for the pan. The first few times I did this, I remember puking up my guts and the little they contained. Then I got used to it. You can get used to anything. There are worse things than the smell of shit. A great many things have no smell at all, and yet they rot senses, hearts, and souls more surely than all the excrement in the world.

The two guards who escorted me back and forth held handkerchiefs soaked in brandy over their noses. They kept a few meters away from me and talked about women, sprinkling their tales with obscene particulars that made them laugh and inflamed their faces. I stepped into the river. I emptied the buckets. And I was always surprised at the frenzy of the hundreds of little fish that arrived in a brownish whirl and wallowed in the filth, flicking their thin silvery bodies in every direction, as though driven mad by their stinking food. But the current quickly diluted it, vile though it was, and soon clear water and the movements of algae were all that could be seen, as well as the reflections of the sunlight, which struck the surface of the river and shattered it into a thousand mirrors.

Sometimes the guards, in their drunken euphoria, allowed me to wash myself in the river. I would pick up a round, smooth stone and use it like a bar of soap, rubbing my skin with it to remove the shit and the dirt. Occasionally, I'd manage to catch some of the little fish that were still lingering around my legs, perhaps hoping for another portion. I'd quickly press their bellies with two fingers to squeeze out their guts and pop the fish into my mouth before the guards had time to see me. We were forbidden under pain of death to eat anything other than the two liters of fetid broth we were served in the evening and the chunk of hard, sour bread we got every morning. I chewed those fish for a good long time, as though they were savory delicacies.

Throughout that period, the odor of shit never left me. It was my true and only clothing. The result was that during the night, I had more room to sleep because no one in the hut wanted to be near me. Man is made thus: He prefers to believe himself a pure spirit, a creator of ideas and ideals, of dreams and marvels. He doesn't like to be reminded that he's also a material being, and that what flows out between his buttocks is as much a part of him as what stirs and germinates in his brain.

Stern wiped his bowl clean with a piece of bread and then, with a brief whistle, made a slender creature appear out of no-where: a ferret, which he'd tamed and which kept him company. The small animal went to him and ate from his hand. Every now and then, while it was gobbling away, it cast a curious glance in my direction, and its round, gleaming little eyes looked like black pearls or ripe mulberries. I'd just told Stern everything I knew about the foxes and all about my visits to Limmat and Mother Pitz.

He got slowly to his feet, disappeared into the darkness on the far side of the room, returned, and spread out on the big table several handsome fox skins, bound together with a piece of hemp cord. "You can add these to your fox count," he said. "Thirteen of them. And I didn't have to kill them. I found them dead, and all in the position you describe."

Stern took a pipe and filled it with a mixture of tobacco and chestnut leaves while I stroked the fox furs, which were glossy and thick. Then I asked him what all this could possibly mean. He shrugged his shoulders, pulled on his pipe, which crackled mer-rily, and exhaled great clouds of smoke that made me cough. "I don't know anything, Brodeck," he said. "I know nothing about it. Foxes—I can't figure out foxes."

He stopped talking and petted his ferret, which began wrap-ping itself around his arm and emitting little whimpers. Then he spoke again: "I don't know anything about foxes. But I remember my grandfather Stern talking about wolves. There were still wolves around here in his time. Nowadays, whenever I see one, if it's not a wolf ghost, it's a stray come from far away. Once old Stern told me the story of a pack, a fine pack according to him, more than twenty animals. He enjoyed spying on them and stalking them a little, just to get on their nerves. And then one day, they're all gone. He stops hearing them and stops seeing them. He tells himself they got tired of his little game and went to stay on the other side of the mountain. The winter passes. A heavy winter, full of snow. Then spring returns. He tramps through all the forests, as though he's inspecting them, and what does he find at the foot of the big Maulenthal rocks? The remains of the entire pack, in an advanced stage of decay. They were all there, every one of them, old and young, males and females, all with their backs or their skulls broken. Now, as a rule, wolves don't fall off rocks. Occasionally, one may take an accidental step into thin air, or slip, or the edge of the cliff may crumble under its feet, but just one. Not a whole pack."

Stern fell silent, looking me right in the eye. I said, "You mean to tell me they all fell to their deaths of their own accord?"

"I'm telling you what old Stern told me, that's all."

"But what's that got to do with the foxes?"

"Wolves, foxes, they're more or less cousins. Family. Maybe man isn't the only animal that thinks too much."

Stern's pipe had gone out. He relit it, grabbed the little ferret, which was now trying to get inside his jacket, and filled our wineglasses.

A great silence passed over us. I don't know what Stern was thinking about, but I was busy trying to make what he'd just told me jibe with what old Limmat had said. I got nowhere. Nothing was clear; there was nothing I could incorporate into a Report that an official in S. would have accepted without scowling at it and thrusting it into the stove.

Stern fed the dying fire a few bundles of dried juniper twigs. We spoke for perhaps an hour longer, about the seasons and the winter, about game and woodcutting, but concerning foxes no more was said. Then, seeing that the light was beginning to fade from the sky and I wanted to get home before night, I bade Stern farewell. He accompanied me outside. The wind had risen and was agitating the tops of the tall firs. This caused the branches to shed some large clumps of snow, but the gusting wind broke them up into fine powder, which covered our shoulders like frozen white ash. We shook hands, and then Stern asked me, "How about the *Gewisshor*? Is he still in the village?"

On the point of asking Stern what he was talking about, I remembered that some people had referred to the *Anderer* like that—the *Gewisshor*, the "Learned Man," the "Scholar"—probably because that was the impression he made. I didn't answer right away, and suddenly I was cold. And I thought that if Stern was asking me that question, then he didn't know anything, and on the famous night of the *Ereigniës*, he wasn't in the inn. So there were at least two of us with no blood on our hands. I didn't know what to say to him.

"He went away . . ."

"Then wait," Stern said and went back into the cabin. When he came out again a few seconds later, he was carrying a package, which he handed to me. "He ordered that from me. It's already paid for. If he doesn't come back, you can keep it."

The package contained an unusual kind of soft hat, a pair of gloves, and a pair of slippers, all in handsome marten fur, beautifully dressed and sewn. I hesitated, but I ended up sticking the package under my arm. That was when Stern looked me in the eye and said, "You know, Brodeck, I don't think there are any foxes anymore. They're all dead. They'll never come back."

And as I made no reply, not knowing what to say, he shook my hand without another word, and after a few moments' hesitation, I started off down the trail.

s I've already related, at the moment when the *Anderer* first arrived in the village and passed through the gate with his animals, night was approaching, creeping down like a cat that's just spotted a mouse and knows she'll soon have it in her jaws.

It's a funny time of day. The streets are deserted, the encroaching darkness turns them into cold, gray blurs, and the houses become shifty silhouettes, full of menace and insinuation. Night has the curious power of changing the most everyday things, the simplest faces. And sometimes it doesn't so much change them as reveal them, as if bringing out the true natures of landscapes and people by covering them in black. The reader might shrug off everything I'm saying here. He might think I'm describing childish fears, or embellishing a novel. But before judging and condemning, one must imagine the scene: that man, come from out of nowhere—for he really did arrive from out of the blue, as Vurtenhau said (now and again Vurtenhau enunciates a few truths amid a great mass of idiocy)—anyway, as I was saying, one must imagine that fellow, dressed like a character from another century, with his strange beasts and his imposing baggage, entering our village, which no stranger had entered for years, and moreover arriving here just like that, without any ado, with the greatest of ease. Who wouldn't have been a little afraid?

"I wasn't afraid of him."

That's the Dörfer boy, the eldest, answering my questions. He was the first person in the village to see the *Anderer* when he arrived.

Our conversation takes place in Pipersheim's café. The boy's father insisted that we should talk in the café rather than in the family home. He must have figured he'd have a better chance here of downing a few shots in peace. Gustav Dörfer's a small, drab creature, always bundled in dirty clothes that give off an odor of boiled turnips. He hires himself to the local farms, and when he has a few pennies, he drinks them up. His wife weighs twice as much as he does, but the size disadvantage doesn't keep him from beating her like a dusty rug when he's drunk, after trashing the premises and breaking a few of the remaining dishes. He's given her five children, all of them puny and glum. The eldest is named Hans.

"And what did he say to you?" I ask Hans. The kid looks at his father, as though requesting an authorization to speak, but Dörfer couldn't care less. He has eyes only for his glass, which is already empty, and he contemplates it, clutching it with both hands and gazing at it with a look of painful melancholy. Pipersheim's watching us from behind the bar, and I signal to him to refill Dörfer's glass. Our host puts a hand to his mouth and removes the toothpick he's constantly sucking, the cause of his punctured, bleeding gums and distressing breath. Then he grabs a bottle, comes to our table, and pours Dörfer another drink. Dörfer's face brightens a little.

"He asked me the way to Schloss's inn."

"Did he know the name, or were you the one who said it?"

"He knew it."

"So what did you say to him?"

"I gave him directions."

"And what did he do?"

"He wrote down what I said in his little notebook."

"And then?"

"And then he gave me four marbles. Pretty ones. He took them out of a bag and said, 'For your trouble.' "

" 'For your trouble'?"

"Yes. I didn't understand at first. People don't say that here."

"How about the marbles? You still have them?"

"Peter Lülli won them off me. He's really good. He's got a whole bagful."

Gustav Dörfer wasn't listening to us. His eyes were riveted on his glass and its liquid contents, which were disappearing too fast. The boy drew his shoulders up around his ears. His forehead bore bruises and scabs and bumps and little scars, some fading, some brand new, and his eyes, when you managed to catch and hold them for a few moments, spoke of blows and suffering, of the wounds that constituted his harsh, inalterable daily lot.

I recalled that notebook, which I'd often seen in the *Anderer*'s hands. He wrote down everything in it, including, for example, the directions to an inn located only about sixty meters from where he was standing. The longer his sojourn among us lasted, the larger his little notebook began to loom in people's minds, and although his producing it on every possible occasion had at first seemed like nothing but an odd compulsion, a comical tic good for smiling at or gossiping about, it quickly became the object of bitter recriminations.

I particularly remember a conversation I overheard on August 3, a market day. It was coming to an end, and the ground was littered with spoiled vegetables, dirty straw, pieces of string, crate fragments, and other inert objects, which seemed to have been left in the market square by the receding waters of an invisible tide.

Poupchette loves the market, and so I take her there with me almost every week. The little animals in their pens—kids, bunnies, chicks, ducklings—make her clap her hands and laugh. And then there are the smells, of fritters and frying and hot wine and roasting chestnuts and grilled meat, and also the sounds, the voices of every pitch and timbre, mingling together as though in a giant basin: the cries, the calls, the chatter of the vendors hawking their wares, the prayers of those selling holy images, the feigned anger essential to proper bargaining. But what Poupchette looks forward to most of all is when Viktor Heidekirch arrives with his accordion and begins to play, filling the air with notes that sound sometimes like laments and sometimes like cries of joy. People make way for him and form a circle around him, and suddenly the noise of the market seems to die out, as if everyone were listening to the music, as if it had become, for the moment, more important than everything else.

Viktor turns up at every party and every wedding. He's the only person in the village who knows music, and also just about the only one in possession of a working musical instrument. I believe there's a piano in the back room of Schloss's inn, the one where the *Erweckens'Bruderschaf* meets, and there may be some brass instruments in there as well. Diodemus affirmed that there were, having seen them, he said, one day when the door wasn't completely closed, and when I teased him about being so well informed, declaring that he must know the room very well and suggesting that maybe he was, in fact, a member of the brotherhood, his face darkened and he told me to shut up. Viktor's accordion and his voice are also a part of our local memory. That day, he made the women weep and the men's eyes turn red with his rendition of "Johanni's Complaint," a song about love and death whose origins are lost in the mists of time. It tells the story of a young girl who loves but isn't loved in return, and who, faced with the prospect of seeing the ruler of her heart in another woman's arms, prefers to step into the Staubi at twilight on a winter day and lie down forever in the cold, moving water.

When de abend gekomm Johanni schlafft en de wasser
Als besser sein en de todt dass alein immer verden
De hertz is a schotke freige who nieman geker
Und ubche madchen kann genug de kusse kaltenen

Sometimes Amelia comes with us. I take her arm. I lead her. She lets herself be guided, and her eyes gaze at things only she can see. On the day of the conversation I want to record, she was sitting on my left, humming her song and moving her head back and forth in a gentle rhythm. On my right, Poupchette was chewing a sausage I'd just bought for her. We leaned against the biggest of the columns supporting the entrance to the covered part of the market. In front of us, a few meters away, old Roswilda Klugenghal, who's half madwoman and half vagrant, was digging around in some garbage, looking for vegetables and offal. She found a twisted carrot, held it up for inspection, and talked to it as if it were an old acquaintance. At that moment, the voices coming from the other side of the column became audible, voices that I recognized at once.

They belonged to four men: Emil Dorcha, a forester; Ludwig Pfimling, a stableboy; Bern Vogel, a tinsmith; and Caspar Hausorn, one of the mayor's clerks. Four men already quite overheated, as they'd been drinking since dawn and the market's festive atmosphere had done nothing to lower their temperatures. They spoke loudly, sometimes stumbling over words, but the tone of their conversation was very clear, and I quickly realized who its subject was.

"Did you see him? Like a weasel, he is, always sniffing around at everything," Dorcha declared.

"That fellow's nothing but *rein schlecht,* 'pure bad,' " Vogel added. "Mark my words—bad and depraved."

"He doesn't hurt anybody," Pfimling pointed out. "He takes walks, he looks around, he smiles all the time."

"Outside smiles hide inside wiles—you forget the proverb. Besides, you're so stupid and nearsighted, you wouldn't see anything wrong with Lucifer himself!"

The speaker was Hausorn, and he'd spat out his words as though they were little pebbles. He went on in a milder tone: "He must have come here for some purpose. Some purpose that isn't very clear and doesn't bode well for us."

"What do you think it is?" Vogel asked him.

"Don't know yet. I'm racking my brains. I don't know what it is, but a lad like him is bound to have something in mind."

"He writes everything in his notebook," Dorcha observed.

"Didn't you all see him a little while ago, sitting in front of Wuzten's lambs?"

"Of course we saw him. He stayed there for minutes and minutes, writing stuff down and looking at the lambs the whole time."

"He wasn't writing," Pfimling submitted. "He was drawing. I saw him, and I know you say I don't see anything, but I saw him drawing. And he was so absorbed in what he was doing that you could've eaten off of the top of his head and he wouldn't have felt anything. I walked up behind him and looked over his shoulder."

"Drawing lambs?" Dorcha asked, apparently addressing Hausorn. "What's that supposed to mean?"

"How should I know? You think I've got all the answers?"

The conversation came to a halt. I imagined it was over for good, not to be taken up again, but I was mistaken. After a while, a voice resumed speaking, but it had become very low and very serious, and I couldn't identify it. "There aren't many lambs around here, not among us, I mean . . . Maybe all that stuff he draws is a bunch of symbols, like in the church Bible, and it's a way for him to say who's who and who's done what and how recently, so he can report it when he goes back where he came from . . ."

I felt the cold running over my back and rasping my spine. I didn't like the voice or what it had said, even if the exact meaning of his words remained obscure.

"But then, if he's using that notebook for what you're talking about, it mustn't ever leave the village!"

It was Dorcha who made that last remark; his was a voice I recognized.

"Maybe you're right," the other voice said. I still couldn't make out whose it was. "Maybe that notebook should never go anywhere. Or maybe the person it belongs to is the one who can't leave, not ever . . ."

After that, nothing. I waited. I didn't dare move. Nevertheless, after a few moments, I leaned to one side and sneaked a look around the column. No one was there. The four had left without my hearing them. They'd disappeared into the air, like the veils of fog the southern breeze snatches off our mountain crests on April mornings. I even wondered whether I'd dreamed the things I'd heard. Poupchette pulled my sleeve. "Home, Daddy? Home?"

Her little lips were shiny with sausage grease, and her pretty eyes gleamed merrily. I gave her a big kiss on the forehead and put her on my shoulders. Her hands held on to my hair and her feet beat against my chest. "Giddyap, Daddy! Giddyap!" I took Amelia's hand and pulled her to her feet. She didn't resist. I hugged her against me, I caressed her beautiful face, I planted a kiss on her cheek, and the three of us returned home like that, while my head still resounded with the voices of the faceless men and the threats they had made, like seeds that asked nothing but time to grow.

Gustav Dörfer eventually passed out on the table in the café, less from drink than from weariness, no doubt: weariness of body, or weariness of life. His kid and I had long since stopped talking about the *Anderer* and changed the subject. It turned out, to my surprise, that the boy had a passion for birds, and he insisted on questioning me about all the species I knew and described in my reports to the administration. And so we talked about the thrushes and their close relatives the fieldfares, and about other birds as well: the March grays, which as their name indicates return to us around the beginning of spring; the crossbills, which abound in the pine forests; the wrens, the titmice, the blackbirds, the ptarmigans, the capercaillies, the mountain pheasants; the blue soldiers, whose unusual name comes from the color of their breast feathers and their propensity for fighting; the crows and ravens; the bullfinches, the eagles, and the owls.

Inside that head of his, which was covered with lumps from paternal beatings, the child—he was about twelve—had a brain filled with knowledge, and his face lit up when he talked about birds. By contrast, his pupils became dull and lusterless again when he turned toward his father and remembered his presence, which our conversation had made the kid forget for a while. Hans paused and contemplated his parent, who was snoring open-mouthed, with one side of his face flattened against the old wood of the tabletop, his cap askew, and white saliva oozing between his lips.

"When I see a dead bird," Hans Dörfer said to me, "and I pick it up in my hand, tears come into my eyes. I can't make them not come. Nothing can justify the death of a bird. But if my father croaked all of a sudden, right here, right next to me, I swear I'd dance around the table and buy you a drink. I swear!"

'm in our kitchen. I've just put the marten fur cap on my head. I'm also wearing the slippers, and I've slipped on the gloves.

An odd sensation of warmth comes over me, bringing with it a comfortable drowsiness, like the state you enter as you drink a glass or two of hot wine after a long walk on a late-autumn afternoon. I feel good and, of course, I'm thinking about the *Anderer*. I'm not claiming that wearing clothes meant for him, items that he himself ordered (how did he manage to meet Stern, who comes to the village so rarely? and how did he know that Stern could sew animal skins?), has made me capable of seeing into his thoughts and penetrating the little world of his mind, but having said that, I still feel that I'm approaching him somehow, that somehow I'm back in his presence, and that maybe he'll give me a sign or a look which will help me learn a little more.

I must confess to being totally at a loss. I've been charged with a mission that far exceeds my capabilities and my intelligence. I'm not a lawyer. I'm not a police officer. I'm not a storyteller. The present account, if anyone ever reads it, will prove I'm not: I keep going backward and forward, jumping over time like a hurdle, getting lost on tangents, and maybe even, without wishing to, concealing what's essential.

When I read the pages of my account thus far, I see that I move around in words like tracked game on the run, sprinting, zigzagging, trying to throw off the dogs and hunters in hot pursuit. This jumble contains everything. I'm emptying my life into it. Writing's a relief to both my heart and my stomach.

With the Report that the others have ordered me to write up, things are different. My tone is neutral and impersonal. I transcribe conversations almost verbatim. I pare everything down. A few days ago, Orschwir informed me that I have to present myself in the village hall next Friday at sunset. "Come see us Friday, Brodeck," he said. "You can give us a reading . . ."

He came in person to my house to tell me that. He placed his great bulk on the chair that Fedorine had pulled up for him without thanking her or even greeting her, took off his cap of otter fur, and refused the offered glass. "Don't have time, thanks. I've got work to do. We have thirty pigs to slaughter this morning, and if I'm not there, my workers are liable to make a mess of them . . ."

We heard steps above our heads. The stepper was Poupchette, who was scurrying around up there like a little mouse. Then there were other footfalls, slower and heavier, and a distant voice, Amelia's voice, humming her song. Orschwir cocked his head back for a moment, and then he looked at me as if he were about to say something, but he changed his mind. He took out his tobacco pouch and rolled himself a cigarette. A great silence, hard as stone, settled over us. Having announced that he was needed at his farm, Orschwir, for no apparent reason, chose to linger. He took two or three puffs on his cigarette, and an aroma of honey and old alcohol permeated the air in the kitchen. Orschwir doesn't smoke just anything. He smokes a rich man's tobacco, very blond and finely cut, which he orders from far away.

He gave the ceiling another look and then once again turned his appalling face to me. No more sounds could be heard, not the footsteps, not Amelia's voice. Fedorine was ignoring us. She'd finished grating some potatoes and was rolling them in her hands, shaping them into little pancakes called *Kartfolknudle;* later she'd fry them in boiling oil and strew them with poppy seeds before serving them to us.

Orschwir cleared his throat. "Not too lonely?"

I shook my head.

He seemed to reflect, took a deep drag on his cigarette, and began wheezing and choking. His skin turned as red as the wild cherries that ripen in June, and tears filled his eyes. At length the coughing subsided.

"You need anything?"

"Nothing."

Orschwir rubbed his two cheeks with one big hand, as if he were shaving them. I wondered what he could possibly be trying to say to me.

"All right, then, I'll be leaving."

He pronounced these words hesitantly. I looked him in the eyes, hoping to see what was behind them, but he quickly cast them down.

I heard myself responding to him, but my words sounded so strange and threatening that they hardly seemed to come from me: "It's really convenient for you to act as if they don't exist, isn't it? As if they're not here, neither one of them. That suits you just fine, right?"

The effect of this sally was that Orschwir fell completely silent. I saw him trying to ponder what I'd just said, and I could tell that he was turning my words over and over in his mind, taking them apart and putting them back together, but his efforts apparently came to naught, for he suddenly leapt from his chair, grabbed his cap, jammed it down over his skull, and left the house. The door closing behind him made its little noise, a high meow. And all at once, thanks to that simple little sound, I was on the other side of that door and it was two years ago, the day I came home.

From the moment I entered the village, all the people I passed stared at me goggle-eyed and opened their mouths wide without producing a single word. Some of them went running to their houses to spread the news of my return, and all of them understood that I must be left alone, that they mustn't ask me any questions yet, that all I wanted to do was to stand before the door of my house, put my hand on the knob, and push the door open, to hear its little noise, to enter my home once more, to find there the woman I loved, who had never left my thoughts, to take her in my arms, to squeeze her so tight it hurt, and to press my lips to hers again at last.

Ah, the vision of those last few meters, culminating in that embrace, how often had I gazed upon it in my dreams! That day, when I opened the door, my door, the door to my house, my body was trembling and my heart was pounding as though about to burst through my chest. I couldn't catch my breath, and I even thought for a moment that I was going to die there, that I was going to step over the threshold and die from too much happiness. But suddenly the face of the *Zeileneseniss* appeared to me, and my happiness stiffened and froze. It was a little as though someone had shoved a big handful of snow between my shirt and my naked skin. But why, at that precise moment, did that woman's face come floating up out of limbo and dancing before my eyes?

In the last weeks of the war, the camp became an even stranger place than it had been before. Unceasing, contradictory rumors shook it like windy blasts, alternately hot and cold. Some recent arrivals murmured that the conflict was nearing its end and that we, who walked bowed down and looked like corpses, were on the winning side. This news restored to our eyes, the eyes of the living dead we had become, a gleam long since extinguished, but the fragile light couldn't last. The guards let their confusion show for a few seconds before they quickly and brutally dispelled it: apparently determined to affirm that they were still the masters, they attacked the first one of us they got their hands on, kicking him, beating him with truncheons and rifle butts, and driving him down into the mud as though trying to make him disappear. Nevertheless, their nervousness and the constantly worried expressions on their faces led us to conclude that something big really was happening.

The guard who was my master stopped paying much attention to me. Whereas every day for weeks on end he'd amused himself by putting a leather collar around my neck, attaching a braided leash to it, and parading me around the camp—me walking on all fours, and him following behind, upright on his two legs and his certitudes—now I never saw him anymore except at mealtime. He came furtively to the kennel that served as my bed and poured two ladles of soup into my bowl, but I could tell that this game no longer amused him. His face had become gray, and two deep wrinkles I'd never seen before now furrowed his forehead.

I knew that he'd been an accountant before the war and that he had a wife, three children—two boys and a girl—and a cat, but no dog. He was an innocuous-looking fellow with a timid manner, shifty eyes, and small, well-groomed hands, which he washed methodically several times a day while whistling a military tune. Unlike a great many of his colleagues, he didn't drink and never visited the windowless huts where female prisoners (whom we never laid an eye on) were made available to the guards. He was a pale, reserved, ordinary man, who always spoke in an even tone, never raising his voice, but who had twice, before my eyes and without a second's hesitation, bludgeoned prisoners to death for forgetting to salute him by lifting their caps. His name was Joss Scheidegger. I've tried hard to banish that name from my memory, but the memory doesn't take orders. The best you can hope for is to deaden it a bit from time to time.

One morning, there was a great deal of commotion in the camp: noises of every sort, shouted orders, questions. The guards scuttled about in all directions, gathering their kits together, loading multifarious objects onto carts. There was a new smell in the air, a sour, pregnant odor that surpassed the stench emanating from our poor bodies: fear had changed sides.

In their great agitation, the guards ignored us completely. Before, we had existed for them as slaves, but that morning, we no longer existed at all.

I was lying in the kennel, keeping warm among the mastiffs and watching the curious spectacle of our keepers preparing to make a rapid exit. I followed each movement. I heard each call and every order, none of which concerned us anymore. At one point, when the majority of the guards had already abandoned the premises, I saw Scheidegger heading for the hut near the kennels where the offices of the prison census authority were located. He stayed briefly in the hut and emerged with a leather pouch, which seemed to contain documents. One of the dogs saw him and barked. Scheidegger looked toward the kennel and stopped. He appeared to hesitate, darting glances all around, and having determined that no one was watching, he walked quickly to my kennel, knelt on the ground beside me, dug in his pocket, took out a little key with which I was quite familiar, and with shaky hands opened the lock on my collar; then, not knowing what to do with the key, he suddenly threw it down as if it were burning his fingers. "Who's going to pay for all this?"

It was a shabby, undignified question—an accountant's question—and as Scheidegger asked it, he looked me in the eye for the first time, perhaps expecting me to give him an answer. His forehead was covered with sweat and his skin even grayer than usual. What was the meaning of his query? Was he hoping for forgiveness? From me? He stared at me for several seconds, imploringly, fearfully. Then I started to bark. My barking was prolonged, lugubrious, melancholy, instantly echoed and extended by the two mastiffs. Scheidegger, terrified, bounded to his feet and ran away.

Within a little less than an hour, there wasn't a guard left in the camp. Silence reigned. Nothing could be heard, and no one could be seen. Then, timidly, one by one, shadows began to step out of the huts, not yet daring to take a real look around, and not saying a word. An unsteady, incredulous army, hesitating figures with sallow skin and hollow cheeks, began to fill the streets of the camp. Soon the former prisoners formed a compact, fragile crowd, still silent, which took the measure of its new circumstances by drifting aimlessly from one place to another, dazzled by the freedom none of them dared name.

When this great tide of suffering flesh and bones turned the corner and moved toward the group of huts that housed the guards and their commanders, something incredible happened. Those in front raised their hands, without a word, and everyone stopped short as though frozen in place. Yes, it was an incredible sight: standing alone, facing hundreds of creatures that were gradually becoming men again, was the *Zeilenesseniss.* Completely alone. Immensely alone.

I don't believe in fate. And I no longer believe in God. I don't believe in anything anymore. But I must admit that there seemed to be more than mere chance in that meeting between a throng of people in extreme misery and the person who was the living symbol of their tormentors.

Why was she still there, when all the guards had left? She too must have left, and then she'd come back, no doubt in haste, to fetch something she'd forgotten. The first thing we heard was her voice. Her ordinary voice, sure of itself, enlivened by her sense of her power and her privileges; the voice of superiority, which sometimes gave the order to hang one of us and sometimes sang nursery rhymes to her child.

I didn't understand what she said—I was standing rather far from her—but I could tell that she was speaking as though nothing had changed. I'm sure she didn't know she was alone in the camp; she didn't know she'd been abandoned. I'm sure she thought there were still guards on hand, ready to execute the least of her orders and to beat us to death if she desired them to do so. But no one answered her call. No one came to her side to serve her or aid her. No one in the crowd facing her made a move. She kept on talking, but little by little, her voice changed. The words came faster and faster at the same time as their intensity decreased; then her voice exploded and became a howl before fading away again.

Today, I imagine her eyes. I imagine the eyes of the *Zeilenesseniss* when she began to realize that she was the last of them, that she was alone, and that perhaps—yes, perhaps—she would never leave the camp, that for her, too, it was going to be transformed into a grave.

I was told that she began to strike the men at the head of the crowd with her fists. No one replied in kind; they simply made way for her. And so she gradually moved deeper into the great river of walking dead, unaware that she would never emerge from it, for the waves closed in again behind her. There was no outcry, no complaint. Her words disappeared with her. She was swallowed up, and she met an end in which there was no hatred, an end that was almost mechanical—a fitting end, in short, an end in her own image. I truly believe, even though I couldn't swear it, that no one laid a hand on her. She died without suffering a blow, without a word addressed to her, without even so much as a glance cast upon her, who had felt such contempt for our glances. I imagine her stumbling at some point and falling to the ground. I imagine her stretching out her hands, trying to catch hold of the shadows moving past her, over her, on her body, on her legs, on her delicate white arms, on her stomach and her powdered face; shadows that paid her no attention, that didn't look at her, that brought her no help but didn't attack her, either; moving shadows that simply passed, passed, passed, treading her underfoot the way one treads dust or earth or ashes.

The next day, I found what remained of her body. It was a poor thing, swollen and blue. All her beauty had vanished. She looked like a *Strohespuppe,* a "straw fairy," one of the big dolls children make by stuffing old dresses with hay; *Strohespuppen* are paraded through the village on the feast of St. John and then, as night falls, tossed into a great fire, while everyone sings and dances to the glory of summer. Her face wasn't there anymore. She no longer had eyes or a mouth or a nose. In their place I saw a single wound, enormous and round, inflated like a balloon, and attached to it was a long mane of blond hair mingled with clumps of mud. It was by her hair that I recognized her. In former days, while I crept along the ground, acting the dog, her hair had appeared to me like filaments of sunlight, blinding and obscene.

Even in death, she kept her fists so tightly clenched that they resembled stones. Part of a prettily worked golden chain dangled from one hand. At the end of that chain, no doubt, there was a medal, one of those delicately engraved medals that represent a male or female saint and are placed around infants' necks when they're baptized. Perhaps that very medal was the reason why she returned; perhaps she'd noticed it was missing from her child's small, soft chest. She'd reentered the camp, counting on leaving it again very quickly. She must not have known that once you abandon Hell, you must never go back there. But in the end, there's no sort of difference between dying from ignorance and dying under the feet of thousands of men who have regained their freedom. You close your eyes, and then there's nothing anymore. And death is never difficult. It requires neither a hero nor a slave. It eats what it's served.

XVII

"Beer leaves no stain, nor does eau-de-vie, but wine!"
Father Peiper was launched on a litany of complaints. He
stood at his stone sink, dressed in his shirt and underpants, scrubbing his white chasuble with a large brush and a bar of soap. "And
right on the cross, to boot! If I can't get this out, idiots and zealots
will see it as a symbol! We're already weighed down with symbols!
We traffic in symbols! It's no use adding to them!"

I watched him work and said not a word. I was in a corner
of his kitchen, sitting on a rickety chair with a frowsy straw bottom. The air in the room was hot and heavy and reeked of dirty
dishes, hardened cooking fat, and cheap wine. Hundreds of empty
bottles stood here and there, dozens of them holding burning
candles, their fragile flames stretching toward the ceiling.

Peiper stopped scrubbing his vestment, tossed it with a gesture of vexation into the stone sink, and turned around. He
looked at me and started, as if he had forgotten my presence.
"Brodeck, Brodeck," he said. "Have a drink?"

I shook my head.

"You don't need it yet. Lucky you . . ."

In his quest for a bottle that still had some wine in it, he
shifted a great many empties, producing a crystalline, incoherent

music before finding the one he sought. He grabbed it by the neck as though his life depended on it and poured himself a glass. Picking it up with both hands, he raised it to eye level, smiled, and said in a solemn voice heavy with irony, "This is my blood. Take and drink ye all of it." Then he downed the contents in one gulp, slammed the glass on the table, and burst into loud laughter.

I had just come from the village hall, where—in compliance with Orschwir's command—I'd gone to discuss the progress of my Report.

Night had fallen suddenly on the village that evening, like an ax striking a chopping block. Over the course of the day, big clouds had moved in from the west and stalled over our valley. Blocked by the mountains as though caught in a trap, the clouds had begun to gyrate madly, and then, around three o'clock in the afternoon, a glacial north wind had arrived and split them wide open. Their gaping bellies released a great deal of dense snow, a deluge of stubborn, numberless flakes, serried like the resolute soldiers of an infinite army and clinging to everything they touched: roofs, walls, paving stones, trees. It was the third of December. All the snowfalls of the previous weeks had been mere tokens, and we knew it; the snow that came down that day, however, was no laughing matter. It was the first of the big snows, to be followed by others, whose company we would have to endure until spring.

In front of the village hall, *Zungfrost*—"Frozen Tongue"— had lit two lanterns and placed them on either side of the door. With the aid of a large shovel, he was piling the snow into two mounds, leaving a path like a trench between them. His clothes were covered with snowflakes, which clustered and clung to him in a way reminiscent of feathers, so that he looked like a large fowl.

"Hello, *Zungfrost!*"

"Hel . . . hel . . . hello, Bro . . . Brodeck! It's real . . . real . . . real . . . really com . . . com . . . coming down!"

"I'm here to see the mayor."

"I . . . I know. He . . . he . . . he's waiting for you upstairs."

Zungfrost is my junior by a few years. He always smiles, but he's not simpleminded. In fact, if you look closely at his smile, it could just as easily be a grimace. His face froze one day long ago; his face, his smile, and his tongue all froze. At the time, he was a kid of seven or eight, and we were in the depths of another frigid winter. All the village children, both young and not so young, had gone to a bend in the Staubi where the surface of the river was completely frozen. We slid around on the ice. We shoved one another. And then someone—it was never clear who—threw *Zungfrost's* afternoon snack, a slice of bacon stuffed into a chunk of bread, far out onto the ice. The kid watched his sandwich skidding across the surface, getting farther and farther away, until it stopped about a meter or two from the other bank of the river. Then he began to cry, shedding big, silent tears as round as mistletoe berries. The rest of us laughed, and then someone yelled, "Stop crying! Just go get it!" There was a silence. We all knew that the ice must be thin where the sandwich had come to rest, but no one said anything. We waited. The kid hesitated; then, maybe out of defiance, to show that he wasn't afraid, or maybe simply because he was very hungry, he started moving out across the ice, crawling slowly on all fours. Everyone held his breath. We sat down on the riverbank, pressing against one another, and watched the kid as he advanced like a cautious little animal. We could tell he was trying to make himself as light as possible, even though he wasn't very heavy to begin with. The closer he got to his sandwich, the more our little group of spectators managed to recover from our original amazement, and we began to cheer him on, beating out a cadence whose rhythm grew faster and faster. At the moment when he stretched out his hand toward the bread and bacon, everything went awry. The ice beneath him suddenly withdrew, like a tablecloth snapped off a table, and he disappeared without a cry into the waters of the river.

A forester named Hobel happened to be passing not far away, and it was he, alerted by our cries, who pulled the boy out of the river some minutes later with the help of a long pole. The kid's face was as white as cream. Even his lips had turned white. His eyes were closed, and he was smiling. Some of us thought he was dead for sure. Nevertheless, he was put under blankets and his skin rubbed with alcohol, and several hours later he came to. Life returned to his veins and blood ran into his cheeks. The first thing he asked for was his afternoon snack, but in the asking, he stumbled over every word, as if the cold, flowing river had frozen his mouth and his tongue had remained enclosed and half dead under a caparison of ice. He received his nickname that day, and thereafter no one ever called him anything other than *Zungfrost*.

When I reached the landing, I could hear voices coming from the council room. My heart started beating a bit faster. I took a deep breath, uncovered my head, and knocked at the door before entering.

The council room is huge. I'd even say it's too big for the little that goes on in it. It's something out of another era, from a time when a community's riches were measured in proportion to its public buildings. The ceiling's improbably high. The walls, which have been simply whitewashed, are covered with ancient maps, framed parchments whereon texts written in sloping, complex scripts record laws, leases, and duties dating back to the time when the village was dependent upon the lords of Molensheim, before the Emperor, by a charter of 1756, accorded it its freedom and declared it released from all servitude. On all these documents, wax seals hang from shriveled ribbons.

Ordinarily the members of the village council sit on either side of the mayor at a large table, facing several rows of benches set out to accommodate the citizens who come to hear the council's deliberations. That evening the table was there, but the benches had been shoved into a corner of the room and piled atop one another in monumental disorder. The only objects in front of the big table were a single chair and a tiny desk.

"Come on in, Brodeck, we're not going to eat you . . ." That was Orschwir, addressing me from his central place at the table. His words elicited from the others a bit of muffled laughter, apparently an expression of their self-assurance and complicity. There were two of them. On the mayor's left, Lawyer Knopf stuffed tobacco into his pipe while looking at me over the smudged lenses of his spectacles. The chair on Orschwir's right was empty, but Göbbler occupied the next seat over. He leaned toward me and turned his head; because his eyes betrayed him more and more with each passing day, he'd apparently decided to try to see people and things with his ears instead. My blood ran cold at the sight of him.

"Are you going to sit down or not?" Orschwir said. The

warmth in his voice sounded forced. "You're among friends, Brodeck. Make yourself at home. You have nothing to fear."

I was on the point of asking the mayor the reason for my neighbor's presence, and for Lawyer Knopf's as well; Knopf may have been one of the village notables, but he wasn't even a member of the council. Why were he and Göbbler there and nobody else? Why precisely those two? What offices did they hold? What were their functions? What qualified them to sit behind the big table?

My brain was boiling with all these questions when I heard the door open behind me. A broad smile lit up Orschwir's face. "Come in, please," he said respectfully, addressing the newcomer, whom I couldn't yet see. "You haven't missed anything. We were just about to get started."

Halting steps, punctuated by the taps of a cane, resounded in the room. The new arrival was approaching, but I still couldn't see him. The sounds at my back came closer. I didn't want to turn around. He paused a few paces from me, and then I heard him say, "Hello, Brodeck." I'd heard that voice tell me hello hundreds and hundreds of times. My heart stopped beating; I closed my eyes; my hands felt damp. A bitter taste flooded my mouth. The steps behind me began again, elegantly slow. Then there was the sound of a chair scraping the floor, followed by silence. I opened my eyes again. Ernst-Peter Limmat, my old schoolmaster, was sitting in the chair on Orschwir's right, looking at me.

"Have you lost your tongue, Brodeck? Come on! We're all here! Read us what you've written so far."

As he spoke these words, Orschwir rubbed his hands together, the way he rubbed them after concluding a shrewd business deal. It wasn't my tongue that had gone missing. That wasn't what I'd lost all of a sudden. It was something else: another portion, perhaps, of faith and hope.

My dear old teacher Limmat, what were you doing there, sitting behind that table like a judge in a tribunal? So you knew, too, didn't you?

XVIII

The faces. Their faces. Was this another of those agonizing dreams, like the ones that used to seize me at night in the camp and fling me into a world where nothing was familiar? Where am I? Will this all come to an end some day? Is this Hell? What wrong have I done? Tell me, Amelia. Why is this happening? Because I left you? Yes, it's true: I left you. I wasn't there. My darling, forgive me, please forgive me. You know they took me away. You know there was nothing I could do. Speak to me. Tell me what I am. Tell me you love me. Stop that humming, I beg you, stop it. Stop droning that tune. It breaks my head and my heart. Open your lips and let words come out. I can hear everything now. I can understand everything. I'm so tired. I'm so insignificant, and there's no light in my life without you. I'm dust, and I know it. I'm futile.

I've drunk a little too much this evening. It's the middle of the night. I'm not afraid of anything anymore. I must write everything down. They could be coming. I'm waiting for them. Yes, I'm waiting for them.

In the council room, I read the few pages—ten at the most— on which I'd recorded witnesses' statements and reconstructed events. I kept my eyes on the lines, never looking up at my audience of four, who sat there and listened. I kept slipping off the chair, whose seat was tilted forward, and the desk was so small that my legs barely fit under it. My position was distinctly uncomfortable, but that's what they wanted: they wanted me to be ill at ease in that vast room, in that trial-like setting.

I read in a lifeless, absent voice. I hadn't yet recovered from the surprise—and the bitter disappointment—of encountering my former schoolmaster there. My eyes and mouth read, but my thoughts were elsewhere. Many memories of him came to my mind, some of them very old: my first day of school, when I stepped inside the door and saw his eyes turn toward me, big eyes of a glacial blue, the blue of deep crevasses; and the times—how I'd loved them!—when he had me stay after school and helped me progress in my studies, helped me make up for the time I'd lost, coaching me with patience and kindness. His voice grew less solemn during those sessions. We were alone together, and he spoke to me gently, corrected my mistakes without anger, encouraged me. I remember back then, when I was still a little boy and I'd lie awake at night trying to evoke my father's face, I would often catch myself giving him the schoolmaster's features, and I also remember that the image was pleasant and comforting.

A short while ago, when I came back home, I pulled down the mushrooms, the trumpets of death that Limmat had given me the other day when I visited him to talk about the foxes, and threw the garlands into the fire.

Fedorine opened one eye and noticed what I was doing. "Are you crazy?" she asked. "What's wrong with them?"

"With them? Nothing. But the hands that strung them together aren't exactly clean."

There was a ball of coarse wool and some knitting needles in her lap. She said, "You're speaking Tibershoï, Brodeck."

Tibershoï is the magic language of the country of Tibipoï, the setting of so many of Fedorine's tales. Elves, gnomes, and trolls speak Tibershoï, but humans can never understand it.

I didn't reply to her. I grabbed the brandy bottle and a glass and went out to the shed. It took me several long minutes to free the door from all the snow piled up against it. And snow was still falling; the night was full of it. The wind had stopped, and the snowflakes, abandoned to their own caprice, came down in unpredictable, graceful swirls.

There was a long silence in the council room when I finished reading what I'd written. It was a question of who would speak first. I raised my eyes to them, which I hadn't done since I'd started to read. Lawyer Knopf was sucking his pipe as though the fate of the world depended on it. He couldn't produce more than a wisp of smoke, and this seemed to irritate him. Göbbler was apparently asleep, and Orschwir was making a note on a piece of paper. Limmat alone was looking at me and smiling. The mayor raised his head. "Good," he said. "Very good, Brodeck. It's very interesting and well written. Keep on going, you're on the right path."

He turned toward the others on either side of him, seeking their assent or authorizing them to state their opinions. Göbbler dived in first. "I was expecting more, Brodeck. I hear your typewriter so much. It seems to me you really write a lot, and yet the Report is far from being finished . . ."

I tried to hide my anger. I tried to reply calmly, without showing surprise at anything, without challenging Göbbler's observation or even his presence. I surely would have liked to tell him that he'd do better to direct his attention to the fire burning in his wife's ass than to my compositions. I replied that writing this sort of Report did not come naturally to me, that I had difficulty finding the right tone and the right words, that collating the statements of the people I'd interviewed, putting together an accurate account, seizing the truth of what had gone on during the last few months constituted an arduous task. Yes, I was constantly at my typewriter, but I labored, I revised, I crossed out, I tore up, I started over, and that was the reason why I wasn't going farther or faster.

"I didn't mean to upset you, Brodeck. What I said was just a passing comment. I apologize," Göbbler said, miming embarrassment.

Orschwir seemed satisfied with my justifications. He turned once more to his colleagues on either hand. Siegfried Knopf looked happy because his pipe was working again. He gazed upon it with benevolent eyes and stroked its bowl with both hands, without paying the least heed to the people around him.

"Schoolmaster Limmat, perhaps you have a question?" the mayor asked respectfully, turning toward the old teacher. I felt the sweat spring to my forehead, as it had done when he quizzed me in front of the whole class. Limmat smiled, allowed some time to pass, and rubbed his long hands together.

"No, not a question, Mr. Mayor, but rather a remark, a simple remark . . . I know Brodeck very well. I've known him a long time. I know he'll conscientiously perform the task we've entrusted to him, but . . . how shall I say it . . . he's a dreamer, and I use that word in no bad sense because I think dreaming is a great and positive thing, but in this particular case, he mustn't make a muddle of everything, he mustn't mix up dreams and reality or confuse what exists with what never took place. I exhort him to pay attention. I exhort him to stay on the straight road and not to let his imagination govern his thoughts and his sentences."

For hours after the meeting, I kept going over Limmat's words in my mind. What were they supposed to mean? I had no idea.

"We won't keep you any longer, Brodeck. I imagine you're in a hurry to get back home." Having said these words, Orschwir rose to his feet, and I immediately followed suit. I bade farewell to the others with a little movement of my head and began walking rapidly toward the door. This was the moment that Lawyer Knopf chose to arouse himself from his reverie. His old nanny-goat's voice caught up with me: "That's a handsome cap you've got there, Brodeck. It must be really warm. I've never seen anything like it . . . Where'd you get it?"

I turned around. Lawyer Knopf was approaching me, hopping a little on his crooked legs. His eyes were fixed on the *Anderer's* cap, which I had just placed on my head. Knopf was now quite close to me, and he reached for the cap with one clawlike hand. I felt his fingers running over the fur. "Very original, and what fine work! Beautiful! Just the thing for the weather that's on the way. I envy you, Brodeck."

Knopf trembled a little as he stroked the cap. I could smell his tobacco-laden breath, and I saw a delirious light dancing in his eyes. Suddenly I wondered whether he hadn't gone mad. Göbbler came over to us and said, "You didn't answer Lawyer Knopf's question, Brodeck. He wants to know who made your cap for you."

I hesitated. I hesitated between silence and a few words I could fling at them like knives. Göbbler was waiting. Limmat joined us, clutching the lapels of his velvet jacket around his skinny neck.

In the end, I summoned up a confident tone and said, "Göbbler, you'll never believe me, but be that as it may, I'm going to tell you the absolute truth. Remember, however, that it's a secret, and please don't repeat it to anyone. You see this cap? Just imagine, the Virgin Mary made it for me and the Holy Ghost delivered it!"

Ernst-Peter Limmat burst out laughing. Knopf laughed, too. Göbbler was the only one scowling. His nearly dead eyes searched for mine, as if he wanted to gouge them out. I left the lot of them standing there and went out the door.

Outside the snow hadn't stopped falling, and the path *Zungfrost* had cleared an hour previously had already vanished. The village streets were deserted. Halos quivered around the lanterns hanging from the gables. The wind had come up again, but very lightly, and it made the snowflakes flutter in every direction. Suddenly I felt a presence against me. It was *Ohnmeist*, who was trying to bury his cold muzzle in my pants. Such familiarity surprised me. I began to wonder whether the dog wasn't mistaking me for someone else, for the *Anderer*, the only other person with whom it had taken such liberties.

We trudged along side by side, the dog and I, surrounded by the smells of the snowy cold and the pinewood smoke that came down from the chimneys in gusts. I no longer remember exactly what I thought about in the course of that strange promenade, but I know that suddenly I found myself very far from those streets, very far from the village, very far from familiar, barbaric faces. I was walking with Amelia. We were holding on to each other, arm in arm. She was wearing a coat of blue cloth with embroidered sleeves and a border of gray rabbit fur around the collar. Her hair, her most beautiful hair, was coiled up under a little red hat. It was very cold. We were very cold. It was our second meeting. I gazed hungrily at her face, at her every gesture, her small hands, her laughter, her eyes.

"So you're a student, you say?"

She had a delicious accent, which slid over her words and gave them all, the pretty ones as well as the ugly ones, a discreet highlight. We were circling the lake for the third time, walking along the Elsi Promenade. We weren't alone. There were other couples like us, groups of two people looking at each other a great deal, speaking little, laughing for no reason, and falling silent again. With the three pennies I'd borrowed off Ulli Rätte, I bought a sizzling hot crêpe from the vendor whose stall was next to the skating rink. He poured a generous extra spoonful of honey over the crêpe and held it out to us, saying, "For the lovers!" We smiled, but we didn't dare look at each other. I offered the crêpe to Amelia. She seized it as though it were a treasure, cut it in half, and handed me my portion. Night was falling, and with it the icy air that turned Amelia's cheeks even rosier and made her hazel eyes shine all the more brightly. We ate the crêpe. We looked at each other. We were at the very beginning of our life.

With a long, drawn-out whine, *Ohnmeist* brought me back to the village. He rubbed his head against me one more time and then went away, taking little steps and wagging his tail as if waving good-bye. I followed him with my eyes until he disappeared behind the woodshed that stands beside the workroom in Gott's smithy. He'd probably found some shelter there for the winter.

I hadn't noticed how much distance the dog and I had covered. We'd gone all the way to the end of the village, close to the church and the cemetery. The snow was coming down as thickly as before. The edge of the forest was invisible, even though it began barely thirty meters away. When the church came into sight, I thought about Father Peiper, and the light in his kitchen window made me decide to knock on his door.

XIX

I spoke and Peiper listened, steadily refilling his glass. I spilled my guts. I went on at length. I didn't talk about the pages I'm writing alongside the Report, but I discussed everything else. I revealed all my doubts and fears. I told him how odd it felt to have fallen into a trap and to be unable to understand who had woven it, who was holding the cords, why I had been pushed into it, and especially how I might manage to get out of it. When I finally stopped, Peiper let a little while pass in silence. Talking had done me good.

"Who are you confiding in, Brodeck? The man, or what's left of the priest?"

I hesitated to reply, simply because I had no idea what my reply should be. Peiper sensed my confusion and said, "I'm asking the question because the two aren't the same. You know they aren't, even though you no longer believe in God. I'm going to help you a bit, and I'll start by telling you something in confidence: I hardly believe in God anymore, either. I spoke to Him for a long time, for years and years, and throughout those years, He really seemed to listen to me and to respond as well, with little signs, with the thoughts that came to me, with the things He inspired me to do. And then, that all stopped. I know now that

He doesn't exist or He's gone away forever, which comes to the same thing. So there it is: we're alone. Nevertheless, I go on with the show. I play my part badly, no doubt, but the theater's still standing. It causes no one any harm, and there are some elderly souls in the audience who would be still more alone and still more abandoned if I closed the place down. You see, every performance gives them a little strength, the strength to go on. And there's another principle I haven't repudiated: the seal of confession. It's my cross, and I bear it. I shall bear it to the end."

All at once, he grabbed my hand and squeezed it tightly. "I know everything, Brodeck. Everything. And you can't even imagine what that *Everything* means."

He stopped talking, having just realized that his glass was empty. He rose to his feet, trembling, and cast anxious looks at the bottles that littered the room. He moved five or six before finding one that still held a little wine. He smiled and clasped the bottle in his arms, the way you embrace a loved one you're happy to see again. He returned to his chair and filled his glass. "Men are strange. They commit the worst crimes without question, but later they can't live anymore with the memory of what they've done. They have to get rid of it. And so they come to me, because they know I'm the only person who can give them relief, and they tell me everything. I'm the sewer, Brodeck. I'm not the priest; I'm the sewer man. I'm the man into whose brain they can pour all their ordure, all their filthy deeds, and then they feel relieved, they feel unburdened. When it's over, they go away as though nothing's happened. They're all new and clean. Ready to start afresh. They know the sewer has closed over what they dumped into it and will never repeat what it's heard to anybody. They can sleep in peace, Brodeck, and at the same time I'm all awash, I'm overflowing, I can't take any more, but I hold on, I try to hold on. I'll die with all these deposits, these horrors, in me. You see this wine? It's my only friend. It puts me to sleep and makes me forget, for a little while, the great, vile mass I carry around inside, the putrid load they've all entrusted to me. I'm not telling you this because I want your pity. I just want you to understand. You feel alone because you must write about hideous things; I feel alone because I must absolve them."

He stopped, and in the multiple, moving light of the candles, I distinctly saw his eyes fill with tears.

"I didn't always drink, Brodeck, as you well know. Before the war, water was my daily beverage, and I knew that God was at my side. The war . . . maybe the peoples of the world need such nightmares. They lay waste to what they've taken centuries to build. They destroy today what they praised yesterday. They authorize what was forbidden. They give preferential treatment to what they used to condemn. War is a great broom that sweeps the world. It's the place where the mediocre triumphs and the criminal receives a saint's halo; people prostrate themselves before him and acclaim him and fawn upon him. Must men find life so gloomy and monotonous that they long for massacre and ruin? I've seen them jump up and down on the edge of the abyss, walk along its crest, and look with fascination upon the horror of the void, where the vilest passions hold sway. Destroy! Defile! Rape! Slash! If you had seen them . . ."

The priest snatched my wrist and pressed it hard. "Why do you think they tolerate my incoherent sermons and my drunken Masses, my cursing and raving? Why do they all come to church?

Why hasn't anyone asked the bishop to recall me? Because they're afraid, Brodeck. It's as simple as that: they're afraid of me and of all the things I know about them. Fear is what governs the world. It holds men by their little balls. It squeezes them from time to time, just to remind their owners that it could annihilate them if it so desired. I see their faces in my church when I'm in the pulpit. I see them through their masks of false calm. I smell their sour sweat. I smell it. It's not holy water running down the cracks of their asses, believe me! They must curse themselves for having told me so much . . . Do you remember when you were an altar boy, Brodeck? Do you remember serving when I said Mass?"

I was very small, and Father Peiper made a great impression on me. He had a deep, silky voice, a voice that wine-bibbing hadn't yet worn down. He never laughed. I wore a white alb and a bright-red collar. I closed my eyes and inhaled the incense, believing God would come into me more readily if I did that. My happiness, my bliss was without flaw. There were no races, no differences among men. I'd forgotten who I was and where I'd come from. I'd never thought about the bit of flesh missing from between my thighs, and no one had ever reproached me for it. We were all God's people. At the altar in our little church, I stood at Father Peiper's side. He turned the pages of the Holy Book. He brandished the host and the chalice. I rang the little bells. I presented him the water and the wine and the white linen cloth he used to wipe his lips. I knew there was a Heaven for the innocent and a Hell for the guilty. Everything seemed simple to me.

"He came to visit me once . . ." Peiper's head was bowed down, and his voice had become colorless. I thought he was talking about God again.

"He came, but I don't think I was capable of understanding him. He was so . . . different. I couldn't . . . I wasn't able to understand him."

Suddenly I realized that the priest was talking about the *Anderer*.

"It couldn't end any other way, Brodeck. That man was like a mirror, you see. He didn't have to say a single word. They each saw their reflection in him. Or maybe he was God's last messenger, before He closes up shop and throws away the keys. I'm the sewer, but that fellow was the mirror. And mirrors, Brodeck— mirrors can only break."

As though underlining his words, Peiper grabbed the bottle in front of him and hurled it against the wall. Then he grabbed another one and another one and another one after that, and as each bottle shattered, launching thousands of glass shards to all corners of the kitchen, he laughed, he laughed like one of the damned and shouted, *"Ziebe Jarh vo Missgesck! Ziebe Jarh vo Missgesck! Ziebe Jarh vo Missgesck!"*—"Seven years of bad luck! Seven years of bad luck! Seven years of bad luck!" Then, abruptly, he stopped, clutched his face in his hands, threw himself forward onto the table, and sobbed like a child.

I stayed with him for a few moments without daring to move or say a word. He sniffled twice, very loudly, and then there was silence. He remained in his chair, his upper body sprawled on the table, his head hidden between his arms. The candles consumed themselves and went out, one by one, and the kitchen gradually grew dark. Peaceful snores emanated from Peiper's body. The church bell sounded ten o'clock. I left the room, closing the door very gently behind me.

I was surprised by the light outdoors. The snow had stopped, and the sky was almost entirely clear. The last clouds were still trying to cling to the Schnikelkopf peaks, but the wind, now blowing from the east, was busy tidying them up, tearing the cloud remnants into small strips. The stars had put on their silver apparel. As I raised my head and looked at them, I felt as though I were plunging into a sea both dark and glittering, its inky depths studded with innumerable bright pearls. They seemed very near. I even made the stupid gesture of stretching out my hand, as if I might seize a handful of them and stick them inside my coat as a present for Poupchette.

Smoke rose straight up from the chimneys. The air had become very dry again, and the cold had formed a hard, sparkling crust on the mounds of snow piled up in front of the houses. I felt in my pocket for the pages I'd read to the others a few hours ago; they were just a few thin sheets of very light paper, but they seemed heavy and hot. I thought over what Peiper had told me about the *Anderer,* and it was hard for me to decide between the ravings of a drunkard and the words of a man accustomed to speaking in parables. More than anything else, I wondered why the *Anderer* had visited the priest, especially considering that our new neighbor quite noticeably avoided the church and never went to Mass. What could he and Peiper have talked about?

As I passed Schloss's inn, I saw that a light was still burning in the main room. And then—I don't know why—I felt a sudden urge to step inside.

Dieter Schloss was behind the bar, talking with Caspar Hausorn. They were both leaning forward, so close to each other that you would have thought they were going to kiss. I let out a greeting that made them jump, and then I went over to the table in the corner, right next to the fireplace, and sat down.

"Do you still have some hot wine?"

Schloss nodded. Hausorn turned in my direction and made a curt movement with his head that might have passed for a "good evening." Then he leaned toward Schloss's ear once more, murmured something the innkeeper seemed to agree with, picked up his cap, finished his beer in one gulp, and left without looking at me again.

It was the second time I'd been in the inn since the *Ereigniës*. And just as I had done the previous time, I found it hard to believe that this very ordinary place was where a man had been put to death. The inn looked like any other village inn: a few tables, chairs, and benches, shelves holding one-liter bottles of wine and liquor, big, framed mirrors so covered with soot they hadn't reflected anything for years, a cabinet for the chess and checkers sets, sawdust on the floor. The rooms were upstairs. There were exactly four of them. Three of them hadn't been used for a long time. As for the fourth room, the biggest and also the prettiest, it had been occupied by the *Anderer.*

On the day following the *Ereigniës,* after my visit to Orschwir, I'd stayed in Mother Pitz's place for nearly an hour in an effort to recover my wits, to calm my mind and my heart, while the old woman sat beside me, turning the pages of a volume of her dried-plant collection and providing a running commentary on all the flowers pressed inside the book. Then, after my head had finally cleared, I thanked her, left her café, and went straight to the inn. I found the door locked and the shutters closed. It was the first time I'd ever seen Schloss's inn in that state. I knocked on the door, dealing it rapid, heavy blows, and waited. Nothing. I knocked again even harder, and this time a shutter opened partway and Schloss appeared at the window, looking suspicious and fearful.

"What do you want, Brodeck?"

"I want to talk to you. Open up."

"This may not be the best time."

"Open up, Schloss. You know I have to make the Report."

The word had come out of my mouth all by itself. Using it for the first time felt utterly strange, but it had an immediate effect on Schloss. He closed the shutter, and I heard him hurrying downstairs. A few seconds later, he was unbolting the big door. He opened it and said, "Come in quick!"

He closed the door behind me so promptly that I couldn't stop myself from asking him if he was worried that a ghost might slip inside. He said, "That's no joking matter, Brodeck," and crossed himself twice. "What do you want?"

"I want you to show me the room."

"What room?"

"Don't play dumb. The room."

Schloss hesitated. He seemed to be thinking over my request. Then he said, "Why do you want to see it?"

"I want to see it right now. I want to be thorough. I don't want to forget anything. I have to tell the whole story."

Schloss ran his hand over his forehead, which was gleaming as though he'd rubbed it with lard. "There's not a lot to see, but if you insist . . . Follow me."

We climbed the stairs to the upper floor. Schloss's big body took up the entire width of the staircase, and every step bent under his weight. He was breathing hard. When we got to the landing, he reached into one of the pockets in his apron, took out a key, and handed it to me, saying, "I'll let you unlock the door, Brodeck."

I had to insert the key three times before I could turn it. I couldn't control my shaking hand. Schloss backed off a few steps and tried to catch his breath. Finally there was a little click, and I pushed the door open. My heart was like a hunted bird. I was afraid of seeing that room again, afraid of encountering a dead man, but what I saw surprised me so much that my anxiety vanished at once.

The room was completely empty. There was no more furniture, no more art objects, no more clothes, no trunks; all that remained was a big wardrobe, which was bolted to the wall. I opened the double doors, but the wardrobe, too, was empty. There was nothing in the room anymore. It was as if the *Anderer* had never occupied it. As if he'd never existed.

"What happened to all his baggage?"

"What are you talking about, Brodeck?"

"Don't insult me, Schloss."

The room smelled like damp wood and soap. The floor had been copiously wetted down and scrubbed. In the place where the bed used to stand, I could make out a big stain, which was darker than the rest of the bare larch-wood planks.

"Was it you who washed the floor?"

"Somebody had to do it . . ."

"And what's that stain?"

"What do you think it is, Brodeck?"

I turned to Schloss.

"What do you think?" he repeated wearily.

_____

XX

I got up very late this morning, with a hammer at work inside my head. I believe I really drank too much last night. The brandy bottle's almost completely empty. My mouth's as dry as tinder, and I have no idea how I found the way to my bed. I wrote late into the night, and I remember being unable to feel my fingers toward the end because the cold had numbed them. I also remember that the keys on the typewriter were sticking more and more. The windowpane was covered with frost shaped like fern fronds, and I was so drunk I thought the forest was on the march, preparing to surround and smother the shed, and me with it.

When I finally got out of bed, Fedorine asked no questions. She brewed an infusion for me, a concoction in which I recognized the aromas of wild thyme, pennyroyal, and houseleek. She simply said, "Drink this. It's good for what you've got." I did what she said, as I used to do when I was little. Then she placed before me a basket Alfred Wurtzwiller had brought a little earlier in the day. It contained potato soup, a loaf of rye bread, half a ham, apples, and leeks—but no money. This wasn't my usual delivery. When the administration in S. deigned to show that it hadn't completely forgotten me, I'd receive a money order, along with three or four stamped, restamped, signed, and countersigned official documents, attesting to the payment made thereby. But in this basket, there was only food. I couldn't help drawing a connection between the food basket and the previous evening's audition in front of the mayor and the others. They were paying me like this. They were paying me a little. For the Report. For what I'd already written, and—especially—for what I hadn't written.

Next, Fedorine bathed Poupchette in the tub. My darling clapped her hands and slapped the hot water, laughing and shouting, "Li'l fish! Li'l fish!" I took her in my arms, pressing her against me, as wet as she was, and kissed her soft, warm, naked skin, which made her laugh all the more. Behind us, at the window, her eyes raised to the distance and the white immensity of the valley, Amelia hummed her song. Poupchette started struggling, and I put her down. She scooped up a handful of suds, ran to her mother, and threw them at her. Amelia turned and looked at the child but kept right on humming. Her dead eyes settled for a few moments on Poupchette's pretty smile, and then she stared out at the whiteness again.

I feel weak and useless. I'm trying to write things down, but who's going to read them? Who? I'd do better to take Amelia and Poupchette in my arms, sling old Fedorine across my back, along with a bundle of provisions, clothes, and a few nice keepsakes, and go far away from here. Start over. Start all over again. In the old days, Nösel said this was mankind's distinguishing feature: "Man is an animal that always starts over." Nösel spoke in slow, cadenced, spellbinding sentences, his two hands flat on his wide desk, and after each pronouncement he left a great silence, which each of us could fill as he chose.

"Man is an animal that always starts over." But what is it he's always starting over? His mistakes, or the fragile scaffolding whose construction sometimes allows him to climb close to heaven? Nösel never said, maybe because he knew that life itself, the life we hadn't completely entered yet, would eventually make us understand. Or maybe because he simply had no idea, or because he was untroubled by doubts, or because he'd fed on books for so long he'd forgotten the real world and those who dwelled in it.

Last night, Schloss brought me my hot wine and then sat down uninvited at my table. I knew he wanted to say something to me, but I had nothing to say to him. I was too absorbed in what Father Peiper had told me. Moreover, I wanted to drink my glass of hot wine and feel the fire reviving my body, and that was all. I wasn't looking for anything else. My skull was teeming with unanswered questions and hundreds of little pieces of a big mechanism I had to invent so that I could put it together.

"I know you don't like me too much, Brodeck," Schloss suddenly murmured. I'd forgotten he was there. "But I'm not the worst, you know."

The innkeeper seemed even bigger and sweatier than usual. He was twisting his fingers and gnawing his plump, cracked lips. "I did what I was told, that's all. I don't want any trouble, but that doesn't stop me from thinking . . . Look, I'm only a simple man. I'm not as intelligent as you are, but whatever you might think, I'm not vicious, either. I'm not the worst. It's true that I served drinks to the *Fratergekeime* while they occupied the village. But what did you want me to do? Serving drinks is my business. I wasn't about to get myself killed for refusing to serve a glass of beer. I've always regretted what happened to you, Brodeck, I swear, and I had nothing to do with it, you can believe me . . . and as for what they did to your wife . . . My God . . ."

I nearly spat in Schloss's face when he referred to Amelia, but what he said after that stopped me.

"I loved my wife, too, you know. Maybe that seems strange to you, because as you may remember she wasn't very beautiful, but now she's not here I feel like I'm living only half a life. Nothing's important anymore. If Gerthe had been here during the war, who knows, maybe I wouldn't have served the *Fratergekeime*. I felt strong in her presence . . . Maybe I would've spat in their faces. Maybe I would've grabbed the big knife I cut onions with and stuck it in their bellies. And then, if she'd been here, maybe . . . maybe the *Murmelnër* would still be alive, maybe I would've got myself killed before I let anything happen to him under my roof . . ."

I felt my stomach churning. A touch of nausea. The hot wine didn't agree with me. It wasn't warming my insides, it was nibbling at them, like a little animal in my stomach, suddenly trying to get a bite of everything within reach. I looked at Schloss as though I'd never seen him before. It was as if a bank of fog had dissolved, bit by bit, and behind it an unsuspected, oddly harmonious landscape was visible. At the same time, I wondered whether Schloss might be trying to fool me. It's always easy to regret what happened after it happens. Regret costs nothing. It allows you to wash your hands and your memory, to cleanse them thoroughly and make them pure and white. But all the same, what Peiper told me about confession and the sewer—that was really something! All the men of the village must have passed through his confessional eventually, and Schloss probably wasn't the last of them. And then I remembered too clearly his attitude and his face on the night of the *Ereigniës*—he hadn't exactly hung back. He didn't seem then to disapprove of the crime committed within his walls, whatever he might say to me now. He hadn't looked like a man seized by the terror and horror of what had just taken place.

I wasn't sure what to think. I'm still not sure what to think. That's evidence of what is, without a doubt, the camp's great victory over its prisoners; that is, over those it didn't kill. The others, the ones who came out of it alive, like me—all of us still carry a part of it, deep down inside, like a stain. We can never again meet the eyes of other people without wondering whether they harbor the desire to hunt us down, to torture us, to kill us. We've become perpetual prey, creatures which, whatever they do, will always look upon the dawning day as the start of a long ordeal of survival and upon nightfall with an odd feeling of relief. Disappointment and disquiet ferment in us. I think we've become, and will remain until the day we die, the memory of humanity destroyed. We're wounds that will never heal.

"Maybe you don't know we had a baby before the war," Schloss went on. "It was when you were far away, studying at the University, and maybe Fedorine didn't write you about it. The baby didn't live long—four days and four nights. It was a boy. The midwife, old Paula Beckenart, may she rest in peace, said he looked just like a little Schloss. She helped him out of Gerthe's belly on the seventh of April. Outside the birds were chirping and the larch buds were becoming as big as plums. The first time Paula placed him in my arms, I thought I wouldn't know how to hold him. I was afraid I'd squeeze him too tight or smother him with my big hands, and I was also afraid of dropping him. I imagined him breaking apart like crystal. Gerthe laughed at me, and the little one hollered and waved his arms and legs. But as soon as he found Gerthe's breast, he started sucking her milk and didn't stop, as if he wanted to empty her completely. I'd had Hans

Douda make a cradle from the trunk of a walnut tree. It was a fine piece of wood he was saving to make a wardrobe, but I put the gold coins on his workbench and the deal was done."

Schloss had big, dirty fingernails. As he told me about his child, he made an effort to clean them—without even looking at them—but they stayed black.

"He really occupied that cradle. He beat the bottom of it with his little feet as hard as he could. He made a pretty noise, like the sound of ax blows coming from deep in the forest. Gerthe wanted to call him Stephan, and I preferred Reichart. To tell the truth, we'd been caught off guard; we'd both persuaded ourselves that the baby had to be a girl. We had a name ready for the little girl who never came: Lisebeth, because Lise was my mother's name, and Gerthe's mother was Bethsie. But when the little man made his appearance and the midwife held him up in the air, we had no name for him. Throughout the four days of his short life, Gerthe and I squabbled constantly over his name, laughing the whole time. I'd say, 'Reichart'; she'd reply, 'Stephan.' It became a game, a game that ended in hugs and kisses. And so when the child died, he didn't have a name. He died nameless, and I've blamed myself for that ever since, as though it was part of what killed him."

Schloss fell silent and bowed his head. He stopped moving entirely, as though he'd ceased to breathe. My mouth tasted like cinnamon and cloves, and the gnawing in my stomach hadn't let up.

"Sometimes I dream about him at night. He reaches out to me with his tiny hands, and then he leaves, he goes away, like there's some force carrying him off, and there's no name I can call out, there's no name I can say to try and hold him back."

Schloss had lifted his head and spoken those last words with his eyes fixed on mine. His eyes were big, overflowing; they took up too much space; I felt as though they were crowding me out. He was surely waiting for me to say something, but what? I knew well that ghosts can cling stubbornly to life and that sometimes they're more present than the living.

"One morning I woke up and Gerthe wasn't in bed anymore. I hadn't heard anything. She was kneeling beside the cradle and not moving. I called her. She didn't reply. She didn't even turn her head toward me. I got up and went over to her, crooning the names, Stephan, Reichart . . . Gerthe leaped to her feet and pounced on me like an animal gone crazy, trying to hit me, tearing at my mouth, scratching my cheeks. I looked into the cradle and saw the baby's face. His eyes were closed, and his skin was the color of clay."

I don't know how long I stayed with Schloss after he told me that. I also can't recall whether he kept talking about his child or just sat there in silence. The fire in the hearth died down. He didn't add more wood. The flames went out, and then the few embers. It got cold. At some point, I stood up and Schloss accompanied me to the door. He clasped my hand at length, and then he thanked me. Twice. For what?

On the way back, my head was buzzing, and I had the feeling that my temples were banging together like cymbals. I found myself saying Poupchette's name aloud, again and again: "Poupchette, Poupchette, Poupchette, Poupchette . . ." It was like throwing little stones into the air, pebbles of sound that would bring me home quickly. I couldn't stop myself from thinking about Schloss's dead baby, about all the things he'd told me, about the few hours the child had spent in our world. Human life is so strange. Once you've plunged into it, you often wonder what you're doing here. Maybe that's why some, a little cleverer than the others, content themselves with opening the door a crack and taking a look around, and when they see what's inside, they want nothing more than to close that door as fast as possible.

Maybe they're right.

XXI

I want to go back to the first day, or rather to the first evening: the evening when the *Anderer* appeared in our village. I've reported his meeting with the oldest Dörfer child, but I haven't described his arrival at the inn a few minutes later. My account is based on the statements I took from three different eyewitnesses: Schloss himself; Menigue Wirfrau, the baker, who'd gone to the inn to drink a glass of wine; and Doris Klattermeier, a young girl with pink skin and hay-colored hair, who was passing in the street when the *Anderer* arrived. There were other witness, both in the inn and outside, but the three named above related the events in almost exactly the same way, except for one or two small details, and I thought it best to rely on them.

The *Anderer* had dismounted to speak to the Dörfer boy, and he walked the rest of the way to the inn, leading his horse by the reins while the donkey followed a few paces behind. He tethered the animals to the ring outside; then, instead of opening the door and entering the inn like everyone else, he knocked three times and waited. This was such an unusual thing to do that he had to stand there for a long time. "I thought it was a prankster," Schloss told me. "Or some kid!" In short, nothing happened. The *Anderer* waited. No one opened the door for him, nor did he open it for himself. Some people, among them young Doris, had already gathered to observe the phenomenon: the horse, the ass, the baggage, and the oddly attired fellow standing outside the door of the inn with a smile on his round, powdered face. After a few minutes, he knocked again, but this time the three blows were harder and sharper. Schloss said, "At that point, I figured something out of the ordinary was going on, and I went to see."

So Schloss opened the door and found himself face-to-face with the *Anderer.* "I nearly choked! Where did this guy come from, I thought, the circus or a fairy tale?" But the *Anderer* didn't give him time to recover. He lifted his funny hat, revealing his very round, very bald pate, made a supple, elegant gesture of salutation, and said, "Greetings, kind sir. My friends"—here he indicated the horse and the donkey—"and I have come a great distance and find ourselves quite exhausted. Would you be kind enough to offer us the hospitality of your establishment? In exchange for our payment, of course."

Schloss is convinced that the *Anderer* said, "Greetings, Mr. Schloss," but young Doris and Wirfrau both swear that this was not the case. Schloss was probably so stunned by the strange apparition and its request that he lost his bearings for a few moments. He said, "I didn't know how to answer him at first. It had been so many years since we'd had any visitors, except for the ones you know about! And besides, the words he used . . . He pronounced them in *Deeperschaft,* not in dialect, and my ear wasn't used to hearing that."

Menigue Wirfrau told me that Schloss hesitated for a few moments, looking at the *Anderer* and scratching his head, before he replied. As for the *Anderer,* it seems he stood motionless, smiling as if all this were perfectly normal and time—which was falling drop by drop into a narrow pipe—was of no importance. Doris Klattermeier remembered that his donkey and his horse didn't move, either. She shivered a little when she told me that, and then she made the sign of the cross, twice. For most of the people in our village, God is a distant being composed of books and incense; the Devil, on the other hand, is a neighbor whom many of them believe they've seen once or twice.

At last, Schloss uttered a few words. "He asked the stranger how many nights he planned to stay," according to Wirfrau. Wirfrau was kneading when I went to see him, naked from the waist up, his chest and the rims of his eyes covered with flour. He seized the big wad of dough with both hands, lifted it, turned it, flung it into the kneading trough, and repeated the process. He spoke without looking at me. I'd found a place to sit between two sacks and the woodpile. The oven had been humming for a good while, and the little room was hot with the smell of burning wood. Wirfrau went on: "For a while, the fellow seemed to be thinking the question over, smiling the whole time. He looked at the ass and the horse, and it was like he was asking them their opinion. Then he answered in his funny voice, 'I should think that our sojourn will be rather extended.' I'm sure Schloss didn't know what to say, but he didn't want to look like a dope, either. So he shook his head several times, and then he invited the stranger to step inside."

Two hours later, the *Anderer* was lodged in the room, which Schloss had dusted in haste. The *Anderer's* bags and trunks had been brought upstairs and his horse and donkey given beds of fresh straw in the stable just across from the inn, the property of one Solzner, an old man about as lovable as a whack from a club.

At the stranger's request, a basin of fresh, pure water and a bucket of oats were placed close to the animals. He went over to make sure they were well accommodated, taking the opportunity to brush their flanks with a handful of hay and whisper in their ears some words no one heard. Then he handed old Solzner three gold pieces, the equivalent of several months' food and shelter for the beasts, bade them farewell, wished them a good night, and left the stable.

In the meanwhile, the inn had filled with people, many of whom had come to gaze upon the prodigy with their own eyes. Although not curious by nature, I must confess that I myself was one of them. The news had flashed along the streets and into the houses at lightning speed, and there were a good thirty or more of us in the inn by the time the lukewarm night settled on the roofs of the village. For all that, our curiosity remained unsatisfied, because the *Anderer* went up to his room and stayed there. Downstairs the discussion was vigorous, as was the consumption of beverages. Schloss didn't have enough hands to keep up with all the drinkers. He must surely have told himself that the arrival of a traveler was, when all was said and done, a good thing. He did as much business on that day as he did when there were fairs or funerals. Menigue Wirfrau couldn't stop describing the arrival of the *Anderer*, his outfit, his horse and his donkey, and little by little, since everyone stood him a drink to loosen his tongue, he began embellishing his account and stumbling on every word at the same time.

But every now and then we could hear footsteps upstairs, and the room would fall silent while everyone held his breath. Our eyes were fixed intently on the ceiling, as if in an effort to pass through it. We imagined the visitor. We gave him form and flesh. We were trying to enter into the labyrinth of his brain when we hadn't even set eyes on him yet.

At one point, Schloss went upstairs to ask him if everything was all right. We tried to overhear their conversation, but in vain; even those who leaned their big ears into the stairwell caught nothing. When Schloss came back down, he was immediately surrounded.

"Well?"

"Well what?"

"What did he say?"

"He said he wanted a 'collation.' "

"A 'collation'? What's that?"

"A light meal, he said."

"What are you going to do?"

"What he asked me to do!"

Everyone was curious to see what a *collation* looked like. Most of the crowd followed Schloss into his kitchen and watched him prepare a large tray, on which he put three thick slices of bacon, a sausage, some marinated gherkins, a pot of custard, a loaf of brown bread, some sweet-and-sour cabbage, and a large piece of goat cheese, together with a jug of wine and a mug of beer. When he passed through the crowd of his customers, he carried the tray devoutly, and everyone made way for him in silence, as though for the passage of a holy relic. Then Wirfrau's voice broke the spell: he was still describing the *Anderer's* arrival at the inn. No one was listening to him anymore, but because of the state he was in, that fact escaped his notice. Similarly, a little later, he failed to observe that he had confused his kneading-trough with his bed; after preparing his dough in the latter, he went to sleep in the former. The following day brought him a raging hangover, while we got a day without bread.

When I returned home, Fedorine was waiting for me: "What's going on, Brodeck?"

I told her what I'd learned. She listened to me attentively, shaking her head. "That's not good. None of it. Not good."

They were just a few simple words, but they irritated me, and I asked her curtly why she'd said them.

"When the flock has finally settled down, it must not be given any reason to start moving again," she replied.

I shrugged my shoulders. I was in a lighthearted mood. I was—I haven't realized this until today—I was probably the only person in the village pleased by the arrival of a stranger. I considered it a sign of rebirth, a return to life. For me, it was as though an iron door that for years had sealed the entrance to a cave had opened wide, and the air of that cave had suddenly received the wind and the beams of a bright sun. But I couldn't imagine that sometimes the sun grows bothersome, and its beams, which light up the world, inadvertently illuminate what people are trying to bury.

Old Fedorine knew me like a pocket she'd put her hand into several thousand times. She planted herself in front of me, looked me straight in the eye, and stroked my cheek with one trembling hand. "I'm very old, my little Brodeck, so very old," she said. "Soon I won't be around anymore. You must be careful. You've already come back once from a place people don't come back from. There's never a second chance. Never. And don't forget: you have other souls in your charge. Think about them, both of them . . ."

I'm not very big, but only at that moment did I grasp how

little Fedorine was. She looked like a child, a child with an old man's face; a bent, wizened, thin, fragile creature with crumpled, wrinkled skin, a creature a small puff of air could have swept away like a collection of dust. Her eyes shone, despite the milky cloud obscuring them, and her lips moved. I took her in my arms and pressed her against me at length, and I thought of birds, little lost birds, the weak, sick, or disconsolate sparrows that can't keep up with their fellows in the great migrations; toward the end of fall, you can see them, with their feathers drooping and panic in their hearts, perching on roofs or in the lower branches of trees, waiting resignedly for the cold that will kill them. I gave Fedorine several kisses, first on her hair, then on her forehead and cheeks, as I did when I was a child, and I recognized her smell, a smell of wax, of stoves, of clean cloth, the smell that has sufficed, almost since my life began, to bring a peaceful smile to my lips, even in my sleep. I held her against me like that for a long time, while scenes from the past flashed through my mind at lightning speed. My memory juxtaposed disparate instants, creating a bizarre mosaic whose only effect was to make me more aware of times that had fled away forever, moments that would never return.

Fedorine was there, I clasped her to me, and I could talk to her. I inhaled her smell; I felt her beating heart. It was as if mine were beating in her. Again I remembered the camp. The only thought that occupied our minds there was the thought of death. We lived in perpetual consciousness of our death, and this was, no doubt, the reason why some of us went mad. Even though man knows he'll die one day, he can't live for long in a world that offers him nothing but the consciousness of his own death, a world pervaded by death and conceived solely for that purpose.

ICH BIN NICHTS read the placard the hanged man wore. We

were quite aware that we were nothing. We knew it all too well. Each of us was a nothing. A nothing handed over to death. Its slave. Its toy. Waiting and resigned. Oddly enough, although I was a creature of nothingness, inhabiting nothingness and by it inhabited, the fact never managed to frighten me. I didn't fear my own death, or if I feared it, it was with a sort of fleeting, animal reflex. By contrast, the thought of death became unbearable when I associated it with Amelia and Fedorine. It's the death of others, of loved ones, not our own, which eats away at us and can destroy us. And that's what I've been bound to struggle against, brandishing faces and features at its black light.

XXII

In the beginning, our village welcomed the *Anderer* as some kind of monarch. Indeed, there was something like magic in the whole affair. People in these parts aren't open by nature. That can no doubt be explained, at least to some extent, by our landscape of valleys and mountains, of dense forests and hemmed-in vales, and our climate of rains and mists, of frosts and snow-storms and unbearable hot spells. And then, of course, there was the war, which failed to improve things. Doors and hearts were closed even more completely and padlocks were carefully affixed, concealing what was inside from the light of day.

But at first, once the incredible surprise of his coming among us had passed, the *Anderer* was able, however involuntarily, to emanate a charm with the power to cajole even the most hostile, for everyone wanted to see him—children, women, and oldsters included—and he happily entered into the spirit of the game, smiling at one and all, lifting his hat to the ladies and inclining his head to the men. However, he never spoke the smallest word, and if there hadn't been people who'd heard him speak the day he arrived, we might have considered him a mute.

He couldn't walk in the streets without being followed by a little band of laughing, idle kids, to whom he gave small gifts that seemed to them treasures: ribbons, glass marbles, lengths of gilded string, sheets of colored paper. He pulled all that out of his pockets, as if they were constantly full of such things; one would have thought there was nothing else in his baggage.

When he went into old man Solzner's stable to visit his two mounts, children came and watched him from the door, not daring to enter, nor did he invite them to do so. He greeted his horse and his donkey by name, always addressing them formally, stroking their coats, and slipping lumps of yellow sugar (which he extracted from a little garnet-colored velvet bag) between their gray lips. The children watched the spectacle with open mouths and staring eyes, wondering what was the language he used when he murmured into the animals' ears.

To tell the truth, he spoke more to his horse and his ass than he did to us. Schloss had received instructions to knock on his guest's door at six o'clock every morning, but not to enter the room, and to place the tray on the floor in front of the threshold. The same items were always arranged on the tray: a round brioche—for which the *Anderer* paid Wirfrau in advance—a raw egg, a pot of hot water, and a large bowl.

"He can't be drinking hot water with nothing in it!" The man who uttered this cry of disbelief one evening was Rudolf Scheuling, whose gullet had admitted no liquid but *schnick* since he was twelve years old. In fact, what the *Anderer* drank was tea, strong tea that left large brown stains on the rims of cups. I tasted that tea once, when he invited me to his room to chat a bit and to show me some books. It left a taste of leather and smoke in the mouth, along with a hint of salt meat. I'd never drunk anything like it.

For dinner, he went down to the big room. There were always a few curiosity seekers who came just to look at him, and especially to observe his manners, his delicate table manners: his distinguished way of holding his fork and knife, of sliding his blade into the breast of a chicken or the flesh of a potato.

In the very beginning, Schloss made a real effort to search his memory for recipes worthy of the visitor, but he quickly gave up, at the request of the *Anderer* himself. Despite his round body and his red cheeks, he ate almost nothing. At the end of a meal, his plate was never empty; half the food was untouched. By contrast, he drank one large glass of water after another, as if always afflicted by a raging thirst. This conduct moved Marcus Graz, a beanpole as lean as a stray dog, to remark that it was a blessing that the *Anderer* didn't piss in the Staubi, which he would have surely caused to overflow its banks.

In the evening, he'd take only a bowl of soup, and even then it was light fare, more a broth than a soup, and after that he'd bow to whoever was in the inn and go upstairs to his room. The light in his window shone late. Some even said they had seen it all night long. In any case, people wondered what he could be doing up there.

Early in his sojourn among us, he spent a good part of each afternoon walking every street in the village, methodically, as if he were making a grid or a survey. No one really noticed, because to see what he was doing you would have had to follow him all the time, and only the children did that.

Dressed like something out of an old, dusty fable full of obsolete words, he trudged along, slightly slew-footed, his left hand on a handsome cane with an ivory pommel and his right clutching the little black notebook which came and went under his fingers like some odd sort of tamed animal.

Sometimes he took one of his beasts out for a bit of air. He chose either the horse or the donkey, never both at the same time, and he led the animal by its bridle, patting its sides as they walked, down to the banks of the Staubi, a little upriver from the Baptisterbrücke, where the grass was fresh and thick and the grazing good. He himself placed his large buttocks on the riverbank and remained unmoving, watching the current and the bright eddies, as if he expected a miracle to rise up out of them. The children stopped some distance behind him, a little higher up on the slope. They all respected his silence, and not one of them threw a stone into the water.

The first event took place two weeks after the *Anderer*'s arrival in our village. I think it was the mayor's idea, even though I couldn't swear it. I've never asked him because that's not important. What *is* important is what happened that evening, the evening of June 10.

By then everyone in the village knew that the *Anderer* was only a transient presence within our walls, but it also seemed clear that he was preparing for an extended sojourn. During the day on June 10, news spread that the village, led by the mayor, was going to welcome the new visitor in a fitting manner. There would be a speech, some music, and even a *Schoppessenwass,* which is the dialect word for a kind of large table, laden with glasses, bottles, and food, which is traditionally set up on certain popular occasions.

Zungfrost got busy near dawn, building a small platform (which looked rather more like a scaffold, to tell the truth) near the covered market. His hammer blows and his screeching saw could be heard even before the sun started to gnaw away at the blackness of the night; the sound pulled many an onlooker from his bed. By eight o'clock, everyone had heard about the reception.

By ten, there were more people in the streets than on a market day. In the afternoon, *Zungfrost* began painting some large, shaky letters on a wide paper banner hung above the platform. They turned out to be an expression of welcome, WI SUND VROH WEN NEU KAMME, an odd formulation which had issued from Diodemus's brain. While *Zungfrost* finished his job, two peddlers, alerted to the opportunity in some unfathomable way, arrived and began offering the villagers gathered around the market blessed medals, rat poison, knives, thread, almanacs, seeds, pictures, and felt hats. I knew the peddlers, having often encountered them on mountain roads or forest paths. Dirty as earthworms, with hair black as ink, the two were father and son. People called them *De Runhgäre,* "the Runners," because they were capable of covering considerable distances in very few hours. The father greeted me. I asked him, "Who told you there was a celebration today?"

"The wind."

"The wind?"

"The wind says a lot, if you know how to listen."

He looked at me mischievously as he rolled himself a cigarette. "Have you been back to S.?"

"I don't have authorization. The road's still closed."

"So what do you live on? The wind?"

"No, not the wind. The night. When you know it well, the night's a fairy cape. All you have to do is put it on, and you can go wherever you want!"

He burst out laughing, and his laughter exposed his four remaining teeth, planted in his jawbone like the memories of trees on a desolate hill. Not far from us, Diodemus was absorbed in watching *Zungfrost,* who was putting the finishing touches on his letters. Diodemus gave me a little wave, but only later, when we were side by side and the ceremony was about to begin, did I ask him the question that was troubling me somewhat: "Was that your idea?"

"What idea?"

"The sentence on the banner."

"Orschwir told me to."

"Told you to what?"

"To come up with something, some words . . ."

"Your sentence is pretty odd. Why didn't you write it in *Deeperschaft*?"

"Orschwir didn't want me to."

"Why not?"

"I don't know."

Right there and then I didn't know, either, but later I had a chance to reflect. The *Anderer* was a mystery. Nobody knew who he was. Nobody knew where he came from or why he was here. And nobody knew whether he understood when people spoke in dialect. The sentence painted on the banner was perhaps a means of discovering the answer to that last question. A most naïve means, to be sure, and in any case it failed in its purpose, for that evening, when the *Anderer* passed the platform and saw the inscription, he paused briefly, ran his eyes over the words, and then continued on his way. Did he understand what he read? No one knows; he said nothing about it.

Although it's possible that Diodemus hadn't intended to be ambiguous, the banner slogan he came up with sounded funny. It means—or rather it can mean—different things, because our dialect is like a springy fabric: it can be stretched in every direction.

"*Wi sund vroh wen neu kamme*" can mean "We're happy

when a new person arrives." But it can also mean "We're happy when something new comes along," which isn't at all the same thing. Strangest of all, the word *vroh* has two meanings, depending on the context: it's equivalent to "glad" or "happy," but it also has a connotation of "wary" or "watchful," and if you favor this second area of meaning, then you find yourself contemplating a bizarre, disquieting statement which nobody perceived at the time but which hasn't stopped resounding in my head ever since, a kind of warning freighted with a small load of threats, a greeting like a knife brandished in a fist, the blade shaken a little and glinting in the sun.

XXIII

In the afternoon of that same day, I brought Amelia and Poupchette along with me on an excursion. We climbed all the way to Lutz's cabin. It was formerly a shepherd's refuge, but it hasn't been used for two decades. Rushes and meadow buttercups have slowly overgrown the surrounding pastures. The grass has retreated before the advancing moss. Some ponds have appeared; at first, they were merely puddles, but eventually they transformed the place into a kind of ghost, the ghost of a meadow not yet completely metamorphosed into a marsh. In an effort to understand and explain this transformation, I'd already written three reports on it, and each year around the same time I returned to the spot to measure the extent and nature of the changes. The cabin is west of the village, about a two-hour walk away. The path leading to it is no longer as clearly marked as it once was, when the tread of hundreds of pairs of clogs gave it renewed depth and form every year. Paths are like men; they die, too. Little by little, they get cluttered and then overwhelmed; they break apart, they're eaten by grass, and in the end they disappear. After only a few years have passed, all that remains is a dim outline, and most people eventually forget that the path ever existed.

Poupchette, riding on my shoulders, chattered to the clouds. She spoke to them as if they could understand her. She told them to get a move on, to suck in their big bellies, and to leave the sun alone in the wide sky. The air coming down off the mountains gave fresh pinkness to her cheeks.

I was holding Amelia's hand. She was beside me, walking along at a good pace. Sometimes her eyes rested on the ground and sometimes they stared off toward the far horizon, which was serrated by the jagged peaks of the Prinzhornï. But in either case, I could tell that her gaze never really came to rest on her surroundings, whether near or far. Her eyes seemed like butterflies, marvelously flitting about for no apparent reason, as though shifted by the wind, by the transparent air, but with no thought to what they were doing or what they saw. She marched on in silence. No doubt, the quickened rhythm of her breathing prevented her from humming her eternal song. Her lips were slightly parted. I clutched her hand and felt her warmth, but she noticed nothing. Perhaps she no longer knew how much the person at her side loved her.

Once we reached the cabin, I had Amelia sit on the stone bench by the door, and then I set Poupchette down next to her. I told Poupchette to be good while I made my rounds and recorded my data. I assured her I wouldn't be long. I promised that after I finished we'd sit there and eat up the *Pressfrütekof* and the applewalnut cake that old Fedorine had wrapped in a big white cloth for us.

I began taking my measurements. I quickly found the landmarks on which I based my findings every year, namely various big stones that had once enclosed the sheepfold and marked property boundaries. By contrast, I had some trouble locating the sandstone trough that stood almost exactly in the center of the pasture. The trough was carved from a single block of stone;

when I saw it for the first time as a child, it had seemed to me like some kind of vessel abandoned there on solid ground, a ship made by the gods and now an encumbrance to men, who were neither clever enough to make use of it nor strong enough to move it.

Eventually, I found the trough in the middle of a big pond whose surface area, curiously enough, had tripled over the course of a year. The mass of stone was completely submerged and nearly hidden from sight. Glimpsed through the transparent prism of the water, the trough no longer put me in mind of a vessel, but rather of a tomb. It looked like a primitive, heavy coffin, long since emptied of any occupant, or perhaps—and this thought gave me chills—awaiting the man or woman destined to lie in it forever.

I jerked my eyes away and looked for the silhouettes of Poupchette and Amelia in the distance, but all I could see were the crumbling cabin walls. My girls were on the other side, invisible, vanished. I abandoned my measuring instruments on the edge of the pond and ran like a madman back to the cabin, calling out their names, seized by a deep, violent, irrational fear. The cabin wasn't very far away, but I felt as though I'd never reach it. My feet slipped on the slick earth. I sank into soggy holes and quagmires, and the soft wet ground, which made sounds like the groans of the dying, seemed determined to suck me in. When I finally got to the cabin, I was exhausted and out of breath. My hands, my pants, and my hobnailed boots were covered with black mud that stank of beechnuts and waterlogged grass. I couldn't even shout out Amelia's and Poupchette's names anymore, even though I had run so hard to reach them. And then I saw a little hand reach around a corner of the wall, pick a buttercup, break off its stem, and move on to another flower. My fear disappeared as quickly as it had overcome me. Poupchette's face came into sight. She looked at me. I could read her astonishment in her eyes. "Dirty Daddy! All dirty, Daddy!" She started laughing, and I laughed, too. I laughed very hard, very, very hard. I wanted everyone and everything to hear my laughter: all the people in the world who wished to reduce me to an ashy silence, and all the things in the world that conspired to swallow me up.

Poupchette was proudly holding the bouquet of buttercups, daisies, and forget-me-nots she'd gathered for her mother. The flowers were still quivering with life, as if they hadn't noticed that they'd just passed the gates of death.

Amelia had strayed away from the cabin, walked to the edge of the pasture, and stopped on a sort of promontory, beyond which the slope splits and shatters into broken rocks. Her face was turned toward the vast landscape of plains spreading out beyond the border, an indistinct expanse that seemed to doze under scraps of fog. Amelia was holding her arms away from her body, a little as though she were preparing to take flight, and her slender silhouette stood out against the distant, pale, blue-tinted background with a grace that was almost inhuman. Poupchette ran to her mother and flung herself against her thighs, trying in vain to get her short arms around them.

Amelia hadn't moved. The wind had undone her hair, which streamed in the wind like a cold brown flame. I approached her with slow steps. The wind carried her perfume to me, as well as snatches of her song, which she'd started humming again. Poupchette jumped up and managed to grab one of her arms. She pressed the flowers into her mother's hand. Amelia made no effort to hold on to the bouquet; her fingers remained open, and one by one the flowers blew away. Poupchette dashed about right and left, trying to catch them, while I kept moving very slowly toward Amelia. Her body, outlined against the sky, seemed to be suspended in it.

Schöner Prinz so lieb
Zu weit fortgegangen
Schöner Prinz so lieb
Nacht um Nacht ohn' Eure Lippen
Schöner Prinz so lieb
Tag um Tag ohn' Euch zu erblicken
Schöner Prinz so lieb
Träumt Ihr was ich träume
Schöner Prinz so lieb
Ihr mit mir immerdar zusammen

Handsome Prince so dear
Gone too far away
Handsome Prince so dear
Night after night without your lips
Handsome Prince so dear
Day after day without seeing you
Handsome Prince so dear
Do you dream of what I dream of
Handsome Prince so dear
You and me, together forever

Amelia was dancing in my arms. We were with other couples under the bare trees of January, drunk on youth in the golden, misty light of the streetlamps in the park, gliding along to the music of the little orchestra playing under the pavilion. The musicians, bundled up in fur clothing, looked like strange animals. It was the instant before the first kiss, preceded and brought on by a few minutes of vertigo. It was in another time. It was before the chaos. That song was playing, the song of the first kiss, a song in the old language that had passed across the centuries as a traveler crosses frontiers. Called in dialect *"Schon ofza prinzer, Gehtes so muchte lan,"* it was a love song blended with bitter words, a song of legend, the song of an evening and a lifetime, and now it's the dreadful refrain inside which Amelia has shut herself up as inside a prison, where she lives without really existing.

I held her tight against me. I kissed her hair, the nape of her neck. I told her in her ear that I loved her, that I would always love her, that I was there for her, close to her, all around her. I took her face in my hands, I turned it toward me, and then, while tears ran down her cheeks, I saw in her eyes something like the smile of a person far, far away.

XXIV

As we made our way back home, we were caught up in the excitement of that particular day, the tenth of June. On the square, men and women were starting to form groups and press against one another, becoming a crowd.

For a long time now, I've fled crowds. I avoid them. I know that everything—or almost—has come from them. I mean the bad things, the war and all the *Kazerskwirs* it opened up in the brains of so many. I've seen how men act when they know they're not alone, when they know they can melt into a crowd and be absorbed into a mass that encompasses and transcends them, a mass comprising thousands of faces fashioned like theirs. One can always tell himself that the fault lies with whoever trains them, exhorts them, makes them dance like a slowworm around a stick, and that crowds are unconscious of their acts, of their future, and of their course. This is all false. The truth is that the crowd itself is a monster. It begets itself, an enormous body composed of thousands of other conscious bodies. Furthermore, I know that there are no happy crowds. There are no peaceful crowds, either. Even when there's laughter, smiles, music, choruses, behind all that there's blood: vexed, overheated, inflamed blood, stirred and maddened in its own vortex.

Signs of what was to come were already visible a long time ago, when I was in the Capital, where I had been sent to complete my studies. My going there was Limmat's idea. He spoke of it to the mayor at the time, Sibelius Craspach, as well as to Father Peiper. All three declared that the village needed at least one of its young people to advance his education beyond the rest, to go out and see a bit of the world before returning home to become a schoolmaster, a health practitioner, or perhaps the successor to Lawyer Knopf, whose powers were beginning to fail; his legal documents and his counsels had astounded more than one recent client. And so the three elders had chosen me.

In a way, you could say it was the village that sent me to the Capital. Limmat, Craspach, and Father Peiper may have had the idea, but just about everybody pitched in and supported me. At the end of every month, *Zungfrost* would take up a collection, going from door to door, ringing a little bell, and repeating the same words: *"Fu Brodeck's Erfosch! Fu Brodeck's Erfosch!"*—"For Brodeck's studies! For Brodeck's studies!" Everyone gave according to his means and inclination. The donation might be a few gold pieces, but it could also be a woolen overcoat, a cap, a handkerchief, a jar of preserves, a little bag of lentils, or some provisions for Fedorine, because as long as I was in the Capital, I couldn't do any work to help her. So I'd receive little money orders along with some strange parcels, which my landlady, Fra Haiternitz, panting from having climbed the six flights of stairs to my room, would hand me with a suspicious air, all the while chewing a wad of black tobacco, which stained her lips and turned her breath into fumes from Hell.

In the beginning, the Capital gave me a headache. I'd never

in my life heard so many noises. The streets seemed like furious mountain torrents, ferrying along an intermingled throng of people and vehicles amid a racket that made me dizzy and often drove me to flatten myself against a wall to avoid being swept away by the uninterrupted flood. I lived in a room whose rusty window wouldn't open more than an inch. There was hardly space for anything except my straw mattress, which I folded up every morning. A board placed atop the folded mattress served as my desk. Apart from some luminous days in high summer or the dead of winter, the city was constantly imprisoned under a fog of coal smoke, which issued from the chimneys in lazy clouds that wrapped themselves around one another and then hung in the air for days and nights, deflecting the sun well beyond us. My first days of city life seemed unbearable. I never stopped thinking about our village, nestled in the valley's conifer forest as in a lap. I even remember crying as I lay in bed.

The University was a large baroque building which, three centuries earlier, had been the palace of a Magyar prince. Looted and wrecked in the revolutionary period, it was then sold to a prosperous grain merchant, who converted it into a warehouse. In 1831, when the great cholera epidemic raged throughout the country like a dog tracking a debilitated prey, the warehouse was requisitioned and served as a public hospital. Some people were treated there. Many died there. Much later, toward the end of the century, the Emperor decided to transform the hospital into a University. The common rooms were cleaned and furnished with benches and rostrums. The morgue became the library and the dissecting room a sort of lounge, where the professors and some students from influential families could sit in large armchairs of tawny leather, smoking their pipes, conversing, and reading news-papers.

Most of the students came from middle-class families. They had pink cheeks, slender hands, and clean fingernails. All their lives, they'd eaten their fill and worn good clothes. There were only a few of us who were virtually penniless. We could be spot-ted right away, identified by the scoured look the mountain air had given our cheeks, by our clothes, by our gauche manners, by our obvious and enduring fear of being in the wrong place. We'd come from far away. We weren't from the city or even from the countryside around it. We slept in badly heated attic rooms. We never, or very rarely, went home. Those who had families and money paid us little attention. But for all that, I don't believe they had contempt for us. They simply couldn't imagine who we were, or where we came from, or the desolate, sublime landscapes we'd grown up in, or our daily existence in the big city. They often walked past us without even seeing us.

After several weeks, I stopped being frightened of the city. I was unaware of its monstrous, hostile aspect; I noticed only its ugliness. And that was easy for me to forget for hours on end be-cause I loved plunging myself into my studies, into books. To tell the truth, I hardly ever left the library, except to go to the lecture halls where the professors gave their courses. I found a compan-ion in the person of Ulli Rätte, who was the same age I was and had likewise been more or less dispatched to the University by his village, in the hope of his returning with an education that would contribute to the greater good. Rätte came from a far corner of the country, the border region around the Galinek hills, and he spoke a rasping language full of expressions I didn't know. In the eyes of many of our fellow students, Rätte's strange tongue proved him either an oddball or a savage. When we weren't in the University library, in class, or in our rooms, we'd walk together along the streets, talking about our dreams and our future lives.

Ulli had a passion for cafés but not enough money to frequent them. He often dragged me along to contemplate them, and the mere sight of those places—where blue gas and wax candles burned, where women's laughter rose to the ceiling amid clouds of cigar and pipe smoke, where the men wore elegant suits, fur coats during the winter months and silk scarves when the weather was fine, where waiters impeccably cinched into white aprons seemed like soldiers of an inoffensive army—sufficed to fill him with a childlike joy. "We're wasting our time on books, Brodeck," he'd say. "This is where real life is!"

Unlike me, Ulli took to the city like a fish to water. He knew all the streets and all the tricks. He loved the dust of the city, its noise, its soot, its violence, its hugeness. He liked everything about it.

"I don't think I'll go back to my village," he often told me. It was no use my pointing out that his village was the reason why he was there or reminding him that it was counting on him; he dismissed such talk with a word or a backhanded wave. "A bunch of brutes and drunkards—that's all there is where I come from. You think they sent me here out of charity? They're motivated by self-interest and nothing else! They want me to return home stuffed with knowledge, like a force-fed animal, and then they'll make me pay for it for the rest of my life. Don't forget, Brodeck: it's ignorance that always triumphs, not knowledge."

Although cafés occupied his thoughts more than University classrooms, Ulli Rätte was far from stupid. Some of the things he said deserved to be printed in books, but he tossed them off as though they were of no importance, as though he were making fun of them and himself as soon as he said them; and then he'd burst out laughing. His laugh was equal parts bellow and vocalise, and passersby never failed to turn their heads when they heard it.

XXV

That conflict between knowledge and ignorance, between solitude and numbers—that's what made me leave the city before I completed my studies. The great, sprawling urban organism was suddenly shaken by gossip, by rumors that had sprung from nothing: two or three conversations, an unsigned article a few lines long in a daily newspaper, the patter of a tumbler in the marketplace, a song of unknown origin whose ferocious refrain was taken up in the twinkling of an eye by all the singers in the streets.

More and more public gatherings took place until they seemed to be everywhere. A few men would stop near a streetlight and speak among themselves; soon they were joined by others and by others after that. Thus, in a few minutes, the group had swelled to forty—forty bodies pressed together, their shoulders a bit hunched, all moving slightly from time to time or assenting concisely to a point made by one of the speakers, though exactly which one was never clear. Then, as if blown away by a gust of wind, those silhouettes suddenly dispersed in every direction, and the empty sidewalk recommenced its monotonous waiting.

Remarkable and contradictory news reached the Capital from the eastern frontier. On the other side of the border, it was said, entire garrisons were on the march by night, as surreptitiously as possible, and witnesses reported troop movements of a scope hitherto unknown. It was also said that people on this side could hear machines at work over there, digging ditches, galleries, trenches, secret tunnels. And finally, it was said that recently perfected weapons of diabolical power and range were being prepared for deployment, and that the Capital was full of spies, ready to set it ablaze when the time came. Meanwhile, widespread hunger was tormenting citizens' bellies and governing their minds. The oven-like heat of the two preceding summers had grilled the vast majority of the crops standing in the fields surrounding the city. Every day, bands of farmers and their families, impoverished and emaciated, flocked to the Capital; their lost eyes settled on everything they saw, as if they were going to steal it. Children—drab little creatures with yellowish complexions—clung to their mother's skirts. Often, barely able to remain upright, youngsters would fall asleep on their feet, leaning against a wall, and many a mother who could go on no longer sat on the ground with a sleeping child lying across her lap.

At the same moment, Professor Nösel would be talking to us about our great poets, who—in days gone by, centuries and centuries ago, when the Capital was still nothing more than a big market town, when our forests were full of bears and wolf packs, aurochs and bison, when hordes of tribesmen from the distant steppes were spreading fire and terror—fashioned the countless verses of our fundamental epic poems. Nösel could decipher Ancient Greek, Latin, Cimbrian, Arabic, Aramaic, Uzbek, Kazakh, and Russian, but he was incapable of looking out his window, or of lifting his nose from his reading as he walked home to his apartment in Jeckenweiss Street. A man most learned in books, he was blind to the world.

One day, the first demonstration took place. After waiting in vain for someone to hire them, about a hundred men, most of them ruined farmers and unemployed workers, left the Alberge-platz market, where those looking for a day's work ordinarily gathered. Walking fast and shouting, they headed for Parliament. Outside the building, they came up against the soldiers on duty, who managed to disperse them without violence. The demonstrators passed Ulli and me on our way to the University. They formed a somewhat noisy procession, nothing more, like students parading to celebrate their diplomas, except that in this case, the taut, ashen faces and the eyes glittering with muffled resentment clearly didn't belong to students.

"They'll get over it soon!" Rätte declared mockingly. He grabbed me by the arm to haul me to a new café, which he had discovered the previous evening and which he wanted to show me. We set out, but from time to time as we walked, I turned around to catch a glimpse of those men disappearing down the street like the tail of a giant serpent, whose invisible head was even bigger in my imagination.

The phenomenon repeated itself the following day and the six days after that; the only difference was that each time the marchers were more numerous and their grumbling louder. Women, perhaps their wives, joined the ranks of the farmers and workers, along with some protesters who came out of nowhere and had never been seen before. They looked like herdsmen or shepherds, except that they wielded neither sticks nor staffs for driving animals but shouts and words. Soon there was a bit of daily bloodshed, caused when the soldiers stationed in front of the Parliament building struck a few skulls with the flats of their swords. Newspaper headlines about the growing numbers of demonstrators began to appear, but the government remained strangely mute. On a Friday evening eight days after the demonstrations began, a soldier was seriously injured when someone threw a paving stone. A few hours later, the entire city was placarded with an announcement declaring that all gatherings were forbidden until further notice and that any demonstrations would be repressed with the greatest firmness.

This volatile mixture was ignited at dawn the following day, when the swollen body of Wighert Ruppach was found near the church of the Ysertinguës. An unemployed typographer known for his revolutionary opinions, he was said to have had a hand in instigating the first demonstrations, and it was true that many people had spotted his bearded, half-moon face at the head of the mob and heard his baritone voice shouting for bread and work. The police very quickly established that he'd been clubbed to death and that he'd been last seen in the slaughterhouse district, half drunk and stumbling as he exited one of the numerous dives that served black wine and contraband liquor. Robbed of his papers, his watch, and every cent in his pocket, Ruppach had doubtless been the victim of one of his drinking companions or of some criminal whose path he'd crossed—or so went the explanation given by the police. But the city, which was starting to show signs of fever, responded to the official story with growls and threats. Within a few hours, Ruppach achieved the status of martyr, the victim of a senile governing power which couldn't feed its children or protect them from the foreign menace swelling with impunity along its borders. In the death of Ruppach, people thought they recognized a foreigner's hand, or the hand of a traitor. By that point, the truth mattered little. Few citizens were disposed to hear it. Over the course of the previous week, the majority had stuffed their heads with plenty of powder, they had plaited a lovely fuse, and now they had their spark.

Everything exploded on Monday, after a Sunday which most citizens had dedicated to fleeing the city. It seemed deserted, abandoned, emptied by a strange and sudden epidemic. Amelia and I had gone for a walk Sunday evening, pretending not to notice that everything around us pointed to an imminent event of an unprecedented kind.

We'd known each other for five weeks. I was entering another world. I'd suddenly discovered that both the earth and my life could move to rhythms different from those I'd previously known, and that the soft, regular sound of the beloved's breathing is the sweetest one can ever hear. We always walked the same streets and passed the same places. Somehow, without meaning to, we'd outlined a pilgrimage that traced the first days of our love. Our way led past the Stüpispiel Theater, then down Under-de-Bogel Avenue to the Elsi Promenade, the music pavilion, the skating rink. Amelia asked me to tell her about my studies, about the books I was reading, about the country I came from. "I'd love to get to know it," she said.

She'd been in the Capital for a year, having arrived with no treasure but her two hands, which knew how to do delicate embroidery, sew complicated stitches, and make lace as fragile as a thread of frost. One evening, when I inquired about her family and the place she'd come from, she told me, "Everything behind me is darkness. Nothing but darkness," and what she said brought me back to my own past, my distant childhood, which featured death, destroyed houses, broken walls, smoking wounds—some of it I remember a little, and some things Fedorine has related to me. After Amelia spoke those words, I began to love her also as a sister, a fellow creature risen from the same depths as I, a fellow creature who, like me, had no other choice but to keep her eyes fixed straight ahead.

On Monday morning, I attended Nösel's lecture in the Hall of Medals. I've never figured out the reason for that name. It was a low-ceilinged, completely undecorated room whose waxed walls reflected our blurred images. The topic of that day's class was the rhythmic structure of the first part of *Kant'z Theus,* the great national poem that's been passed down from generation to generation for nearly a thousand years. Nösel was speaking without looking at us. I believe he spoke mostly to himself when he lectured, carrying on an odd conversation for solo voice without much concern for our presence and even less for our opinions. As he expounded passionately upon pentasyllables and hexameters, he applied cream to his hair and mustache, filled his pipe, methodically scratched at the various food particles on his jacket lapels, and cleaned his fingernails with a pocketknife. Barely ten of us were paying attention to him; most of the others were dozing or examining the cracks in the ceiling. Nösel stood up, went to the blackboard, and wrote two verses that are still in my memory because the old language of the poem resembles our dialect in so many ways:

Stu pekart in dei mümerie gesachetet
Komm de Nebe un de Osterne vohin

They shall arrive in a murmur
And shall disappear into fog and earth

At that moment, the door of the lecture room opened violently and slammed against the wall, making an enormous, reverberating noise. We all snapped our heads around and saw bug-eyed faces, gesticulating arms, and mouths screaming at us: "Everybody outside! Everybody outside! Vengeance for Ruppach! The traitors will pay!" There weren't more than four or five individuals in the doorway, no doubt students—their features seemed vaguely familiar—but we heard behind them the murmur of a considerable crowd, pushing and supporting those in the front line. Then they disappeared as suddenly as they had come, leaving the door open like the hole in a stone sink, and almost all the students in the room, who a few seconds earlier had been sitting around me, were sucked out through that hole as though by some imperious physical force. There was a great racket of overturned chairs and benches, shouts, insults, cries, and then, suddenly, nothing. The wave had rolled on and was now getting farther and farther away, carrying off brutality to spread it throughout the city.

There were only five of us left in the Hall of Medals: Fritz Schoeffel, an obese fellow with very short arms, who couldn't climb three steps without gasping for air; Julius Kakenegg, who never spoke to anyone at all and always breathed through a perfumed handkerchief; Barthéleo Mietza, who was deaf as a post; me; and, of course, Nösel himself, who'd observed the entire scene with one hand raised, still holding the chalk. He shrugged his shoulders and went on with the class as if nothing had happened.

XXVI

I spent the rest of that strange day inside the walls of the University. I felt protected there. I didn't want to leave. I heard horrible sounds coming from outside, followed by great silences which dragged on and on, giving rise to uneasiness as intense as what was caused by the noise. I stayed in the library the whole afternoon. I knew Amelia was safe at her place, the furnished room she shared with another embroiderer named Gudrun Osterick, a ruddy-faced young woman with hair like sheep's wool. The previous evening, I'd promised them I wouldn't venture out.

I don't remember much about the book I was trying to read during those bizarre hours in the library. It was the work of a physician, Doctor Klaus Reinhold Maria Messner, on the propagation of the plague across the centuries. The book contained tables, charts, and figures, as well as striking illustrations that contrasted with the scientific detachment of the inquiry, for they illuminated it with a sort of macabre and precious romanticism. One of the illustrations that I found particularly unsettling showed a narrow, poor city street. Uneven paving stones constituted the roadway, and the doors of all the houses were wide open. Dozens of big, black, hirsute rats ran grimacing from the houses while three men dressed in long, dark robes, their heads hidden by peaked hoods, piled stiff corpses onto the bed of a handcart. In the distance, plumes of smoke streaked the horizon, while in the foreground, as if he wished to escape from the picture, a child in rags sat on the ground with his face in his hands. Curiously, none of the three men paid any attention to him, already considering him as good as dead. The only creature contemplating him was a rat. Standing on its rear legs, it seemed to be addressing a malicious, ironic question to the child's hidden face. I stared at the picture for a long time, wondering what its engraver's real purpose had been and why Doctor Messner had wanted it reproduced in his book.

Around four o'clock, the daylight suddenly grew dim. Snow clouds had filled the sky, and they began dumping their load on the city. I opened one of the library's windows. Big flakes immediately struck my cheeks and melted. I saw silhouettes coming and going in the streets, walking at a normal pace; the city seemed to have regained its ordinary appearance. I collected my jacket and left the University. At that moment, I didn't know that I would never set foot in it again.

To return to my room, I had to cross Salzwach Square, go down Sibelius-Vo-Recht Avenue, traverse the Kolesh quarter—the oldest part of the city, a maze of narrow streets lined by innumerable storefronts—skirt Wilhem Park, and walk past the lugubrious buildings that housed the thermal baths. I stepped ahead briskly, not raising my head too much. I passed many shadows that were doing the same thing and then a group of men who seemed rather drunk, talking very loud and laughing a lot.

In Salzwach Square and on Sibelius-Vo-Recht Avenue the snow was already sticking to the ground, and the pedestrians left black tracks as they moved along, scurrying like insects. Looking at those places, one could have believed that nothing had happened, that the city had experienced an ordinary Monday, and that the untimely emptiness of the streets was due to nothing more than the cold, the bad weather, and the night itself, which had fallen a little too early.

But to realize that none of that was true, one had only to enter the labyrinth of the Kolesh quarter. What I noticed first was a sound. The sound of glass, of the broken glass I was treading on. I was on a narrow street littered with broken glass, and glinting shards, here and there half buried by snow, covered the ground as far as my eyes could see. I couldn't stop myself from imagining that someone had scattered precious stones by the handful all over the Kolesh quarter. The thought gave the little street a new dimension, sparkling, marvelous, magical, like the setting of a fairy tale; my task was to find the plot and the princess. But that first vision vanished at once when my eyes focused on the shop windows gaping like the jaws of dead animals, the looted interiors of the stores, the smashed barrels spilling out marinated herrings, dried meats, gherkins, and wine, the befouled stalls, the strewn merchandise. The sounds of groans and weeping mingled with the crunch of footsteps on the glass carpet. I couldn't tell where the human sounds were coming from, as there wasn't a living creature in sight. By contrast, three corpses, their heads grotesquely swollen and bruised from the blows they'd been struck, were stretched out in front of a tailor's shop. Stuck on the door, which was hanging from the frame by its single remaining hinge, was a piece of paper with the words SCHMUTZ FREMDËR, "dirty foreigner" (but the word *Fremdër* is ambiguous, as it can also mean "traitor," or in a more colloquial usage, "scumbag," "filth"), crudely lettered in red paint. The paint had run on many of the letters, which looked as though they were dripping blood. Rolls of cloth had been piled up anyhow and an attempt made to set them on fire. Some shards of glass were still attached to the window jambs, forming a star with incredibly slender, fragile rays.

That inscription, SCHMUTZ FREMDËR, was visible in many places, usually accompanied by another, RACHE FÜR RUPPACH, "Revenge for Ruppach." My mind's eye kept returning to the three corpses. Dizziness overcame me, and the vision of those dead bodies made confused images return to my memory, images of other corpses sprawled out like puppets, with no trace of humanity left in their features. I became again the little boy who wandered amid the ruins, abandoned among the debris and the rubble, surrounded by small fires, and not knowing whether he was the plaything of an unending nightmare or a victim of the times, which had decided to toy with him like a cat with a mouse. At the same time as those fragments of my past life arose before me, I could also see every detail of the engraving in Doctor Messner's volume—the plumes of smoke, the countless rats, the child, the robed men, the heap of corpses—and it was as though I were staring at the awful spectacle in the narrow street, the memories of my childhood, and the details of the illustration in Doctor Messner's book, all superimposed on one another and triply horrible. I staggered and almost fell, but I heard someone calling me; I heard a voice calling me, a weak, broken voice, a voice like the thousands of glass shards on the ground.

The caller was an old man, crouched in a doorway a little farther on. He was painfully thin, and his long white beard tugged his face downward, making it look still thinner. He trembled as he stretched out an arm toward me. I hurried to his side, and while he kept repeating the same words—"Madmen. Madmen. They've gone mad. Madmen"—in the old language that was Fedorine's native tongue, I tried to set him on his feet.

"Where do you live?" I asked him. "Do you live on this street?"

His eyes connected with mine for a few seconds, but he didn't seem to understand my questions and took up his litany again. His clothes were ripped in many places; his right hand was covered with blood and appeared useless. I put my arms around his waist to lift him, but I'd barely managed to prop him against the door when voices erupted behind us.

"They're still moving! They're taunting us! They're on their feet, and our Ruppach's dead!"

Three men were coming toward us. They carried long billy clubs, and I could make out two intertwined letters, *W R*, on the black armbands they wore on their left sleeves. They were talking loud and guffawing. Insofar as I could see them—the visors of their caps cast a shadow over their features—one face looked familiar to me, but fear gripped me and my thoughts became confused. At first glance, I thought they might be drunk—and yet they didn't smell of alcohol. Anger and hatred suffice to scramble human brains more thoroughly than brandy can. Alas, I was able to verify this observation on several later occasions, in the camp.

The old man kept up his droning. In fact, I think he hadn't even noticed the presence of the other three. One of them placed the end of his stick against the old fellow's chest and said, "You will repeat after me: 'I'm a *Fremdër*, a worthless piece of shit!' Now! Say it!"

But the old man neither heard nor saw him. I said, "I don't think he understands you. He's hurt—"

The words had sprung unbidden to my lips, and I already regretted them. The stick moved to my chest.

"Did you say something? Did you dare to say something? Who are you, with that nasty mug? You stink like a *Fremdër,* too!" And he struck me a blow on the side that knocked the wind out of me. At that moment, one of his comrades, the one who reminded me of someone, intervened and said, "No, I know him. His name's Brodeck."

He brought his face quite close to mine, and suddenly I recognized him. He was a third-year student who, like me, frequented the library. I didn't know his name, but I remembered that he often consulted volumes of astronomy and spent a lot of time contemplating star charts.

"Brodeck, Brodeck," the one who seemed to be the leader repeated. "A real *Fremdër* name! And look at this faggot's nose! The nose is what gives them away! And their big eyes, popping out of their heads, so they can see everything, so they can take everything!" He kept shoving his stick into my ribs, the way you do to a balky animal.

"Felix, leave him alone! The old guy's the one we want. He's one of them, for sure, the old bastard, and that's his shop over there, I know it! He's a real crook! He gets rich off giving credit!"

The third member of the group, who hadn't spoken yet, made himself heard: "He's mine! It's my turn! You've already bashed two apiece!"

He'd stayed in the shadows so far, but now he came rushing up and I could see him. I could see that he was a boy, a child, in fact, maybe thirteen years old, hardly more. He had fresh, delicate skin, his teeth gleamed in the night, and he was smiling like a lunatic.

"Well, look here, tiny Ulrich wants to join the party! But you're too tender, little brother. The milk's still running out of your ears!"

The old man seemed to have fallen asleep. His eyes were closed. He'd stopped talking. The boy gave his older brother a furious push, prodded me to one side with the end of his club, and stationed himself in front of the feeble mass crouched on the ground. A great silence fell. The night had become as thick as mud. A gust of wind swept through the narrow street, kicking up a bit of snow. Nobody moved. I must be dreaming, I thought, or maybe I'm on the stage at the little Stüpispiel Theater, which put on a great many grotesque and sometimes atrocious spectacles that made no sense whatsoever and always ended in farce—but suddenly the boy went into action. He raised his club above his head and brought it down on the old man with a scream. The victim didn't cry out, but he opened his eyes wide and began trembling as if he'd been flung into an icy river. The child dealt him a second blow, on the forehead, then a third, on a shoulder, then a fourth and a fifth . . . He didn't stop, and he laughed as he swung his club. His comrades encouraged him, clapping their hands and chanting *"Oy! Oy! Oy! Oy!"* to give him the rhythm. The old man's skull split open with a sharp sound like a hazelnut cracked between two stones. The child kept on striking, harder and harder, still laughing like a madman, but gradually, even though his blows didn't cease raining down and he continued to laugh as he looked upon what was left of his victim and his comrades were still clapping time, his blood-spattered face changed. The horror of what he'd just done seemed to penetrate his veins, spread out to his limbs, his muscles, his nerves, invade his brain, and wash away all its foulness. His blows slowed and then stopped. Horrified, he contemplated his club, which was covered with blood and fragments of bone, and his hands, as if they didn't belong to him. Then his eyes returned to the old man, whose face was now unrecognizable, the closed eyelids appallingly swollen, each as big as an apple.

The child dropped his club abruptly, as if it were burning his palm. He was seized by a sudden spasm and vomited a quantity of yellow liquid in two heaves; then he ran away, and the night absorbed him into its belly while his two comrades laughed uproariously. The leader, his brother, shouted after him: "Good work, little Ulrich! The old guy got what he deserved! Now you're a man!"

He prodded the old man's corpse with one foot, turned around, and casually walked away, arm in arm with his comrade, whistling a little love song that was quite popular at the time.

I hadn't moved. It was the first time I'd witnessed a murder. I felt empty. Empty of all thought. And my mouth was full of the bitterest bile. I couldn't take my eyes off the old man's body. His blood mingled with the snow. As soon as the big flakes touched the ground, they were tinged with red, like notched petals of an unknown flower. Once again, the sound of footsteps made me jump. Someone was approaching. I thought they'd decided to come back and kill me, too.

"Get the hell out, Brodeck!"

It was the voice of the student, the one who spent hours gazing at constellations and galaxies reproduced in large books with giant pages. I raised my eyes to him. He was looking at me without hatred but with a kind of contempt. He spoke calmly. "Get the hell out! I won't always be there to save you."

Then he spat on the ground, turned, and walked away.

XXVII

The following day, rumor put the number of corpses recovered from the streets at sixty-seven. It was said that the police had made no effort to prevent criminal activity, even when it was in their power to do so. A new demonstration was scheduled to take place that very afternoon. The city was on the verge of going up in flames.

I rose at dawn after a sleepless night, during which my memory constantly recalled the faces of the murderous child and his aged victim; and I heard again the boy's shouting, the old man's droning, the dull thumping sound of the blows, and the sharper crack of breaking bones. I made a bundle of my few belongings, returned my room key to the landlady, Fra Haiternitz, who accepted them without a word, and whose only response to my few words of farewell was a sort of contemptuous, rotten-toothed smile. She was browning some onions and bacon in a skillet. Her cubbyhole was filled with greasy smoke that stung my eyes. She hung the key on a nail and acted as though I no longer existed.

I walked the streets quickly. There were few people about. Many areas still showed signs of the previous night's vandalism. Some men with frightened faces were talking among themselves, brusquely snapping their heads around at the slightest noise. The doors of several buildings were painted with the inscription SCHMUTZ FREMDËR, and in many places the roadway was still covered with a glass carpet which crunched under my feet and made me shiver.

In case I failed to find Ulli Rätte in his room, I'd written him a good-bye letter, but the precaution was unnecessary. He was there, but he'd gotten so drunk he'd fallen asleep with all his clothes on. He was still holding a half-full bottle in his hand, and he stank of tobacco, sweat, and cheap grain alcohol. The right sleeve of his jacket was torn and marked with a large stain. It was blood. I thought my friend might be wounded, but when I bared his arm I could see that he was unharmed. Suddenly I felt very cold. I didn't want to think. I forced myself to stop thinking. Ulli slept on, openmouthed and snoring. Loudly. I slipped my letter of farewell into his shirt pocket and left the room.

I never saw Ulli Rätte again.

Why did I just write that sentence, which isn't the whole truth? I did see Ulli Rätte—or rather, I'm pretty certain I saw him—once again. In the camp. On the other side. I mean, he was on the side of those who guarded us, not on our side, the side of suffering and submission.

It was a frosty morning. I was Brodeck the Dog. Scheidegger, my master, was walking me. I was wearing the collar, and attached to the collar was the leash. I had to walk on all fours. I had to snort like a dog, eat like a dog, piss like a dog. Scheidegger strutted beside me, looking like a prim office worker. That day, we went all the way to the camp infirmary. Before going in, Scheidegger tied the leash to an iron ring embedded in the wall. I curled up in the dust, lay my head on my hands, and tried to forget the bitter cold.

That was the moment when I thought I saw Ulli Rätte. When I saw Ulli Rätte. When I heard his laugh, his very peculiar laugh, which sounded like a combination of high-pitched sleigh bells and gaily rasping wooden rattles. He was standing with two other guards a few meters away, and his back was turned to me. All three were trying to keep warm by pounding their hands together, and Ulli, or his phantom double, was speaking: "Yes, I'm telling you, it's a little slice of heaven, but right here on earth, not two miles from this shitty place. They've got a lovely stove that purrs and whistles all the time, and they serve their beer cold, with a thick head of white foam. The waitress is round as a ham, and not at all shy! You can sit there and smoke your pipe for hours, lost in a dream, and forget all about this grubby vermin here, ruining our lives!"

He finished his speech with a loud laugh, which was taken up by the others. Then he started to turn around, and I buried my face in my hands. It wasn't that I was afraid he'd recognize me. No, it wasn't that. It was me. I didn't want to see him. I didn't want to meet his eye. What I wanted was to preserve, deep inside my mind, the illusion that this tall, stout man, so happy in his role as torturer, this man who was standing so close to me but who actually lived in a different world from mine, the world of the living, could be someone other than Ulli Rätte, my Ulli, with whom I had spent so much time in former days, with whom I'd shared crusts of bread, dishes of potatoes, happy hours, dreams, and countless arm-in-arm promenades. I preferred doubt to the truth, even the thinnest, most fragile doubt. Yes, that's what I preferred, because I thought the truth might kill me.

Life's funny. I mean the currents of life, the ones that bear us along more than we follow them and then, after a strange journey, deposit us on the right bank or the left bank. I don't know how the student Ulli Rätte became a camp guard, that is, one of the perfectly oiled and obedient cogs in the great death machine we were being fed to. I don't know what trials he'd had to endure or what changes he'd had to go through in order to wind up where he was. The Ulli I'd known wouldn't have hurt a fly. How could he have become the servant of a system that crushed people, that reduced them to the lowest form of existence?

The camp's only advantage was its vast size. I never saw the guard who could have been Ulli Rätte or heard his laugh again. Was the frozen morning scene nothing but one of the many nightmares that visited me and not a memory at all? Perhaps so, but that particular nightmare seemed exceedingly real. So much so that on the day when the camp was liberated, I wandered all over it, going from one mound of corpses to another. There were many such piles. The dead were mostly prisoners, but there were a few guards as well. I turned their bodies over one by one, thinking maybe I'd come upon Ulli, but he wasn't among them. I found only the remains of the *Zeilenesseniss.* I contemplated them for a long time, the way one contemplates an abyss or the memory of unspeakable suffering.

On the morning following what later came to be called *Pürische Nacht,* after I slipped my letter into the unconscious Ulli's pocket, I hurried to Amelia's. She was sitting calmly near the window of her room, absorbed in her embroidery. Her comrade Gudrun Osterick was similarly occupied. They looked at me surprised, both of them. They'd stayed inside for the past two days, just as I'd requested, working steadily in order to finish an important commission on time, a large tablecloth destined for a bridal trousseau. Across the white linen background, Amelia and her friend had scattered hundreds of tiny lilies mingled with large stars, and when I saw those stars, I felt my body go numb. Gudrun and Amelia had clearly heard the sounds of the crowd, the shrieking and howling, but their neighborhood was some distance from the Kolesh quarter, the scene of most of the murders and devastation. The two women knew nothing about the violence that had taken place.

I took Amelia in my arms and held her tight. I told her that I was going away, I was going away and never coming back. Above all, I told her that I had come for her, that I wanted to take her with me to my home, to my village in the mountains. It was another world there, I said, we'd be protected from everything; that land of crests and pastures and forests would be for us the safest of bulwarks. And I told her I wanted her to be my wife.

I felt her shivering against me, and it was as though I held a trembling bird in my arms. Her tremors seemed to reach into the deepest part of my body and make it more vibrant and alive. She turned her beautiful face to me, smiled, and gave me a long kiss.

An hour later, we left the city. We walked quickly, hand in hand. We weren't alone. Men, women, children, old people, entire families were fleeing, too, bringing with them a great deal of baggage. Some carried suitcases crammed to overflowing and impossible to close, so that the linen and crockery they contained were visible. Others pushed carts loaded with trunks and badly tied bundles. Everyone looked serious, fearful, uncertain. Nobody spoke. We all marched along in great haste, as if compelled to put as much distance as possible between us and what we were leaving behind.

But what was actually driving us away? Other men, or the course of events? I'm still a young man, still in my prime, and yet, when I think about my life, it's like a bottle too small to hold everything that's been poured into it. Is this the case with every human life, or was I born into a time that has abolished all limits, that shuffles human lives like cards in a great game of chance?

I didn't ask for very much. I would have liked to remain in the village and never leave. The mountains, the forests, our rivers—all that would have been enough for me. I would have liked to stay far from the noise of the world, but people in these parts have killed one another in large numbers throughout History. Many nations have died and are now only names in books. Some countries have devoured others, eviscerated them, violated them, defiled them. And justice hasn't always triumphed over nastiness.

Why did I, like thousands of others, have to carry a cross I hadn't chosen, a cross which was not made for my shoulders and which didn't concern me? Who decided to come rummaging around in my obscure existence, invade my gray anonymity, my meager tranquillity, and bowl me like a little ball in a great game of skittles? God? Well, in that case, if He exists, if He really exists, let Him hide His face. Let Him put His two hands on His head, and let Him bow down. It may be, as Peiper used to teach us, that many men are unworthy of Him, but now I know that He, too, is unworthy of most of us, and that if the creature is capable of producing horror, it's solely because his Creator has slipped him the recipe for it.

XXVIII

Ⅰ 've just read over my account from the beginning. I'm not talking about the official Report; I mean this whole long confession. It lacks order. I go off in all directions. But I don't have to justify myself. The words come to my mind like iron shavings to a magnet, and I shake them onto the page without worrying too much about emending them. If my tale looks deformed or monstrous, that's because it's made in the image of my life, which I've been unable to contain, and which is in disarray.

On June 10, the day of the *Schoppessenwass* in honor of the *Anderer,* everyone in the village and quite a few people from outside gathered in the market square and waited in front of the little platform *Zungfrost* had built. As I've said, it had been a long time since I'd gazed upon such a dense concentration of humanity in so restricted a space. I saw only merry, laughing, peaceful folk, but I couldn't help thinking about the crowds I'd seen back in the days when the Capital was seized by madness, right before *Pürische Nacht,* and with that thought in mind, I perceived the tranquil countenances around me as masks hiding bloody faces, constantly open mouths, demented eyes.

Viktor Heidekirch's accordion was playing every tune we knew, and in the warm, soft air of that late afternoon, various strong aromas—of fried food, of grilled sausages, of doughnuts, of waffles, of *Wärmspeck*—mingled with the more delicate perfumes given off by the hay drying in the fields around the village. Poupchette inhaled them all with delight and clapped her hands at every old song that came out of Heidekirch's squeezebox. Amelia and Fedorine had stayed home. The sun was in no hurry to disappear behind the crests of the Hörni. It seemed to be taking its time, extending the day a little so as not to miss the party.

All at once, you could tell that the ceremony was about to begin. Something like a wave ran through the crowd, gently moving it like the leaves of an ash tree stirred by a breeze. Viktor Heidekirch, perhaps at a signal arranged in advance, silenced his instrument. You could still hear a few voices, a few laughs, a few shouts, but they gradually died down, fading into a great silence. That was when I smelled the henhouse odor. I turned around and saw Göbbler standing two steps away. He greeted me by raising his odd beret, which was made of woven straw. "Going to the show, neighbor?"

"What show?" I asked.

With a slight wave of his hand, Göbbler indicated everything around us. He sniggered. I made no reply. Poupchette pulled my hair: "Black curls, Daddy, black curls!" Suddenly, about ten meters away on my right, there was movement, the sounds of shoes scraping the ground and shuffling as people stepped aside. We could see Orschwir's great bulk cleaving the crowd, and behind him, following in his wake, a hat, a hat we'd come to know over the course of the previous two weeks: a sort of black, shiny bowler outside of age and time, unconnected to places or people, for it seemed to float freely in the air, as if there were no head beneath it. The mayor reached the platform and mounted it without a moment's hesitation; then, as it were from on high, he made a ceremonious gesture, inviting the person under the hat, which was all we could see, to join him.

Very cautiously, accompanied by cracking sounds from the green wood, the *Anderer* climbed up and stood at Orschwir's side. The platform was only a few meters high—less than three, in fact—and the stair that *Zungfrost* had nailed together comprised only six steps, but as you watched the *Anderer* hoist himself from one to the next, you might have thought he was scaling the highest peak of the Hörni mountains, so slow and effortful was his progress. When he finally reached the mayor's side, the crowd uttered a murmur of surprise, because it must be said that many of those present were seeing for the first time the person they'd heard so much about—seeing him in flesh and blood and clothes. The platform was neither very wide nor very deep. *Zungfrost,* who was as thin as a lath, had made a guess as to the appropriate dimensions, probably basing his estimates on his own body. But Orschwir was something of a giant, tall and broad, and the *Anderer* was as round as a barrel.

The mayor was wearing his fanciest getup, which he generally put on three times a year for the grandest occasions—the village festival, St. Matthew's Fair, All Souls' Day. The only feature that distinguished this outfit from his everyday attire was a green braided jacket fastened by six frogged buttons. In order to survive where we live, it's better to blend in, to not let anything stand out too far, to be as simple and crude as a block of granite emerging from a stubble field. This is a truth which Orschwir has long since understood. He keeps the pomp to a minimum.

The *Anderer*'s attitude was obviously different. He'd dropped in from the moon or somewhere even farther away; he knew nothing about our ways or what went on inside our heads. Maybe if he'd worn less perfume and pomade, and fewer ribbons, we would have found him less distressing. Maybe if he'd been dressed in coarse cloth and corduroy and an old woolen overcoat, he would have blended in more with our walls, and then, little by little, the village would have—not accepted him; acceptance requires at least five generations—at least tolerated him, as one tolerates certain cats or dogs that arrive out of nowhere, from the depths of the forest, most likely, and enliven our streets with their silent movements and their measured cries.

But the *Anderer*'s toilette, especially on that day, achieved the opposite of blending in: white jabot, frothing between two black satin lapels; watch chain, key chain, and chains for I don't know what else covering his paunch with golden hardware; dazzling cuffs and matching buttons; navy-blue frock coat, woven belt, impeccable gibrette, braided trousers; polished shoes and garnet gaiters; not to mention the rouge on his cheeks—his fat cheeks, as full as perfectly ripe apples—his shiny mustache, his brushed side whiskers, or his rosy lips.

He and the mayor, squeezed together on the little platform, formed an odd couple better suited to a circus big top than to a village square. The *Anderer* was smiling. He'd doffed his hat and was holding it with both hands. He smiled at nothing and looked at no one. People around me began whispering: "*Teuflåsgot!* What kind of a queer duck is this?"

"Is it a man or a balloon?"

"A big ape, I'd say!"

"Maybe that's the fashion where he comes from."

"He's a *Dumkof,* that's what he is. Off his rocker!"

"Quiet down, the mayor's about to speak!"

"Let him speak. We can still admire the prodigy next to him!"

With great difficulty, Orschwir had extracted from one of his pockets two pieces of paper, each folded four times. He smoothed them out for a long moment, trying to put on an air of self-assurance, because it was obvious to his audience that he was somewhat overwhelmed and even uneasy. The speech he read was worth its weight in gold, and I'm going to reproduce it in its entirety. Not that I remember it verbatim; however, a few days ago I simply asked Orschwir for it, because I know he archives everything relating to his office. His reply was, "What do you want it for?"

"For the Report."

"Why are you going back so far? We didn't ask you to do all that."

He made that last observation in a mistrustful tone, as if he suspected a trap. I said, "It's just that I thought it would be a good idea to show what a friendly welcome our village gave him."

Orschwir pushed his ledger aside, took the pitcher and the two glasses that the No-Eyed Girl handed him, poured two glasses of beer, and shoved one over to me. It was plain that my request annoyed him. He hesitated for a while, but in the end he said, "If you think it'll be good for us, then do it."

He took a little piece of paper, slowly wrote a few words on it, and held it out to me: "Go to the village hall and show that to Hausorn. He'll find the speech and give it to you."

"Did you write it?"

Orschwir put his beer glass down and gave me a look that managed to be both irritated and sympathetic. Then he spoke to *Die Keinauge* in a gentle voice I'd never heard him use before: "Leave us, Lise, will you?"

The little blind girl inclined her head in a slight bow and

withdrew. Orschwir waited to answer me until after she'd closed the door behind her. "You see that child, Brodeck? Her eyes, as you know, are dead. She was born with dead eyes. Of all the things you can contemplate around you—that sideboard, that clock, this table my great-grandfather made, that corner of the Tannäringen forest you can glimpse through the window—of all that she can see nothing. Of course, she knows it all exists because she feels it, she inhales it, she touches it, but she can't see it. And even if she should ask to see it, she wouldn't be able to see it. So she doesn't ask. She doesn't waste time making such a request because she knows no one can fulfill it."

He stopped and took a long pull on his beer.

"You ought to make an effort to be a little like her, Brodeck. You ought to content yourself with asking for what you can have and for what can serve your purpose. The rest is useless. All it can do is distract you and put I don't know what kinds of ideas in your head and set them boiling in your brain, and all for nothing! I'm going to tell you something. That night when you agreed to write the Report, you said you would say 'I,' but 'I' would mean all of us. You remember saying that, right? Well, tell yourself that all of us wrote that speech. Maybe I read it, but we all thought it up together. Be content with that, Brodeck. Another glass?"

At the village hall, Caspar Hausorn made a face when I handed him the mayor's note. He was about to say something, but he restrained himself at the last instant. He turned his back to me and opened two large drawers. After shifting several registers, he took out a dark-brown cardboard box, which contained dozens of sheets of paper in various sizes. He glanced at them quickly, one by one, until he came to the pages with the speech, which he handed to me without a word. I took them and was about to stick them in my pocket, but he stopped me abruptly. "The mayor's message says you have the right to read the pages and copy them, but not to remove them."

With a movement of his head, Hausorn indicated a chair and a small table. Then he adjusted the eyeglasses on his nose and returned to his desk and whatever he'd been writing. I sat down and started copying the speech, taking great care to record every word. From time to time, Hausorn raised his head and gazed at me. The lenses of his glasses were so thick that if you looked through them they made his eyes seem disproportionately large, the size of pigeons' eggs, and although he was a man whose fine, well-modeled features women had always appreciated, when I saw him like that I thought about an enormous insect, a kind of giant, furious fly attached to the neck of a decapitated human body.

"My dear friends, both those from our village and those visiting from elsewhere in the vicinity, and you, my dear sir, Mister . . . It is with great pleasure that we welcome you within our walls."

Before going on to reproduce the rest of what Orschwir said on this occasion, standing on the platform and speaking in the twilight of a mild day so far removed from the cold and the feeling of terror on the night of the *Ereigniës,* I must allude to the mayor's moment of confusion and embarrassment when, early in his speech, he said "my dear sir, Mister . . . ," paused, looked at the *Anderer,* and waited for him to supply his name, the name that nobody knew. But the *Anderer* remained mute, smiling without parting his lips, so that the mayor, after repeating "Mister . . . Mister . . . ?" several times in a gently questioning tone, was obliged to continue his speech without having obtained any satisfaction.

"You are the first, and for the time being the only, person to visit our village since the long, grievous months when the war held this part of the world in its atrocious grip. In former days, and for centuries, our region was traversed by travelers who came up from the great plains of the south and took the mountain route on their way to the distant northern coasts and the port cities. Such travelers always found this village a pleasant, auspicious stopping place, and the old chronicles refer to it by the ancient name *Wohlwollend Trast,* 'Kindly Halt.' We don't know whether such a halt is the purpose of your stay here. But however that may be, you honor us by your sojourn in the bosom of our modest community. You are as it were the first sign of a springtime of humanity, returning to us after too long a winter, and we hope that after you others will come to visit us and that we will thus gradually reestablish our connection with the community of mankind. Please, my dear Mister . . ."—and here, once again, Orschwir stopped and looked at the *Anderer,* giving him the opportunity to say his name, but that name was not spoken, and Orschwir, after clearing his throat one more time, returned to his text—"my dear sir, please don't judge us too severely or too quickly. We have gone through much adversity, and our isolation has no doubt reduced us to living on the margins of civilization. Nevertheless, to those who really know us, we're better than we might appear to be. We have known suffering and death, and we must learn again how to live. We must also learn not to forget the past but to overcome it, by banishing it far from us and making sure that it no longer overflows into our present and even less into our future. In the name of every man, woman, and child, and in the name of our beautiful village, which I have the honor to administer, I therefore bid you welcome, my dear"—and this time, the mayor did not pause—"sir, and now I shall yield the floor to you."

Orschwir looked at the crowd, refolded his pages, and shook the *Anderer*'s hand, while the applause mounted up to the pink-and-blue sky, where some apparently drunken swallows were challenging one another to speed trials along incoherent courses. The applause gradually died down and silence fell again, heavily. The *Anderer* smiled, but no one could say at whom or what. At the countryfolk crowded into the first row, who hadn't understood much of the speech and couldn't wait to drink the wine and beer? At Orschwir, whose mounting anxiety grew more and more palpable as the silence persisted? At the sky? Maybe at the swallows. He had yet to pronounce a single word when there came a sudden, violent gust of wind, of very balmy, even hot wind, the kind that makes animals nervous in their stalls and sometimes irritates them so much that they begin kicking wildly at walls and doors. The wind assailed the welcome banner, tore it in half, and wrapped itself in the two parts, twisting and ripping off large sections, which swiftly flew away toward the birds, the clouds, the setting sun. The wind departed as it had come, like a thief. What was left of the banner sagged down. Only two words remained: "*Wi sund*"—"We are." The rest of the sentence had disappeared into thin air, vaporized, forgotten, destroyed. Once again I noticed a chicken smell, very close to me. Göbbler was at my side, and he spoke into my ear. "We *are!* What are we, Brodeck? I wonder what we are . . ."

I made no reply. Poupchette hummed as she sat on my shoulders. She'd clapped very hard during every round of applause. The incident with the banner had distracted the crowd for a few seconds, but now it had calmed down again, and it was waiting. Orschwir was waiting, too, and if you knew him even slightly, you knew that he wouldn't be able to wait much longer. Maybe the *Anderer* could sense that as well, for he moved a little, rubbing and stretching his cheeks with both hands; then he brought them down in front of him, joined them as if he were going to pray, nodded his head to left and right, smiling all the while, and said, "Thank you." That was it: "Thank you." Then he bowed ceremoniously, three times, like an actor on the stage at the end of a play. People looked at one another. Some of them opened their mouths so wide that a round loaf of bread could have slipped in without difficulty. Others elbowed their neighbors and exchanged questioning looks. Still others shrugged their shoulders or scratched their heads. Then someone started applauding. It was as good a way as any to ease the embarrassment. Others imitated him. Poupchette was happy again. "Fun, Daddy, fun!"

As for the *Anderer*, he replaced his hat on his head, climbed down the steps to the platform as slowly as he'd mounted them, and disappeared into the crowd before the eyes of the mayor, who stood there dumbfounded and unmoving, his arms hanging at his sides, while the surviving fragment of the banner teased the fur of his cap and the people at his feet abandoned him, moving briskly toward the trestle tables, the mugs, the glasses, the pitchers, the sausages, and the brioches.

XXIX

Someone's been in the shed! Someone's been in the shed! It was Göbbler, I know it was! I'd swear to it! It couldn't be anybody but him! Besides, there are tracks, footsteps in the snow, big, muddy tracks going toward his house! He didn't even hide them! They think they're so powerful, they don't even bother to hide the fact that they're all spying on me, that they've got their eyes on me every moment.

It was enough for me to be away for barely an hour, off to buy three balls of wool for Fedorine in Frida Pertzer's tiny shop, which offers a little of everything—gold braid, needles, thread, gossip, buttons, cloth by the meter—and that gave him enough time to enter the shed and rummage through everything! Everything's upside down! Everything's been overturned, opened, moved! He didn't even try to put things back in order after he went through them! And he forced the desk drawer open, the one in Diodemus's desk—he broke the drawer and left it on the floor! What was he looking for? He wanted what I'm writing, that's certain. He hears the typewriter too much. He suspects I'm writing something other than the Report! But he didn't find anything! He couldn't find anything! My hiding place is too sure.

A short while ago, when I discovered what had happened, I was furious. I didn't stop to think. I saw the tracks, I rushed over to Göbbler's, and I banged on his door with the flat of my hand. The night was rather advanced, and the village was sleeping, but there was a light in Göbbler's house, and I knew he wasn't asleep. His wife answered the door. She was wearing a nightgown, and when she saw that it was me, she smiled. Against the light from inside, I could distinguish the outlines of her big hips and her immense breasts. She'd taken down her hair.

"Good evening, Brodeck," she said, repeatedly passing her tongue over her lips.

"I want to see your husband!"

"Aren't you feeling well? Are you sick?"

I shouted his name at the top of my voice. I kept shouting it. There was movement upstairs, and soon Göbbler made his appearance, with a candle in his hand and a nightcap on his head.

"Why, Brodeck, what's going on?"

"You tell me! Why did you ransack my shed? Why did you break the desk drawer?"

"I assure you, I haven't done any—"

"Don't take me for an idiot! I know it was you! You're always spying on me! Have the others put you up to it? The footprints lead to your house!"

"The footprints? What footprints? Brodeck . . . Do you want to come in and have some herb tea? I think you're—"

"If you ever do it again, Göbbler, I swear I'll—"

"You'll what?"

He stepped close to me. His face was a few inches from mine. He was trying to see me through the whitish veil that covers his eyes a little more every day. "Be reasonable," he said. "It's nighttime. Take my advice and go to bed. Take my advice."

Suddenly Göbbler's eyes frightened me. There was nothing

human about them anymore. They looked like ice eyes, frozen
eyes, like the eyes I saw once when I was eleven years old and a
caravan of men from the village had gone to collect the bodies of
two foresters from the hamlet of Froxkeim who had been carried
off by a snowslide on the Schnikelkopf slopes. The villagers had
brought down the remains in large sheets suspended from poles.
I saw them pass not far from our cabin while I was out getting
water from the stream. I noticed that the arm of one corpse was
hanging out of the sheet and beating time on the ground, and I
also saw the other man's head through a tear in the cloth. His
stare was fixed and white, with a flat, full whiteness, as if all the
snow that killed him had poured itself into his eyes. I cried out,
dropped the water jug, and went running back to the cabin to
fling myself against Fedorine.

"Don't ever tell me again what I have to do, Göbbler."

I left without giving him time to reply.

I've spent the last hour putting the shed back in order.
Nothing's been stolen, and for a good reason: there's nothing to
steal. My manuscript is too well hidden; no one will ever be able
to find it. I'm holding the pages in my hands. They're still warm,
and when I bring them up to my face and inhale, I smell paper,
ink, and another scent, the smell of skin. No, no one will ever
find my hiding place.

Diodemus had a hiding place, too, and I've just discovered
it, completely by chance, when I was trying to fix the desk drawer.
I turned the desk over and laid it on the floor feet up, and that's
when I saw, on the underside of the desktop, a large envelope. It
was glued there, right over the drawer that was supposed to hide
it. When the desk was upright, the drawer was empty, but above
it, glued and impossible to suspect, was the envelope.

Its contents were really quite varied. I've just sorted through them. To begin with, there's a long list in two columns, one headed "Novels Written" and the other "Novels to Be Written." The first list includes five titles: *The Young Girl by the Water, The Amorous Captain, Flowers in Winter, Mirna's Bouquets,* and *Agitated Hearts.* Not only do I recognize those titles but I also know all about the novels themselves because Diodemus used to read to me from them. We'd sit in his little house, which was cluttered with books, registers, and loose sheets of paper liable at any moment to catch fire from the candles, and I'd always have to struggle against drowsiness, but Diodemus was so enraptured by his stories and his words that he wouldn't even notice my frequent dozes.

I smiled as I read the list, for those titles brought back all those times I'd spent in Diodemus's company, and I envisioned his handsome face—like something on a medal—and the way it became animated when he read. When I perused the other part of the list, the "Novels to Be Written," I couldn't help bursting into laughter at the thought of what I'd escaped. Diodemus had put down the names of more than sixty novels-to-be! Most of the titles resembled one another and gave off a distinct whiff of rose water. But two of them stood out, and Diodemus had underlined them both several times: *The Treason of the Just* and *Remorse.* This last title, in fact, had been copied four times over, each time in bigger letters, as if his pencil had stammered.

On another sheet of paper, he'd drawn up a sort of genealogical tree for his own family. There were the names of his parents, his grandparents, and his great-grandparents, along with their dates and their places of birth. There were also uncles, aunts, cousins, and distant ancestors. But there were likewise some great voids, some holes, some lines that stopped suddenly at a blank space or a question mark. Thus the tree contained both full, abundant branches, almost cracking under their load of names, and naked limbs, reduced to a simple line that died out unadorned. I thought about the strange forests of symbols and dead lives that our trees would compose if they were all lined up together side by side. My tree would disappear under the suffocating branches of the many families that for centuries have safeguarded their memory as their most precious inheritance. In fact, mine wouldn't be a tree at all, just a puny trunk. Above my name, there would simply be two stems, cut very short, bare, leafless, and resolutely mute. But could I possibly, all the same, find a place for Fedorine, the way one can sometimes graft a sturdier plant onto a sickly one in order to give it some of the other's strength and sap?

The envelope also contained two letters. They had been read and reread so often that the paper they were written on was reduced to a thin film about to fall apart at the creases. They were signed "Magdalena" and had been sent to Diodemus a long time ago, well before he came to settle in the village. Both were love letters, but the second spoke of the end of love. It spoke of it in simple terms, without grand phrases, without mawkish expressions or effects. It spoke of the end of love as a truth of existence, an event which cannot be striven against and which forces man to bow his neck and accept his fate.

I don't wish to transcribe here all or even part of those two letters. They don't belong to me. They aren't part of my story. As I read them, I thought that perhaps they had been the cause of

Diodemus's arrival among us, the reason why he put so much distance between his former existence and the daily life he'd built for himself, little by little, in the village. I don't know if he succeeded in healing his wound, nor do I know if he really wanted to. Sometimes you love your own scars.

I was holding in my hands fragments of Diodemus's life, small but essential pieces which, if put together, offered insights into his departed spirit. And as I thought about his life, about mine and Amelia's and Fedorine's, and also about the *Anderer's*—concerning which, to tell the truth, I knew almost nothing, and which I only imagined—the village appeared before me in a new light. I suddenly saw it as the final place, reached by those who leave the night and the void behind them; not the place for new beginnings but simply the place where everything may end, where everything must end.

But there was still something else in the big brown envelope.

There was another letter, a letter addressed to me. I seized it with great curiosity, for it's not often you can hear a dead man speak to you. Diodemus's letter began with these words: "Forgive me, Brodeck, please forgive me . . ." and ended with them as well.

I've just finished reading that long letter.
Yes, I've just read it.

I don't know if I'll be able to give an idea of what I felt as I read the letter. Besides, I'm not certain I felt anything. In any case, however, I can swear that there was no suffering. I didn't suffer as I read Diodemus's letter, which is in fact a long confession, because I'm missing the essential organs for experiencing suffering. I don't possess them anymore. They were removed from me, one by one, in the camp. And—alas—they've never grown back since.

XXX

I'm sure Diodemus assumed I'd wind up thoroughly detesting him after reading the letter he wrote me. Diodemus believed that I was still a participant in the human order, but he was mistaken.

Yesterday evening, after straightening up the shed and accidentally finding Diodemus's hiding place and going through the contents of the brown envelope, I joined Amelia in our bed. It was late. I nestled myself against her. I embraced her warmth and the shape of her body and fell asleep very quickly. I didn't even think about what I'd just read. My heart felt curiously light, while my body was heavy with weariness and disentangled knots. I dropped happily into sleep, as one does every night of his childhood. And I had dreams, not the dreams that ordinarily torment me, the black crater of the *Kazerskwir* and me circling around it, circling and circling—no; my dreams were peaceful.

I found the student Kelmar again. He was very much alive and wearing his beautiful white linen shirt with the embroidered front. The immaculate shirt set off his suntanned skin and his elegant neck. We weren't on the road to the camp. Nor were we in the railway car where we spent so many days and nights, crammed in with the others. We were in a place that recalled to me nothing that I knew; I couldn't even say if it was inside a house or outdoors. I'd never known Kelmar this way. He bore no trace of any blow. His cheeks were fresh and clean-shaven. His clothes smelled good. He smiled. He talked to me. He talked to me at length, and I listened without interrupting him. After some time, he stood up, and I understood, without his having to tell me, that he had to go. He looked at me and smiled, and I have a clear memory of the last words we exchanged.

"After what they did to us in the railway car, Kelmar, I should have stopped like you. I should have quit running and sat on the road."

"You did what you thought you should do, Brodeck."

"No, you were right. It's what we deserved. I was a coward."

"I'm not sure I was right. The death of one man never makes amends for the sacrifice of another, Brodeck. That would be too simple. And then, it's not up to you to judge yourself. Nor to me, either. It's not up to men to judge one another. They're not made for that."

"Kelmar, do you think it's time for me to join you now?"

"Stay on the other side, Brodeck. Your place is still over there."

Those are the last words I remember him speaking. Then I tried to get close to him, I wanted to take him in my arms and hold him tight, but I embraced only the wind.

Contrary to what some claim, I don't think dreams foreshadow anything at all. I just think they come at the right moment, and they tell us, in the hollow of the night, what we perhaps dare not admit to ourselves in the light of day.

I'm not going to reproduce Diodemus's entire letter. For one thing, I don't have it anymore. I'm aware of what it must have cost him to write it.

I didn't leave for the camp of my own accord. I was arrested and transported there. The *Fratergekeime* had entered our village barely a week previously. The war had begun three months before that. We were cut off from the world, and we didn't know very much about what was happening. The mountains often protect us from commotion and turmoil, but at the same time they isolate us from a part of life.

One morning we saw them coming, a lengthy, dusty column marching up the border road. Nobody tried to slow their progress, and in any case such an effort would have been futile; furthermore, I think the deaths of Orschwir's two sons were on everyone's mind, and if there was one thing everyone wanted to avoid, it was any more death.

Besides, the most important fact, the one necessary for understanding the rest, was that those troops who were coming to our village, helmeted, armed, and emboldened by the crushing victories they'd inflicted on every force they'd encountered, were much closer to the inhabitants of our region than the great majority of our own country's population. As far as the men around here were concerned, our nation barely existed. It was a bit like a woman who occasionally reminded them of her presence with a gentle word or a request, but whose eyes and lips they never really saw. The soldiers entering our village as conquerors shared our customs and spoke a language so close to ours that a minimum of effort sufficed for us to understand and use it. The age-old history of our region was mingled with that of their country. We had in common legends, songs, poets, refrains, a way of preparing meats and making soups, an identical melancholy, and a similar propensity to lapse into drunkenness. When all's said and done, borders are only pencil strokes on maps. They slice through worlds, but they don't separate them. Sometimes borders can be forgotten as quickly as they're drawn.

The unit that took over the village comprised about a hundred men under the command of a captain named Adolf Buller. I saw very little of him. I remember him as a man of small stature, very thin, and afflicted with a tic that caused him to jerk his chin abruptly to the left every twenty seconds or so. He was riding a filthy, mud-covered horse, and he never let go of his riding crop, a short riding crop with a braided tip. Orschwir and Father Peiper had stationed themselves at the entrance to the village to welcome the conquerors and implore them to spare its people and its houses, while doors and shutters were closed and locked everywhere and all the inhabitants of the village held their breath.

Captain Buller listened to Orschwir's muttering without getting off his horse. A soldier at his side bore a lance at the end of which a red-and-black standard was attached. The following day, that standard replaced the flag mounted atop the village hall. You could read the name of the regiment the company belonged to, DER UNVERWUNDBARE ANLAUF ("The Invulnerable Surge"), as well as its motto, HINTER UNS, NIEMAND—"After Us, No One."

Buller didn't reply to Orschwir. He jerked his chin twice, gently moved the mayor aside with his riding crop, and advanced, followed by his soldiers.

One might have thought he was going to demand that his men be given beds and warm lodging within the thick walls of the houses, but he did no such thing. The troop moved into the marketplace, unpacked some large tents, and pitched them in the twinkling of an eye. Then the soldiers knocked on all the doors with orders to collect and confiscate all weapons, which mostly turned out to be hunting rifles. They did it without the least brutality and with the greatest politeness. By contrast, when Aloïs Cathor, a crockery mender who always liked playing crafty, told them there were no weapons in his house, they aimed theirs at him, ransacked the rabbit cage he lived in from top to bottom, and wound up discovering an old rifle. They waved it in front of his nose and brought them, Cathor and the rifle, before Captain Buller, who was sipping an eau-de-vie in front of his tent while his orderly stood behind him with the flask, ready to serve a refill. The soldiers explained the affair. Cathor adopted a mocking tone. Buller sized him up from head to foot, drained his glass of brandy, suffered his little nervous tic, pointed his riding crop to summon a lieutenant with pink skin and hay-colored hair, and whispered a few words in his ear. The young man assented, clicked his heels, saluted, and left, taking with him the two soldiers and their prisoner.

A few hours later, a drummer passed through the streets, crying out an announcement: The entire population, without exception, was to gather in front of the church at seven o'clock in order to assist at an event of the greatest importance. Attendance was obligatory for all, under pain of sanctions.

Shortly before the stipulated hour, everyone left his house. In silence. The streets were soon filled with a strange procession; no one said a word, and people didn't dare to raise their heads, to look around them, to meet others' eyes. We walked along together, Amelia and me, holding hands tightly. We were afraid. Everyone was afraid. Captain Buller was waiting for us, riding crop in hand, on the parvis in front of the church, surrounded by his two lieutenants, the one I've already mentioned and another one, squat and black-haired. When the little church square was full, everyone was standing motionless, and all noise had stopped, he spoke.

"Villagers, ladies and gentlemen, we have not come here to defile or to destroy. One does not defile or destroy what belongs to him—what is his—unless he is afflicted with madness. And we are not mad. As of today, your village has the supremely good fortune of forming part of the Greater Territory. You are in your homeland here, and this homeland is our homeland, too. We are henceforth united for a millennial future. Our race is the first among races, immemorial and unstained, and so will yours be, if you consent to rid yourselves of the impure elements which are still to be found among you. Thus it is imperative that we live in perfect mutual understanding and total frankness. Lying to us is not good. Attempting to deceive us is not good. One man has made such an attempt today. We trust that his example will not be followed."

Buller had a delicate, almost feminine voice, and the curious thing was that the uncontrolled chin movement that made him look like a robot gone haywire disappeared while he spoke. He'd hardly finished his speech when, with flawless protocol, as if everything had been rehearsed numerous times, Aloïs Cathor was brought into the square, escorted by the two soldiers who had him in their charge, and led before the captain. Another soldier walked close behind them, carrying something heavy that we couldn't make out very well. When he placed it on the ground, we could see that it was a timber log, a section about a meter high cut from the trunk of a fir tree. Then everything went very fast. The soldiers grabbed Cathor, forced him to his knees, laid his head on the log, stepped back. They were quickly replaced by a fourth soldier, whom no one had yet seen. A big apron of dark leather was strapped to his chest and legs. In his hands he held a large ax. He moved very close to Cathor, raised the ax, and—before anyone even had time to catch his breath—brought the blade down forcefully on the pottery mender's neck. The cleanly severed head hit the ground near the block and rolled a little. A great stream of blood gushed out of Cathor's body, which jerked about spasmodically for several seconds like a decapitated goose before all movement ceased and the corpse lay inert. From the ground, Cathor's head looked at us. His eyes and mouth were wide open, as if he'd just asked us a question and none of us had answered it.

It had happened so quickly; the awful scene had transfixed us all. Stunned as we were, the sound of the captain's voice cleared our heads, only to plunge us into even greater astonishment: "This is the fate of those who wish to play games with us. Think about it, villagers! Ladies and gentlemen, think about it! And in order to assist your reflections, the head and the body of this *Fremdër* will remain here! Burial is forbidden under pain of suffering a similar punishment! And one further word of advice: Cleanse your village! Do not wait for us to do it ourselves. Cleanse it while there's still time! And now disperse, go back to your houses! I wish you a good evening!"

His chin gave a little jerk to the left, as if to shoo a fly. He smacked his riding crop against the seam of his trousers, did an about-face, and departed, followed by his lieutenants. Amelia was trembling against me and sobbing. I held her to my chest as best I could. In a very soft voice, she kept repeating, "It's a bad dream, Brodeck, isn't it? Isn't it just a bad dream?" She kept staring at Cathor's headless body, slumped against the block.

"Come on," I said, putting my hand over her eyes.

Later, when we were already in bed, someone knocked at our door. I felt Amelia flinch. I knew she wasn't asleep. I kissed her on the nape of her neck and went downstairs. Fedorine had already admitted the visitor; it was Diodemus. She was extremely fond of him. She called him the *Klübeigge,* which means "scholar" in her old language. He and I sat at the table. Fedorine brought us two cups and poured us some herbal tea that she'd just prepared with wild thyme, mint, lemon balm, and fir-tree buds.

"What do you intend to do?" Diodemus asked me.

"What do you mean, what do I intend to do?"

"I don't know, look, you were there, you saw what they did to Cathor!"

"I saw it."

"And you heard what the officer said."

"That it's forbidden to touch the body? It reminds me of a Greek story Nösel used to tell back in the University, about a princess who—"

"Forget the Greek princesses! That's not what I want to talk about," Diodemus blurted out, interrupting me. He hadn't stopped wringing his hands since he sat down. "When he said we have to 'cleanse the village,' what do you think he meant?"

"Those people are madmen. I watched them at work when I was in the Capital. Why do you think I came back to the village?"

"They may be mad, but they are nevertheless the masters, ever since they deposed their Emperor and crossed our borders."

"They'll leave, Diodemus. In the end, they'll leave. Why would they want to stay with us? There's nothing here. It's the ends of the earth. They wanted to show us that they have the power now. They've shown us. They wanted to terrorize us. They've done it. They're going to stay a few days, and then they'll go somewhere else, somewhere farther along."

"But the captain threatened us. He said we're supposed to 'cleanse the village.' "

"So? What do you propose to do? Get a bucket of water and a broom and tidy up the streets?"

"Don't joke, Brodeck! You think they're joking? There wasn't anything innocent about what he said. He wasn't speaking at random! He chose every word carefully. Like the word *Fremdër* he used to refer to poor Cathor."

"That's the word they use to talk about anybody they don't like. They're all *Fremdër*, all 'scumbags.' I saw that word painted on many a door during *Pürische Nacht.*"

"As you well know, it means 'foreigner,' too!"

"Cathor wasn't a foreigner! His family's as old as the village!"

Diodemus loosened his shirt collar, which seemed to be strangling him. He wiped his sweaty forehead with the back of his hand, gave me a fearful look, turned his eyes to his cup, took a quick sip, looked at me furtively once more, cast his eyes down again, and then said, almost in a murmur, "But you, Brodeck? You?"

XXXI

I know how fear can transform a man.

I didn't always know that, but I learned it. In the camp. I saw men scream, beat their heads against stone walls, hurl themselves on wire with barbs as sharp as razors. I saw them vomit, soil their pants, empty their bowels entirely, expel all the liquids, all the humors, all the gases their bodies contained. I saw some pray, while others renounced the name of God and covered it with obscene insults. I even saw a man die of it—of fear, I mean. One morning, our guards played their little game and picked him as the next to be hanged, but when one of them stopped in front of him, laughed, and said *"Du!"* the prisoner didn't move. His face betrayed no emotion, no distress, no thought. And as the guard started to lose his smile and lift his club, the man fell down dead, all at once, before the other even touched him.

The camp taught me this paradox: man is great, but he can never measure up to his full greatness. It's an impossibility inherent in our nature. When I made my vertiginous journey, when I descended one by one the rungs of the sordid ladder that carried me ever deeper into the *Kazerskwir,* I was not only moving toward the negation of my own person but also, at the same time, proceeding toward full awareness of my tormentors' motivations and full awareness of the motivations of those who had delivered me into their hands. And thus, somehow, toward a rough outline of forgiveness.

It was the fear others felt, much more than hatred or some other emotion, that had made a victim of me. It was because fear had seized some of them by the throat that I was handed over to torturers and executioners, and it was also fear that had turned those same torturers, formerly men like me, into monsters; fear that had caused the seeds of evil, which we all carry, to germinate inside them.

There's no doubt that I badly misjudged the consequences of Aloïs Cathor's execution. I'd grasped its horror, its odious cruelty, but I hadn't envisioned the inroads it was going to make in people's minds, nor had I understood how much Captain Buller's words, examined and sifted through dozens and dozens of brains, would distress them; I hadn't considered that those words could induce the others to make a decision whose victim would be me. And there was also, of course, Cathor's remains, his head lying on the ground a couple of meters from his body, with the sun shining down and all the ephemeral insects which in those days of early fall were born in the morning, died at night, and spent the hours of their brief existence zooming around the corpse, reveling in the banquet, whirling, zigzagging, buzzing, driven wild by the great mass of flesh putrefying in the heat.

The nauseating smell permeated the whole village. The wind seemed to be on Buller's side. It went to the church square, loaded itself with the miasmal exhalations of carrion, and then rushed gusting and swirling down every street, dancing a jig, slipping under doors, penetrating incompletely closed windows and disjointed tiles, and bringing all of us the fetid spoor of Cathor's death.

Throughout this time, the soldiers behaved with the most perfect propriety, as if everything were normal. There was no thieving, no plundering, no violence, no demands. They paid for whatever they took from the shops. Whenever they encountered women, young or old, they raised their caps. They chopped wood for elderly widows. They joked with the children, who got scared and ran off. They saluted the mayor, the priest, and Diodemus.

Captain Buller, always displaying his tic and flanked by his two lieutenants, took a walk through the village streets every morning and every night, striding along on his short, thin legs. He walked fast, as if someone were waiting for him somewhere, and paid no attention to those he met on his way. Sometimes, wielding his riding crop, he flailed the air or drove off bees.

The inhabitants of the village were all dazed. There was very little in the way of conversation. Communication was kept to a minimum. Heads were bowed. We weltered in our astonishment.

After Diodemus left my house on the night of the execution, I never saw him again. I've learned everything I'm about to write from the long letter he left me.

One evening, the third evening of the *Fratergekeime*'s presence in the village, Buller summoned Orschwir and Diodemus. Orschwir was sent for, obviously, because he was the mayor, but Diodemus was a surprising choice. Anticipating a question Diodemus would never have dared to ask, Buller observed that the village teacher must necessarily be less stupid than the other villagers and could even be capable of understanding him.

Buller received the two men in his tent. It contained a camp bed, a desk, a chair, a sort of traveling chest, and a canvas wardrobe like a slipcover under which were hanging what looked like a few articles of clothing. On the desk, there was some paper printed with the regimental letterhead, along with ink, pens, blotting paper, and a framed photograph showing a thickset woman surrounded by six children ranging in age from about two to about fifteen.

Buller was writing a letter at his desk with his back to Orschwir and Diodemus. He took his time finishing the letter, reread it, slipped it into an envelope, sealed the envelope, and placed it on the desk; then, finally, he turned to face his guests, who—it goes without saying—were still on their feet and hadn't moved a muscle. Buller gazed at them in silence for a long time, obviously trying to divine something about the men he'd be dealing with. Diodemus felt his heart beating as though it would burst, and his palms were clammy with sweat. He wondered what he was doing there and how long the ordeal would last. Buller's tic made his chin jerk at regular intervals. He picked up his riding crop, which lay handy on the bed beside him, and stroked it slowly, gently, as if it were a pet. At last he said, "Well?"

Orschwir opened his mouth wide, found no reply, and looked at Diodemus, who couldn't even swallow, much less speak.

"Well?" Buller said again, without indicating any genuine impatience.

Gathering all his courage, Orschwir managed to ask in a strangled voice, "Well what, Captain?"

This question elicited a smile from Buller, who said, "The cleansing, Mr. Mayor! What else would I be talking to you about? How much progress have you made with the cleansing?"

Once again, Orschwir stared at Diodemus, who lowered his head and tried to avoid his companion's eyes. Then the mayor, who's ordinarily so sure of himself, whose words sometimes sting like whips, whom nothing impresses, who naturally behaves like the rich, powerful man he is, began to stammer and fall apart in the face of a uniformed creature little more than half his size, a minuscule fellow afflicted with a grotesque tic, who sat there caressing his riding crop like a simpering woman. "The thing is, Captain," Orschwir said. "The thing is, we . . . we didn't entirely . . . understand. Yes. We didn't understand . . . what you . . . what you meant."

Orschwir drooped, his shoulders sagging, like a man who's made too great an effort. Buller laughed softly, stood up, and started walking around inside the tent, pacing back and forth as if deep in thought. Then he came to a stop in front of his two visitors. "Have you ever observed butterflies closely, Mr. Mayor? Or you, Mr. Schoolmaster? Yes, butterflies, any sort of butterflies at all. No? Never? That's a shame . . . a great shame! I've dedicated my life to butterflies, you see. Some people focus on chemistry, medicine, mineralogy, philosophy, history; in my case, my entire existence has been devoted to butterflies. They fully deserve such devotion, but not many people are able to see that. It's a sad state of affairs, because one could learn some lessons of extraordinary importance for the human race by contemplating these splendid, fragile creatures. Consider this, for example: the earliest observers of one species of Lepidoptera, known by the name of *Rex flammae,* noted certain behavior that seemed baseless at first; after further observations were made, however, it proved to be perfectly logical. I don't hesitate to use the word 'logical' when speaking about butterflies, which are endowed with remarkable intelligence. The *Rex flammae* live in groups of about twenty individuals. It's believed that some sort of solidarity exists among them; when one of them finds a quantity of food large enough to nourish the entire group, they all gather for the feast. They frequently tolerate the presence among them of butterflies not of their species, but when a predator suddenly appears, it seems that the *Rex flammae* warn one another, in who knows what form of language, and take cover. The other butterflies that were integrated with the group an instant earlier apparently fail to receive the information, and they're the ones that get eaten by the bird. By providing their predators with prey, the *Rex flammae* guarantee their own survival. When everything's going well for them, the presence of one or more foreign individuals in their group doesn't bother them. Perhaps they even profit from it one way or another. But when a danger arises, when it's a question of the group's integrity and survival, they don't hesitate to sacrifice an individual which is none of their own."

Buller stopped talking and went back to pacing, but he didn't take his eyes off Orschwir and Diodemus, who were sweating profusely. Then he spoke again: "Narrow-minded persons might find the conduct of these butterflies lacking in morality, but what's morality, and what's the use of it? The single prevailing ethic is life. Only the dead are always wrong."

The captain sat at his desk again and paid no more attention to the mayor and Diodemus, who silently left the tent.

A few hours later, my fate was sealed.

De Erweckens'Bruderschaf—"The Brotherhood of the Awakening" I spoke of earlier—held a meeting in the little room reserved for it in the back of Schloss's inn. Diodemus was there, too. In his letter, he swears to me that he wasn't a member of the brotherhood and that this was the first time they'd ever invited him to a meeting. I don't see why that's important. First time, last time, what's the difference? Diodemus doesn't give the names of those who were present, just their number: six of them, not counting him. He doesn't say it, but I believe that Orschwir must have been one of the others, and that it was he who reported Adolf Buller's monologue on butterflies. The group weighed the captain's words. They understood what there was to understand, or rather, they understood what they were willing to understand. They convinced themselves that they were the *Rex flammae,* the brilliant butterflies the captain had talked about, and that in order to survive, they would have to remove from their community those who didn't belong to their species. Each of them took a piece of paper and wrote down the names of the alien butterflies. I presume that it was the mayor who gathered up the papers and read them.

All the pieces of paper bore two names: Simon Frippman's and mine. Diodemus swears he didn't put down my name, but I don't believe him. And even if that were true, the others couldn't have had much difficulty persuading him to include my name in the end.

Frippman and I had many things in common: we hadn't been born in the village, we didn't look like the people around here (hair too black, skin too swarthy), and we came from far away, from an obscure past and a painful, wandering, age-old history. I've related my arrival in the village, riding in Fedorine's cart after having made my way amid ruins and corpses, orphaned of my parents and orphaned of my memory. As for Frippman, he'd arrived ten years ago, babbling a few words of the local dialect mixed with the old language Fedorine had taught me. Since many found him impossible to understand, I was asked to serve as interpreter. It seemed likely that Frippman had suffered a severe blow to the head. He kept repeating his last name followed by his first name, but apart from that, he didn't know a lot about himself. As he appeared to be a gentle sort, people didn't drive him away. A bed was found for him in a barn attached to Vurtenhau's farm. Frippman was full of heart. He did day labor for this or that employer—haymaking, plowing, milking, woodcutting—without ever seeming to grow tired and received his wages in food. He didn't complain. He whistled tunes unknown to us. The village adopted him; he let himself be tamed without difficulty.

Simon Frippman and I were thus *Fremdër*—"scumbags" and "foreigners"—the butterflies that are tolerated for a while when everything's going well and offered as expiatory victims when everything's going badly. What was odd was that the men who decided to turn us over to Buller—that is, to send us to our deaths, as they must certainly have known!—agreed to spare Fedorine and Amelia, even though they were alien butterflies, too. I don't know that one should speak of courage when referring to this omission, to this desire to spare the two women. I think rather that the gesture was like an attempt at expiation. Those who denounced us needed to keep a region of their conscience pure and intact, a portion that would be free from the taint of evil and would therefore allow them to forget what they'd done or at least give them the ability to live with it, in spite of everything.

The soldiers kicked in the door of our house shortly before midnight. Not long before that, the men who'd participated in the meeting of the brotherhood had gone to see Captain Buller and given him the two names. Diodemus was there. In his letter, he says that he was crying. He was crying, but he was there.

Before I had time to realize what was happening, the soldiers were already in our bedroom. They grabbed me by the arms and dragged me outside while Amelia screamed, clung to me, tried to beat them with her weak fists. They didn't even pay attention to her. Tears were running down Fedorine's old cheeks. I felt as though I'd become the little lost boy again, and I knew that Fedorine was thinking the same thing. We were already in the street. I saw Simon Frippman, his hands tied behind his back, waiting between two soldiers. He smiled at me, wished me a good evening as if nothing were wrong, and remarked that it wasn't too warm. Amelia tried to embrace me, but someone pushed her away and she fell on the ground.

"You'll come back, Brodeck! You'll come back!" she screamed, and her words made the soldiers burst out laughing.

don't feel any hatred toward Diodemus. I bear him no grudge. As I read his letter, I imagined his suffering more vividly than I remembered my own. And I understood, too. I understood why he'd been so assiduous in taking care of Fedorine and Amelia, visiting them every day, constantly doing things for them, and helping them all the more after Amelia entered into her great silence. And I also understood why, once he got over his initial astonishment, he greeted my return from the camp with such an explosion of joy, hugging me, making me dance, spinning around with me in his arms, laughing all the while and wheeling me faster and faster, until in the end I passed out. I had returned from the dead, but he was the one who could finally live again.

Brodeck, all my life I've tried to be a man, but I haven't always succeeded. It's not God's forgiveness I want; it's yours. You'll find this letter. I know if something happens to me, you'll keep my desk, and that's why I'm going to hide the letter in it. I know you'll keep the desk because you talk about it so much—it must be lovely to write at that desk, you say, and I write all the time. So sooner or later, you'll find this. And you'll read it, all of it. All of it. About Amelia, too, Brodeck. I've uncovered everything; I owed you that much.

And now I know who did it. It wasn't only soldiers—Dör-
fermesch, men from the village, were in on it, too. Their
names are on the back of this sheet. There's no possibility of
a mistake. Do what you want with this information,
Brodeck. And forgive me, Brodeck, forgive me, I beg you . . .

I read the end of the letter several times, bumping up against
those last words, unable to comply with Diodemus; I couldn't
turn the page over and look at the names. The names of men
whom I necessarily knew, because our village is very small. Amelia
and Poupchette were sleeping only a few dozen meters from
where I was. My Amelia, and my adorable Poupchette.

I remember telling the *Anderer* the story. It was two weeks
after I'd come upon him sitting on the *Lingen* rock, contemplating the landscape and making sketches. I was returning home
from a long hike I'd taken to check the state of the paths connect-
ing the pastures in the high stubble. I'd left at dawn and walked
a lot, and now I was hungry and thirsty and glad to be back in
the village. I encountered him just as he was leaving Solzner's stable, where he'd gone to visit his donkey and his horse. We greeted
each other. I went on my way, but after a few steps I heard him
speak: "Would this be an appropriate time for you to accept my
recent invitation?"

I was on the point of telling him I was exhausted and eager
to get home to my wife and daughter, but all I had to do was look
at him as he stood there expectantly, a broad smile on his round
face, and I found myself saying exactly the opposite. My response
seemed to make him happy, and he asked me to follow him.

When we entered the inn, Schloss was washing down the
floor, using a great deal of water. There were no customers. The

innkeeper started to ask me what I was having, but he changed his mind when he realized I was following the *Anderer* up the stairs to his lodging. Schloss leaned on his broom and gave me a funny look, and then, seizing the handle of his bucket as if in anger, he violently flung the remaining water onto the wooden floor.

A suffocating smell of incense and rose water pervaded the air in the *Anderer's* room. Some open trunks stood in one corner, and I could see that they contained a quantity of books with gold-embossed bindings and a variety of fabrics, including silks, velvets, brocades, and gauzes. Other fabrics hanging on the walls hid the drab, cracked plaster and gave the place an Oriental flair, like a nomad encampment. Next to the trunks were two big, bulging portfolios, each apparently containing a great deal of material, but the ribbons binding them were abundantly knotted and the portfolios' contents invisible. On the little table that served as his desk, some old, colored maps were spread out, maps that had nothing to do with our region; they depicted elevations and watercourses unknown. There was also a big copper compass, a telescope, a smaller compass, and another measuring instrument that looked like a theodolite, but of a diminutive size. His little black notebook lay closed on the table.

The *Anderer* invited me to sit in the only armchair after removing from it three volumes of what I thought was an encyclopedia. From an ivory case, he took two extremely delicate cups, probably of Chinese or Indian workmanship, decorated with motifs of warriors armed with bows and arrows and princesses on their knees. He placed the cups on matching saucers. On the headboard of the bed was a big, silver-plated samovar with a neck like the neck of a swan. The *Anderer* poured boiling water into our cups and then added some dry, shriveled, very dark brown leaves. They unfolded into a star shape, floated for an instant on the surface of the water, and then slowly sank to the bottom of the cup. I realized that I'd watched the phenomenon as if it were a magic trick, and I also realized that my host had observed me with a look of amusement in his eyes.

"A lot of effect for not much," he said, handing me one of the cups. "You can fool whole populations with less than that." He sat facing me on the desk chair. It was so small that his broad buttocks hung over both sides of the seat. He brought the cup to his lips, breathed on the brew to cool it, and drank it in little sips with apparent delight. Then he put down his cup, rose to his feet, rummaged around in the largest trunk, the one that contained the biggest books, and returned with a folio volume whose worn covers gave evidence of much handling. Among all the volumes in the trunk, all the books gleaming with gold and brilliant colors, the one in his hand was easily the dullest of the lot. The *Anderer* held it out to me. "Have a look," he said. "I'm sure it will be of interest to you."

I took a quick peek, and I couldn't believe my eyes. The book was the *Liber florae montanarum* by Brother Abigaël Sturens, printed at Müns in 1702, illustrated with hundreds of colored engravings. I'd searched in all the libraries of the Capital without ever finding it. Later I'd learned that only four copies were believed to be in existence. Its market value was immense; many rich literary types would have given a fortune to possess it. As for its scientific value, it was inestimable because it listed all the flora of the mountain, including the rarest and most curious species that have since disappeared.

The *Anderer* obviously perceived my confusion, which I

made no effort to conceal. "Please," he said. "Feel free to examine it. Go on, go on . . ."

Then, like a child who's just had a marvelous toy placed in front of him, I took hold of the book, opened it, and started turning the pages.

It was like plunging into a treasure trove. Brother Abigaël had taken his inventory with extreme precision, and the extensive notes on each flower, each plant, not only recapitulated all the known lore but also added many details I'd never read anywhere else.

But the most extraordinary part of the work, the primary reason for its reputation, was to be found in its illustrations, in the beauty and delicacy of the plates that accompanied the commentaries. Mother Pitz's herbaria were a precious resource that had often helped me to revise or complete my reports and sometimes even to focus and direct them. All the same, what I found there had lost all life, all color, all grace. Imagination and memory were required to envision that entombed, dry world as it once had been, full of sap and suppleness and colors. Here, on the other hand, in the *Liber florae,* it seemed as though an intelligence combined with a diabolical talent had succeeded in capturing the very truth of flowers. The disturbing precision of lines and hues made each subject appear to have been picked and placed on the page just a few seconds before. Summer snowflake, lady's slipper orchid, snow gentian, healing wolfsbane, coltsfoot, amber lily, iridescent bellflower, shepherd's spurge, genepy, lady's mantle, fritillary, potentilla, mountain aven, stonecrop, black hellebore, androsace, silver snowbell—they danced before me in an endless round and made my head spin.

I'd forgotten the *Anderer.* I'd forgotten where I was. But suddenly, the spinning stopped short. I turned a page, and there before my eyes, as fragile as gossamer, so minuscule that it seemed almost unreal, its blue, pink-edged petals surrounding and protecting a crown of golden stamens, was the valley periwinkle.

I'm certain I cried out. There in front of me, in the ancient, sumptuous volume lying across my knees, was a painting of that flower, a testament to its reality, and there was also, peering over my shoulder, the face of the student Kelmar, who had spoken so much of the valley periwinkle and made me promise to find it.

"Interesting, isn't it?"

The *Anderer's* voice drew me out of my reverie. "I've been looking for this flower for so long . . ." I heard myself saying, in a voice I didn't recognize as my own.

The *Anderer* looked at me with his delicate smile, the otherworldly smile that was always on his face. He finished his cup of tea, set it down, and then said, in an almost lighthearted tone, "Things in books don't always exist. Books lie sometimes, don't you think?"

"I hardly ever read them anymore."

A silence fell that neither of us sought to break. I closed the book and clasped it to me. I thought about Kelmar. I saw us getting down from the railway car. I heard the uproar again, the cries of our companions in misery, the bawling guards, the barking dogs. And then Amelia's face appeared before me, her beautiful, wordless face, her lips humming their never-ending refrain. I felt the *Anderer's* kindly eyes on me. And then it all came out of its own accord. I started talking to him about Amelia. Why did I speak of her to him? Why did I tell him, whom I knew not at all, things I'd never confessed to anyone? No doubt I needed to talk more than I was willing to admit, even to myself; I needed to re-

lieve the burden that was weighing down my heart. Had Father
Peiper remained the same, had he not turned into a wine-soaked
specter since the end of the war, would I perhaps have confided
in him? I'm not so sure.

I've suggested that the *Anderer*'s smile didn't seem to belong
to our world. But that was simply because he himself didn't seem
to belong to our world. He wasn't part of our history. He wasn't
part of History. He came out of nowhere, and today, when there's
no more trace of him, it's as if he never existed. So what better
person for me to tell my story to? He wasn't on any side.

I told him about my departure, about being led away by the
two soldiers, while Amelia lay on the ground behind me, weeping and screaming. I also told him about Frippman's good humor,
his heedless assessment of what was happening to us and of what
would be our inevitable fate.

We left the village that same evening, bound by the hands
to the same tether, walking under the watchful eyes of the two
soldiers on horseback. The journey took four days, during which
the guards gave us nothing but water and the remains of their
meals. Frippman was far from despair. He kept talking about the
same things as we trudged along, doling out advice concerning
sowing, the phases of the moon, and cats, which, he declared, often chased him through the streets. He told me all this in his gob-
bledygook, a mélange of dialect and the old language. It was only
over the course of those few days I spent with him that I realized
he was simpleminded; before, I'd just considered him a bit whim-
sical. Everything filled him with wonder: the motions of our
guards' horses, the sheen of our guards' polished boots, the glint
of their uniform buttons in the sunlight, the landscape, the bird-
song. The two soldiers didn't mistreat us. They hauled us along

like parcels. They never addressed a word to us, but they didn't beat us, either.

When we reached S., it was in chaos. Half the city had been destroyed; its streets were filled with rubble and charred ruins. For a week, we were penned up in the train station with many other people of all sorts—men, women, children, entire families—some of them poor, some still wearing the symbols of their past riches and looking down on the others. There were hundreds of us. We were all *Fremdër*—in fact, that name had become our name. The soldiers never called us anything but that, indiscriminately. Little by little, we were already losing our individual existences. We all had the same name, and we had to obey whenever that name—which wasn't a name—was spoken. We didn't know what was awaiting us. Frippman stayed close to me, never leaving my side, sometimes holding my arm for many long minutes at a stretch, squeezing it between his hands like a frightened child. I let him do whatever he wanted. Facing the unknown is always better when you do it with someone else. One morning, the camp authorities carried out a selection process. Frippman was put in the column on the left, and they assigned me to the one on the right.

"Schussa Brodeck! Au baldiegeï en Dörfe!"—"Good-bye, Brodeck! See you soon in the village!"—Frippman called out, his face beaming, as his column was marched away. I couldn't respond to him. I simply waved; I gave him a little wave of my hand so he'd suspect nothing, and especially not the great nothing I had a premonition of. I was sure we were both heading there, him first and me later, to the accompaniment of cudgel blows. He turned and walked away at a good pace, whistling.

I never saw Frippman again. He didn't come back to the village. Baerensbourg, the road mender, inscribed his name on the monument. Unlike mine, there was no need to erase it.

Amelia and Fedorine remained alone in the house. The rest of the village avoided them, as if they'd suddenly caught some kind of plague. Diodemus was the only person who concerned himself with them, out of friendship and out of shame, as I've said. In any case, he tried to take care of them.

Amelia practically stopped receiving commissions for her embroidery, but even though she no longer spent much time working on trousseaus and tablecloths and curtains and handkerchiefs, she hardly remained idle. She and Fedorine had to have food and warmth. I'd shown Amelia all the useful things the woods and stubble fields contained: branches, roots, berries, mushrooms, herbs, wild salads. Fedorine taught her how to trap birds with birdlime and string, how to snare rabbits, how to station herself under a tall fir tree, lure down a squirrel, and stun it with a thrown rock. The two of them didn't go hungry.

Every evening, Amelia jotted down in a little notebook—which I've since found—some words meant for me. Her sentences were always simple and sweet, and she wrote about me, about us, as if I were going to return in the next instant. She recounted her day and began every entry the same way: "My little Brodeck . . ." There was never any bitterness in what she wrote. She didn't mention the *Fratergekeime*. I'm sure she omitted them on purpose. It was an excellent method of denying their existence. Of course, I still have her notebook. I often reread passages from it. It's a long, touching account, in which days of absence unspool, one after another. It's our story, Amelia's and mine. Her words are like lights, counterpoints to all my vast darkness. I want to keep them for myself, for myself alone, the last traces of Amelia's voice before she stepped into the night.

Orschwir didn't shift himself to visit them. One morning, he had half a pig delivered to them, and they found it outside the door. Peiper came to visit them two or three times, but Fedorine found him hard to bear. He would sit for hours next to the stove, emptying the bottle of plum brandy she brought out for him, while his speech became steadily more confused. One evening she went so far as to chase him out of the house with a broom.

Adolf Buller and his troops continued to occupy the village. A week after Frippman and I were arrested, Buller finally gave the authorization to bury Cathor. The deceased had no family apart from Beckenfür, who had married his sister, and so Beckenfür took charge of the burial. "A filthy job, Brodeck, let me tell you . . . Not pretty, really not pretty . . . His head was twice its former size, like some strange balloon, with the skin all black and splitting, and then the rest, my God, the rest—let's not talk about it anymore . . ."

Aside from Cathor's execution and our arrest, the *Fratergekeime* behaved most civilly toward the locals, so much so that the two events were quickly forgotten, or rather, people did all they could to forget them. It was during this time that Göbbler returned to the village with his fat wife. He moved back into his house, which he'd left fifteen years before, and was received with open arms by the whole village, and in particular by Orschwir; the two of them had been conscripts together.

I'm prepared to swear that it was Göbbler's counsels which gradually sent the village over the edge. He pointed out to everyone how advantageous it was to be occupied by foreign troops, how there was nothing hostile about the occupation, no, quite the opposite; it guaranteed peace and security, and it made the village and the surrounding region a massacre-free zone. Admittedly, it wasn't hard for him to convince people that it was in everyone's interest for Buller and his men to stay in the village as long as possible. Clearly, a hundred men eating and drinking and smoking and having their clothes washed and mended bring a community a considerable infusion of money.

With the consent of the whole village and Orschwir's blessing, Göbbler became a sort of deputy mayor. He was often seen in Buller's tent. In the beginning, the captain had viewed him with suspicion, but then, seeing the benefits to be derived from the feckless fellow and the rapprochement he championed, Buller began treating him almost like a comrade. As for Boulla, she opened her thighs wide to the whole troop and distributed her favors to officers as well as to the rank and file.

"Well, what can I say? We got used to it." Schloss told me that the day he came over to my table and sat across from me and got all teary-eyed while he talked to me. "It became natural for them to be here. After all, they were men like us, cut from the same block. We spoke about the same things in the same language, or close to it. Eventually, we knew almost all of them by their first names. A lot of them did favors for the old folks, and others played with the kids. Every morning, ten of them cleaned the streets. Others took care of the roads and the paths, cut wood, cleared away the piles of dung. The village has never been so clean, not before or since! What can I tell you? When they came in here, I filled their glasses—I sure wasn't going to spit in their faces! How many of us do you think wanted to wind up like Cathor or vanish like you and Frippman?"

The *Fratergekeime* stayed in the village for nearly ten months. There were no notable incidents, but the atmosphere worsened during the final weeks. Later, the reason why became clear. The war was changing both its location and its mind. Like a fire in spring, when the acrid smoke, agitated by the wind, panics and abruptly shifts direction, military victories abandoned one side and went over to the other. No news came to the village—not to the villagers, that is. If they were kept ignorant, they couldn't become dangerous. But Buller, of course, knew everything. I like to imagine his face, ravaged by his tic more and more frequently in proportion as the messages arrive with their tidings of defeat, of disaster, of the collapse of the Greater Territory, which was meant to extend its sway over the whole world and last for thousands of years.

Like dogs, the occupying troops sensed their leader's confusion and became increasingly nervous. The masks fell again. The old reflexes returned. Brochiert, the butcher, was beaten before Diodemus's eyes for teasing a corporal about his fondness for tripe. Limmat, having neglected to salute two soldiers on the street, was shoved around, and only the intervention of Göbbler, who happened to be passing at that moment, saved him from a severe clubbing. A dozen incidents of this type made everyone realize that the monsters had never left them, that they had simply fallen asleep for a while, and that now their slumbers were over. Then the fear came back, and with it the desire to keep it at bay.

One afternoon—in fact, it must have been the day before the troops' departure—some *Dörfermesch,* some "men from the village," who had gone off with a sledge to the Borensfall forest to transport some timber, made a discovery near Lichmal clearing: under a jumble of fir branches, arranged to form a sort of shelter, three panic-stricken young girls, adolescents who clung to one another when they saw the men coming. They wore clothes that weren't the same as those peasant women wore. Nor did their shoes bear any resemblance to clogs or boots. The girls had a little suitcase. They'd come from far, very far. They'd obviously been on the run for weeks, and then—God knows how—they'd reached that forest in the midst of a strange universe in which they were completely lost.

The *Dörfermesch* gave them food and drink. They flung themselves on the food as though they hadn't swallowed a bite for days. Then they followed the men trustingly to the village. Diodemus thought that the men didn't yet know, as they made their way back to the village, what they were going to do with those girls. I'd like to believe him. In any case, however, they realized that the girls were *Fremdër*, and they knew that each step, each meter along the path that led to the village brought them closer to their fate. As I've said, Göbbler had become an important man, the only person in the village whom Captain Buller had really accepted, and so the men brought the three girls to Göbbler's house. He was the one who convinced the *Dörfermesch* that they should hand the three over to the *Fratergekeime* as a means of gaining their favor, calming them down, taming them. While Göbbler dispensed this advice, the three young girls waited outside, in front of his house. They were still waiting when rain suddenly began to come down in torrents.

The heavens sport with us. I've often thought that if the rain hadn't started beating down on the roof tiles so hard, maybe Amelia would never have looked out the window. And in that case, she wouldn't have seen the three drenched, trembling, thin, exhausted young girls. She wouldn't have gone outside and invited them to come in and sit by the fire. She wouldn't have been out there with them when the two soldiers, alerted by *one of the men from the village,* appeared and took hold of the girls. Therefore, she wouldn't have protested. She wouldn't have screamed at Göbbler, as I'm sure she did, that what he was doing was inhuman, and she wouldn't have slapped his face. The soldiers wouldn't have seized her. They wouldn't have taken her away with the three girls. And so she wouldn't have taken that first step toward the abyss.

Rain. Just rain, pelting the roof tiles and the windowpanes.

The *Anderer* listened to me. From time to time, he poured some hot water into his glass and added a few tea leaves. All the while I talked, I clutched the old *Liber florae montanarum* in my arms as if it were a person. The *Anderer's* benevolent silence and his smile encouraged me to continue. It soothed me to talk about all that for the first time, to speak of it to that stranger, with his queer looks and his queer clothes, and in that place, which so little resembled a room.

I told him the rest in a few words. There wasn't much left to say. Buller and his men were breaking camp, and despite the driving rain, there was much feverish activity in the market square. The air was filled with orders, shouts, and the sound of shattering glass as dozens of drunken men, laughing, stumbling, and exchanging insults, drank their bottles dry and dashed them to the ground. Buller, his head jolted by his tic with ever-increasing frequency, was observing the whole tumult, standing rigid like a picket just inside the flap of his tent. At that paradoxical moment, the *Fratergekeime* were still the masters, even though it was already clear to them that they had lost. They were fallen gods, mighty warriors with a premonition that soon they'd be stripped of their weapons and their armor. With their feet still in their dream, they knew they were hanging upside down.

Such was the scene when the little procession arrived: the three girls and Amelia, escorted by the *Dörfermesch* and the two soldiers. Very quickly, Amelia and the girls became prey; all four were surrounded, shoved, touched, groped. Accompanied by great outbursts of laughter, they disappeared into the center of a circle that closed behind them, a circle of inebriated, violent men, who drove them toward Otto Mischenbaum's barn amid shouted obscenities and crass jokes. Mischenbaum, a farmer nearly a hundred years old, had never engendered any progeny—*"Hab nie Zei gehab, nieman Zei gehab!"* ("Never had the time, never ever had the time!")—and spent most of his days shut up in his kitchen.

Amelia and the girls vanished into the barn.

They were swallowed up in there.

And then, nothing more.

The next day, the square was deserted but littered with innumerable shards of glass. The *Fratergekeime* had left. All that remained of them was a sour odor of wine, vomited brandy, and thick beer, which lay in puddles all over the square. After that sickening night, during which some soldiers and a few *men from the village,* with Buller's mute blessing, had done great harm to bodies and souls, the doors of all the houses were shut. Nobody yet dared to go outside. And old Fedorine went knocking, knocking, knocking at all those doors. Until she came to the barn.

"I went inside, Brodeck." That's Fedorine, telling me the whole story while she feeds me with a spoon. My hands are covered with wounds. My lips hurt so badly. My broken teeth hurt so badly, as if their fragments were still cutting into my gums. I've just come back after two years out of the world. I left the camp, I walked along highways and byways, and now I'm home again, but I'm still half dead. And so weak. A few days ago, when I finally stepped into my house, I found Fedorine there, and the sight of me made her drop the big earthenware dish she was wiping. Its pattern of red flowers was dispersed to the four corners of the room. I found Amelia, too, more beautiful than ever, yes, even more beautiful than she was in all my memories, and those aren't empty words. She was sitting by the stove, and despite the noise of the breaking dish, despite the sound of my voice calling her name, despite my hand on her shoulder, she didn't raise her eyes to me but kept humming a song that pained my heart, "*Schöner Prinz so lieb / Zu weit fortgegangen,*" the song of our first kiss. And as I said her name, as I said it once more with the great joy I felt at seeing her again, as my hand patted her shoulder and stroked her cheek and her hair, I saw that her eyes didn't see me, I understood that she didn't hear me, I understood that Amelia's body and Amelia's wonderful face were there before my eyes, but that her soul was wandering somewhere else, I didn't know where, but in some unknown place, and I swore to myself that I'd go to that place and bring her back, and it was at that precise moment, at the moment when I made that vow, that I heard for the first time a little voice I'd never heard before and didn't know, a child's little voice, coming from our bedroom and rubbing the syllables against one another, the way you rub flint to make sparks fly, and producing a joyous, free, disorderly cascade of melody, a playful babbling that I now know must be the closest thing to the language of the angels.

"I went into the barn, Brodeck. I went inside. It was very

silent and very dark. I saw some shapes on the floor, little shapes lying in a heap, not moving. I knelt beside them. I know death too well not to recognize it. There were the young girls, so young—none of them was twenty—and all three had their eyes wide open. I closed their eyelids. And there was Amelia. She was the only one still breathing, but weakly. She'd been left for dead, but she didn't want to die, Brodeck, she didn't want to die, because she knew you'd come back one day, she knew it, Brodeck . . . After I went over to her, while I was kneeling with her face pressed against my belly, she started to hum that song she hasn't stopped humming since . . . I rocked her in my arms, I rocked her and rocked her for a long, long time . . ."

There was no more water in the samovar. Gingerly, I put the *Liber florae* down beside me. It was almost dark outside. The *Anderer* opened a window, and a scent of hot resin and humus permeated the room. I'd talked for a long time, no doubt for hours, but he hadn't interrupted me. I was on the point of apologizing for having opened my heart to him like that, without shame and without permission, when chimes sounded directly behind me. I spun around brusquely, as if someone had fired a shot. It was an odd sort of old-fashioned clock, the size of a large watch, made in days gone by to be hung inside carriages. I hadn't noticed it before. Its delicate golden hands indicated eight o'clock. The watchcase was made of ebony and gold, and the numbers of the hours were of blue enamel on an ivory background. Under the axis of the hands, the watchmaker, Benedik Fürstenfelder, whose name was engraved on the bottom of the frame, had inscribed a motto in fine, slanted, intertwining letters: ALLE VERWUNDEN, EINE TÖDTET—"They all wound; one kills."

*   *   *

As I stood up, I read the motto aloud. The *Anderer* likewise got to his feet. I'd talked a lot. Too much, perhaps. It was time for me to go home. Somewhat confused, I told him he mustn't think that . . . He interrupted me by swiftly raising his small, chubby hand, like the hand of a slightly overweight woman. "Don't apologize," he said, his voice nearly as imperceptible as a breath. "I know that talking is the best medicine."

XXXIII

I don't know whether the *Anderer* was right.

I don't know if it's possible to be cured of certain things. Maybe talking's not such good medicine, after all. Maybe talking has the opposite effect. Maybe it only serves to keep wounds open, the way we keep the embers of a fire alive so that when we want it to, when we're ready for it, it can blaze up again.

I burned Diodemus's letter. Of course I burned it. Writing hadn't cured him of a thing, not him. And it wouldn't have done me any good to turn over the last page and read the names of the *Dörfermesch* he'd written there. No good at all. I don't have the spirit of revenge. Some part of me will always remain Brodeck the Dog, a creature that prefers prostration in the dust to biting, and maybe it's better that way.

That evening, I didn't go directly home. I made a long detour. The night was soft. The stars were like silver nails hammered into the growing blackness of the vanishing sky. There are hours on the earth when everything is unbearably beautiful, with a beauty whose scope and sweetness seem uniquely meant to emphasize the ugliness of our condition. I walked to the bank of the Staubi and then upstream from the Baptisterbrücke until I came to a grove of white willows which Baerensbourg tortures every January by cutting off all their branches. That's where the three young girls are buried. I know, because Diodemus told me so. He showed me the exact spot. There's no grave marker, no cross, nothing at all. But I know the three girls are there, under the grass: Marisa, Therne, and Judith. Names are important, and those are their names. The names I've given them. Because in addition to having killed them, the *Dörfermesch* made all trace of them disappear so thoroughly that no one knows what their names were, or where they came from, or who they really were.

That stretch of the Staubi is so beautiful. Its clear waters roll over a bed of gray pebbles. It murmurs and babbles, almost like a human voice. To those willing to lend an ear and sit for a moment on the grass, the Staubi offers a subtle music.

The *Anderer* often sat on that grassy bank, taking notes in his little notebook and drawing. I think some of the people who saw him there persuaded themselves that he wasn't dallying in that place merely by chance, not precisely there, so close to the young girls' mute graves. And it was no doubt over the course of his stops by the willow grove that the *Anderer's* doom, unbeknownst to him, began to be sealed, and that the *Dörfermesch* gradually determined on his death. One must never, not even inadvertently, not even against his will, resurrect horror, for then it revives and spreads. It bores into brains; it grows; and it gives birth to itself again.

Diodemus also found his death not far from there. *Found his death*—a strange expression, when you think about it, but I think it suits Diodemus's case: in order to find something, you must seek it, and I really believe that Diodemus sought his end.

I know he left his room. I know he left the village. I know he walked along the banks of the Staubi, and I know that as he headed upstream, in the opposite direction of the river current, his thoughts flowed backward, against the current of his life. He thought about our long walks, about all the things we'd said to each other, about our friendship. He'd just finished writing his letter, and as he walked along the riverbank, his mind was on what he'd written. He passed by the white willows, he thought about the young girls, he walked on, he kept walking, he tried to drive the ghosts away, he tried to talk to me one last time, I'm sure of it, yes, I'm certain he spoke my name; he climbed up to the top of the Tizenthal rocks, and that very short ascent did him good because the higher he climbed, the lighter he felt. When he reached the summit, he looked at the roofs of the village, he looked at the moon's reflection on the margins of the river, he looked one last time at his life, he felt the night breeze caressing his beard and his hair. He closed his eyes; he let himself drop. His fall lasted for a while. Maybe, wherever he is now, he still hasn't stopped falling.

On the night of the *Ereigniës,* Diodemus wasn't in Schloss's inn. Along with Alfred Wurtzwiller, our harelipped postmaster, Diodemus had gone to S., where Orschwir had sent him with some important papers. I think the mayor gave Diodemus that mission on purpose, to get him out of the way. When he came back to the village three days later, I tried to tell him what had happened, but he quickly cut me off: "I don't want to hear it, Brodeck. You can keep all that to yourself. Besides, you don't know anything for sure. Maybe he left without saying anything to anyone. Maybe he tipped his hat and made a bow and went off the way he came. You didn't see anything, you said so yourself! Did he even exist, this *Anderer* of yours?"

His words took my breath away. I said, "But Diodemus, you can't possibly—"

"Shut up, Brodeck. Don't tell me what I can and can't do. Leave me alone! There's enough trouble in this village!"

Then he rushed away, leaving me at the corner of Silke Lane. I think it was that very evening when Diodemus started writing his letter to me. The *Anderer*'s death had stirred up too many things, more things than he could bear.

I repaired the desk and the broken drawer. I did a good job, I think. Then I rubbed the desk with beeswax, which makes it smell good and gleam in the candlelight. And here I am, sitting at the desk and writing again. It's cold in the shed, but the pages hold the heat from Amelia's belly for a long time. I hide all these words I've written against Amelia's belly. Every morning, I wash and dress Amelia, and every evening, I undress her. Every morning, after writing almost all night long, I slip the pages into a finely woven linen pouch and tie it around her stomach, under her shirt. Every night, when I put her to bed, I remove the pouch, which is warm and impregnated with her scent.

I tell myself that Poupchette grew in Amelia's belly, and that in a way, the story I'm writing comes out of it, too. I like this encouraging analogy.

I've almost finished the Report that Orschwir and the others are waiting for. I have just a few more things to say, and then it's done. But I don't want to give it to them before I finish my own story. I still have certain paths to go down. I still have several pieces to put together. I still have a few doors to open. So they won't be getting their Report yet, not right away. First I have to continue describing the days that led up to the *Ereigniës*. Imagine a bowstring being pulled tauter and tauter, every hour a little more. Such an image gives a good idea of the weeks that preceded the *Ereigniës* because the whole village was drawn like a bow; but no one knew what arrow it would let fly, nor what its true target would be.

The summer heat was baking us like an oven. Old folks declared that they couldn't remember such sweltering temperatures. Even in the heart of the forest, among the rocks where in mid-August the cool breath of buried glaciers usually rises up from the depths, the only breezes were searing hot. Insects whirled around madly above the dry mosses, rubbing their elytra together with an unnerving sound like an orchestra of out-of-tune violins and filling woodcutters' brains with steadily mounting irritation. Springs dried up. The wells were at their lowest level. The Staubi turned into a narrow, feeble stream in which brown trout, brook trout, and char died by the score. Cows panted for air, and their withered teats yielded a small amount of clear, bitter milk. The animals were brought back to their stables and only let out again at nightfall. They lay on their sides, lowering their big eyelids over their shiny eyes and lolling their tongues, which were as white as plaster. Anyone in search of a cool spot had to climb up to the high stubble fields, and the happiest creatures of all were undoubtedly the flocks of sheep and goats, the shepherds, and the goatherds on the heights, heartily drinking the fresh wind. Down below, in the village streets and in the houses, all conversations revolved around the blazing sun, which we watched in despair as it rose every morning and quickly climbed to its zenith in a blue and absolutely empty sky that stayed that way the whole day long. We moved very little. We ruminated. The smallest glasses of wine went to men's heads, and their owners needed no pretext to fly off the handle. No one's to blame for a drought. No one can be condemned for it. And so anger builds and must be taken out on something, or someone.

Let the reader make no mistake. I'm not saying that the *Ereigniës* occurred because we had scorching weather in the weeks preceding it and heads were on the boil like potatoes in a pot. I think it would have taken place even at the end of a rainy summer. In that case, of course, it would have required more time. There would not have been the haste, the tensed bow I mentioned earlier. The thing would have happened differently, but it would have happened.

People are afraid of someone who keeps quiet. Someone who says nothing. Someone who looks and says nothing. If he stays mute, how can we know what he's thinking? No one was pleased about the *Anderer*'s scant, two-word reply to the mayor's speech. The next day, once the joy of the celebration—the free wine, the dancing—was past, people talked about the stranger's attitude, about his smile, his outfits, and the pink cream on his cheeks, about his donkey and his horse, about the various nicknames he'd been given, about why he'd come to our village and why he was still here.

And it can't be said that the *Anderer* made up any lost ground over the course of the following days. I have no doubt that I'm the person he talked to most—apart from Father Peiper, but in that regard I've never been able to find out which of them talked more than the other, and about what—and one may judge the *Anderer*'s verbosity from the fact that I've already recorded in these pages every word he ever said to me. A total of about ten lines, hardly more. It's not that he ignored people. When he passed someone, he raised his hat, inclined his large head (upon which the remaining hair was sparse, but very long and frizzy), and smiled, but he never opened his lips.

And then, of course, there was his black notebook and all the notes people saw him taking, all the sketches and drawings he made. That conversation I overheard, when Dorcha, Pfimling, Vogel, and Hausorn were talking at the end of a market day—I didn't make that up! And those four weren't the only ones aggravated by that notebook! Why was he doing all that scribbling and scratching? What was the purpose of all that? What was it going to lead to?

We would eventually learn the answers to those questions. On August 24.

And that day, for him, was really the beginning of the end.

XXXIV

On the morning of August 24, everyone found a little card under his door. The card was fragrant with the essence of roses, and written on it, very elegantly and in violet ink, were the following words:

This evening, at seven o'clock,
in Schloss's Inn,
portraits and landscapes

More than one villager examined his card from every angle, turning it over and over, sniffing it, reading and rereading the brief text. By seven in the morning, the inn was already thick with people. With men. Only men, obviously, but some of them had been sent by their wives to see what they could find out. There were so many extended arms and empty glasses that Schloss had trouble keeping everyone served.

"So, Schloss, tell us what this foolishness is about!"

Elbow to elbow, they were all knocking back wine, *schorick,* or beer. Outside, the sun was already beating down hard. Schloss's customers pressed against one another and pricked up their ears.

"Did your lodger fall and hit his head?"

"What's he up to?"

"It's *Scheitekliche,* right? Or what?"

"Come on, Schloss, say something! Tell us!"

"How long is this queer duck going to hang around here?"

"Where does he think he is, with his smelly little card?"

"Does he take us for neophytes?"

"What's a neophyte?"

"How should I know? I didn't say it!"

"Damn it, Schloss, answer! Tell us something!"

There was a steady barrage of questions, which Schloss received as if they were inoffensive pellets. His only perceptible response to the general curiosity was the malicious little smile on his thick face. He let the tension mount. It was good for his business, all of it. Talking about it made people thirsty.

"Come on, Schloss, out with it! Hell, you're not going to keep quiet until this evening, are you?"

"Is he upstairs?"

"Can't you move over a little?"

"Well, Schloss?"

"All right, all right, shut up! Schloss is going to speak!"

Everyone held his breath. The two or three who hadn't noticed anything and were continuing their private conversation were quickly called to order. All eyes—some of them already a bit out of focus—converged on the innkeeper, who was enjoying his little show and taking his time. Finally, he said, "Since you insist, I'm going to tell you . . ."

A collective sound of happiness and relief greeted these first words.

"I'm going to tell you everything I know," Schloss continued.

Necks were screwed around and stretched as far as possible

in his direction. He slapped his towel on the bar, put both hands flat on top of the towel, and stared at the ceiling for a long time, amid absolute silence. Everyone imitated him, and had someone entered the inn at that moment, he would surely have wondered why approximately forty men were standing there mute, their heads tilted back and their eyes fixed on the ceiling, staring feverishly at the filthy, sooty, blackened beams as though asking them an important question.

"This is what I know," Schloss went on in a confidential tone. His voice was very low, and everyone drank his words as if they were the finest eau-de-vie. "What I know is—well—it's that I don't know very much!"

A big sound rose from the gathering again, but this time it was full of disappointment and a touch of anger, accompanied by the crash of fists striking the bar, several choice insults, and so forth. Schloss raised his arms in an attempt to calm everyone down, but he had to shout in order to be heard: "He simply asked me for permission to have the whole room to himself, starting at six o'clock, so he can make his preparations."

"Preparations for what?"

"I have no idea! One thing I can tell you is he's going to pay for everyone's drinks."

The crowd recovered their good humor. The prospect of quenching their thirst at little or no expense sufficed to sweep away all their questions. Slowly but surely, the inn emptied out. I myself was on the point of leaving when I felt a hand on my shoulder. It was Schloss.

"Brodeck, you didn't say anything."

"I let the others talk—"

"But how about you? You have no questions to ask? If you

don't have any questions, maybe that's because you have the answers. Maybe you're in on the secret."

"Why would I be?"

"I saw you go up to his room the other day and stay in there for hours. So, obviously, you must have found some things to talk about during all that time, right?"

Schloss's face was very close to mine. It was already so hot that his skin was perspiring everywhere, like fat bacon in a hot skillet.

"Leave me alone, Schloss. I've got things to do."

"You shouldn't talk to me like that, Brodeck. You shouldn't!"

At the time, I considered his words a threat. But after the other day, when he sat at my table and got weepy talking about his dead infant son, I don't know anymore. Some men are so maladroit that you take them for the opposite of what they really are.

The only thing I'd learned at Schloss's inn that morning was that the *Anderer*'s little perfumed cards had succeeded in focusing everyone's attention on him even more closely. Now it wasn't yet seven o'clock, and the last breath of air was already gone. The swallows in the sky looked exhausted and flew slowly. High aloft, one very small, nearly transparent cloud in the shape of a holly leaf drifted alone. Even the animals were quiet. The cocks hadn't crowed. Silent and unmoving, trying to stay cool, hens languished in holes dug in the dusty earth of farmyards. Cats dozed in the shadows of carriage entrances, lying on their sides with their limbs outstretched and their pointy tongues lolling out of their half-open mouths.

When I passed Gott's forge, I heard a great commotion inside. The diabolical racket was being made by Gott himself, who was tidying up the place a little. He noticed me, gave me a sign to stop, and walked over to me. His forge was at rest. No fire burned in it, and the blacksmith was freshly bathed, clean-shaven, and combed. He wasn't wearing his eternal leather apron, nor were his shoulders bare; he had on a clean shirt, high-waisted pants, and a pair of suspenders.

"So what do you think about this, Brodeck?"

Not taking any chances, I shrugged my shoulders, as I really didn't know what he was talking about: the heat, the *Anderer*, his little rosewater-scented card, or something else.

"I say it's going to blow up, all at once, and it's going to be violent, believe you me!"

As he spoke, Gott clenched his fists and his jaws. His cleft lip moved like a muscle, and his red beard made me think of a burning bush. He was three heads taller than I was and had to stoop to speak in my ear.

"This can't last, and I'm not the only one who thinks so! You're educated, you know more about such things than we do. How's it going to end?"

"I don't know, Gott. We just have to wait until this evening. Then we'll see."

"Why this evening?"

"You got a card like everyone else. We're all invited at seven o'clock."

Gott stepped back and scrutinized me as if I'd gone mad. "Why are you talking to me about a card? I mean this fucking sun! It's been grilling our skulls for three weeks! I'm practically suffocating, I can't even work anymore, and you want to talk to me about a card!"

A moan from the depths of the forge made us turn our heads. It was *Ohnmeist,* skinnier than a nail, stretching and yawning.

"He's still the happiest," I said to Gott.

"I don't know if he's the happiest, but in any case, he's surely the idlest!"

And as if wishing to demonstrate that the blacksmith with whom he'd temporarily chosen to dwell had the correct view of the matter, the dog lay his head on his forepaws and calmly went back to sleep.

The day was another in an unbroken series of scorchers, yet it seemed peculiar, hollowed out inside, as if its center and its hours were unimportant and only the evening worth thinking about, waiting for, yearning toward. As I recall, after I returned from the inn that day, I didn't leave the house again. I worked at putting the notes I'd taken for the past several months in order. My scribblings covered a variety of subjects: the exploitation of our forests; sections already cut and scheduled to be cut; assessments for all the parcels of land; replanting; sowing; timberland most in need of cleaning up next year; distribution of firewood-cutting privileges; reversals of debt. Hoping to find relief from the heat, I'd chosen the cellar for my workplace, but even there, where an icy perspiration usually dampens the walls, I found nothing but heavy, dusty air, barely cooler than in the other rooms in the house. From time to time, I heard the sound of Poupchette's laughter above my head. Fedorine had placed her naked in a big wooden basin filled with fresh water. She could stay in there for hours, tirelessly playing the little fish while Amelia sat at the window near her, hands flat on her knees, staring out at nothing and intoning her melancholy refrain.

When I came up from the cellar, Poupchette, rubbed, dried,

and entirely pink, was having a big bowl of clear soup, a broth of carrots and chervil. She called to me as I was preparing to go out: "Leave, Daddy? Leave?" She bounded off her chair and ran to throw herself in my arms.

"I'll be back soon," I said. "I'll come and kiss you in bed. Be good!"

"Good! Good! Good!" she repeated, laughing and spinning around like someone dancing a waltz.

O little Poupchette, some will tell you you're nobody's child, a child of defilement, a child begotten in hatred and horror. Some will tell you you're a child of abomination conceived in abomination, a tainted child, a child polluted long before you were born. Don't pay attention to them, my little sweetheart, please don't listen to them; listen to me. I say you're my child and I love you. I say beauty and purity and grace are sometimes born out of horror. I say I'm your father forever. I say the loveliest roses can bloom in contaminated soil. I say you're the dawn, the light of all my tomorrows, and the only thing that matters is the promise you contain. I say you're my luck and my forgiveness. My darling Poupchette, I say you're my whole life.

Göbbler and I closed our doors behind us at the same moment, and we were both so surprised that we simultaneously looked heavenward. Our houses, fashioned for winter, are naturally dark, and we often have to burn one or two candles, even on bright, sunny days, in order to see. When I stepped out of the dark interior, I expected to find, as soon as I crossed my threshold, the leonine sun that had roared down at us unremittingly for the past several weeks. But it was as if an immense, drab, grayish-beige blanket, streaked with black, had been cast over the whole sky. On the eastern horizon, the crests of the Hörni were disappearing into a thick, metallic magma, speckled with fleecy blotches, which gave the suffocating impression of gradually sinking, lower and lower, as if it would eventually crush the forests and stave in the roofs of houses. Fitful patches of brightness mottled the dense mass here and there with a false, yellowish light, like aborted, soundless flashes of lightning. The heat had grown sticky and seized our throats like criminals' hands, slowly but surely strangling us.

After our first surprise had passed, Göbbler and I started walking: at the same time, in the same tempo, side by side, trudging like a pair of robots down the dusty road. Bathed in that strange illumination, it looked as though it were covered with birch ashes. The smell of chicken feathers and chicken droppings floated around me, a sickening, corrupt odor as of flower stems rotting in vases and neglected for days.

I had no desire to talk to Göbbler, and the silence didn't bother me. I expected him to start a conversation at any moment, but he uttered no sound. We walked through the streets like that, mute, rather like two men on their way to a funeral who know that all words are useless in the face of death.

In proportion as we drew near the inn, more and more silhouettes joined us, gliding out of side streets and lanes, slipping out of alleyways and doorways, and walking beside us, as silent as we were. It may be that the general silence was due not to the prospect of discovering what we were going to be shown in the inn but to the sudden change in the weather, to the thick metallic cope which had brought the afternoon to a dark, winterish end and was still covering the sky.

There was no woman in that stream of men, which swelled with every step. We were all men, nothing but men, men among men. And yet, there are women in the village, as there are everywhere else, women of every sort, young, old, pretty, and very ugly women, all of whom know things, all of whom think. Women who have brought us into the world and who watch us destroy it, who give us life and often have occasion to regret it. I don't know why, but that's what I thought about at that moment, as I walked along without saying anything, in the midst of all those men who were walking along without saying anything, either, and I thought especially about my mother. About her who does not exist, whereas I exist. Who has no face, whereas I have one.

Sometimes I look at myself in the little mirror that hangs above the stone sink in our house. I observe my nose, the shape and color of my eyes, the color of my hair, the outline of my lips, the formation of my ears, the shade of my skin. And aided by all that, I attempt to compose a portrait of my absent mother, of the woman who one day saw the little body emerge from between her thighs, who cradled it to her breast, who caressed it, who gave it her warmth and her milk, who talked to it, who gave it a name, and who no doubt smiled a smile of happiness. I know what I'm doing is futile. I'll never be able to compose her features or draw them out of the night she entered so long ago.

Everything had been turned upside down inside Schloss's inn. The place was unrecognizable. It was as if it had put on a new skin. We went in on tiptoe, almost not daring to enter at all. Even those ordinarily incapable of keeping their mouths shut remained speechless. Many turned toward Orschwir, apparently under the impression that the mayor was different from them and would show them what was to be done, how they should behave, what to say and not to say. But Orschwir was like everybody else. Not any cleverer, not any wiser.

The tables had been pushed against one wall, covered with clean cloths, and laden with dozens of bottles and glasses, lined up like soldiers before a battle. There were also big platters piled with sliced sausages, pieces of cheese, strips of lean bacon, slices of ham, loaves of bread, and brioches, enough sustenance to nourish a regiment. At first, all eyes were attracted by that array of food and drink, which was lavish to a degree that is rarely seen among us, except at certain weddings where well-to-do peasants unite their progeny and seek to impress their guests. And so it was only later that we noticed the cloths hanging on the walls, covering what appeared to be about twenty picture frames. Members of the company pointed out these objects to one another with quick chin movements, but there was no time to say or do anything else, because the staircase steps began to creak and the *Anderer* appeared.

He didn't have on any of the bizarre clothing that people had willy-nilly grown accustomed to—no frilly shirt, no jabot, no frock coat, no stovepipe trousers. He was simply wearing a sort of large, ample robe, which covered his entire body and fell to his feet, baring his big neck in a way that made it look disembodied, as though an executioner had neatly lopped off his head.

The *Anderer* walked down a few steps. He made an odd impression, for his robe was so long that even his feet were hidden; he seemed to glide along a few inches above the floor, like a ghost. No one who saw him said a word, and he precluded any reaction by beginning to speak himself, in his discreet, slightly reedy voice: "I have long searched for a way to thank you all for your welcome and your hospitality. The conclusion I reached was that I should do what I know how to do: look, listen, and capture the souls of people and things. I have done much traveling, all over the world. Perhaps that is the reason why my eyes see more and my ears hear better. I believe, without presumption, that I have comprehended you yourselves to a great degree, and likewise this landscape which you inhabit. Accept my little works as homages. See nothing more in them. Mr. Schloss, if you please!"

The innkeeper had been standing at attention, awaiting only this signal before going into action. On the double, he sped around the perimeter of his inn's main room, whipping off the cloths covering the pictures. As if the scene were not yet sufficiently strange, this was the moment when the first thunderclap sounded, loud and sharp, like a whip cracking on an old nag's rump.

The perfumed card had told the truth: there were *portraits,* and there were *landscapes.* They weren't, properly speaking, paintings, but rather ink drawings, sometimes composed in broad brushstrokes, sometimes in extremely delicate lines jostling, covering, and crossing one another. To see the pictures up close, we passed before them in procession, as though making a strange Way of the Cross. Some in attendance, such as Göbbler and Lawyer Knopf, who were both blind as bats, practically pressed their noses against the pictures; others did the opposite, backing away to take the full measure of a drawing and falling behind the rest of the company. The first cries of surprise and the first nervous laughs came when some of the men recognized themselves or others in the portraits. The *Anderer* had made his selection. How was not clear, but the portrait subjects he had chosen were Orschwir, Hausorn, Father Peiper, Göbbler, Dorcha, Vurtenhau, Röppel, Ulrich Yackob (the verger), Schloss, and me. The "landscapes" included the church square and the low houses around its perimeter, the *Lingen,* Orschwir's farm, the Tizenthal rocks, the Baptisterbrücke with the grove of white willows in the background, Lichmal clearing, and the main room in Schloss's inn.

What was really curious was that although we recognized faces and places, no one could say that the drawings were perfect likenesses. It was almost as though they elicited familiar echoes, impressions, resonances that came to mind to complete the portraits which were merely suggested in the pictures before us.

Once everyone had completed his little round, things began to get serious. The company turned its back to the drawings as though they had never existed. There was a general movement toward the laden tables. You would have thought that most of the men in the inn had neither eaten nor drunk for days, so savage was their assault on the refreshments. In no time at all, everything that had been put out disappeared, but Schloss must have had orders to provide a steady supply of full bottles and platters because the buffet never seemed to be depleted. Cheeks grew flushed, foreheads began to sweat, words became louder, and the first oaths reverberated off the walls. Many in the group had doubtless already forgotten why they had come, and no one was looking at the pictures anymore. The only thing that counted was what they could get down their throats. As for the *Anderer,* he had disappeared. It was Diodemus who pointed this out to me: "Right after his little speech, he went back up to his room. What do you think about that?"

"About what?"

"About this whole affair . . ." Diodemus waved a hand at the exposition on the walls. I believe I shrugged my shoulders. "It's funny," he said. "Your portrait, I mean. It doesn't look very much

like you, and yet, it's completely you. I don't know how to describe it. Come have a look."

Not wanting to be disagreeable to Diodemus, I followed
him. We slipped past the bodies in our way, with their emanations,
their smells, their sweat, their beery or vinous breath. Voices were
growing heated and so were heads; many of the company were
talking very loud. Orschwir had removed his velour hat. Lawyer
Knopf was whistling. *Zungfrost,* who ordinarily drank only water,
had downed three glasses under compulsion and was starting to
dance. Three laughing men held back Lulla Carpak, a vagrant
with yellow hair and the complexion of a radish, who as soon as
he got drunk always felt an absolute need to break someone's face.

"Take a good look," Diodemus said. We were standing before my portrait. I did what he suggested. At length. Initially, I
didn't fix my attention too closely on the lines the *Anderer* had
traced there, but then, little by little, and without understanding
why or how, I went deeper and deeper into the drawing.

The first time I'd seen it—a few minutes earlier—I hadn't
noticed anything. My name was written under it, and maybe I
felt a bit embarrassed about being portrayed, because I'd quickly
turned my head away and hurried on to the next picture. But
when I saw it again, when I stood in front of it and considered it,
it was as if it sucked me in, as if it came alive, and what I saw were
no longer lines and curves and points and little blots, but entire
pieces of my life. The portrait the *Anderer* had composed was, so
to speak, alive. It was my life. It confronted me with myself, with
my sorrows, my follies, my fears, my desires. I saw my extinguished childhood, my long months in the camp. I saw my home-
coming. I saw my mute Amelia. I saw everything. The drawing

was an opaque mirror that threw back into my face all that I'd been and all that I was. Diodemus, once again, brought me back to reality.

"Well?"

"It's peculiar," I said.

"If you look, if you really look, it's like that for everyone: not really faithful, but very true."

Maybe it was Diodemus's passion for novels that made him always peer into the deepest folds of words and caused his imagination to run ten times faster than he did. But on that particular occasion, what he said to me wasn't stupid. I made one more tour around the room, studying the drawings the *Anderer* had put up on the walls of the inn. The landscapes, which had at first struck me as run-of-the-mill, came to life, and the faces in the portraits told of secrets, of torments, of heinousness, of mistakes, of confusion, of baseness. I'd touched neither wine nor beer, and yet I tottered and my head spun. In Göbbler's portrait, for example, there was a mischievousness of execution which caused the viewer, if he looked at the image from the left, to see the face of a smiling man with faraway eyes and serene features, whereas if he looked at it from the right side, the same lines fixed the expressions of the mouth, eyes, and forehead in a venomous scowl, a sort of horrible grimace, haughty and cruel. Orschwir's portrait spoke of cowardice, of dishonorable conduct, of spinelessness and moral stain. Dorcha's evoked violence, bloody actions, unpardonable deeds. Vurtenhau's displayed meanness, stupidity, envy, rage. Peiper's suggested renunciation, shame, weakness. It was the same for all the faces; the *Anderer*'s portraits acted like magic revelators that brought their subjects' hidden truths to light. His show was a gallery of the flayed.

And then there were the landscapes! That doesn't seem like much, a landscape. It has nothing to say. At best, it sends us back to ourselves, nothing more. But there, as sketched by the *Anderer,* landscapes could talk. They recounted their history. They carried traces of what they had known. They bore witness to events that had unfolded there. In the church square, on the ground, an ink stain, located in the very spot where the execution of Aloïs Cathor had taken place, evoked all the blood that had flowed out of his beheaded body, and in the same drawing, if you looked at the houses bordering the square, all their doors were closed. The picture displayed only one open door, the one to Otto Mischenbaum's barn. I'm not making anything up, I swear it! For example, if you tilted your head a little while looking at the drawing of the Baptisterbrücke, you could see that the roots of the white willows figured the shapes of three faces, the faces of three young girls. In the same way, if you squinted slightly when you looked at the picture of the Lichmal clearing, you could make out the shapes of the girls' faces in the oak branches. And if I was unable at the moment to discover what was to be seen in some of the other drawings, that was simply because the events they alluded to hadn't yet taken place. At the time, for example, the Tizenthal rocks were just that, dumb rocks, neither pretty nor ugly, figuring in neither history nor legend, but it was before the *Anderer's* drawing of those very rocks that I found Diodemus. He was planted in front of it like a milestone in a field. Transfixed. I had to say his name three times before he turned a bit and looked at me.

"What do you see in this one?" I asked.

"Several things," he said dreamily. "Several things . . ."

He added nothing more. Later, when he was dead, I had

(needless to say) time to reflect. I thought about the *Anderer*'s drawing again.

I suppose it could be said that I've got a hot head and a broken brain. That the entire rigmarole with the drawings was pure nonsense. That an unsound mind and deranged senses would be required for someone to see in those simple doodles everything that I saw. And that it's surely easy to bring all this up for consideration now, when there's no proof of anything, when the drawings no longer exist, when they've all been destroyed. Yes, exactly right, they were all destroyed! That very evening, no less! If that's not proof, then what is it? The drawings were ripped into a thousand pieces, scattered to the four winds, or reduced to ashes, because they said, in their fashion, things that should never have been said, and they revealed truths that had been carefully smothered.

As for me, I'd had more than enough.

I left the inn when drinking was proceeding at a steadily increasing pace and men were bellowing like beasts, but they were still happy beasts, merrily carousing. Diodemus, for his part, stayed until the end, and I got my account of what happened from him. Schloss continued to bring out pitchers and bottles for about an hour after I left, and then, the ammunition having run out, an armistice was abruptly declared; evidently, the sum agreed between him and the *Anderer* had been reached. From this point on, everything went sour. At first, there were words, followed by a few deeds, but nothing really nasty as yet—general grumbling, a bit of breakage, nothing more serious than that. But then the nature of the grumbling changed, as when a calf is separated from its mother's teats; at first it whimpers, but then it resigns itself and looks around for some other amusement, some small raison d'être. The change came when everyone recalled the reason why they were all there in the first place. They turned back to the drawings and considered them again. Or differently. Or with the scales fallen from their eyes, if you will. In any case, they took another look at the pictures and saw themselves. Exposed. They saw what they were and what they had done. They saw in the *Anderer's* drawings everything that Diodemus and I had seen. And, of course, they couldn't bear it. Who could have borne it?

"A real mess! I never quite understood who started it, and in any case that's not important, because everyone joined in, and nobody tried to restrain anyone else at all. The priest had long since passed out. He was sleeping under a table with a bit of his cassock in his mouth, like a child sucking his thumb. The older fellows had gone home shortly after you did. As for Orschwir, he didn't take part in the spectacle, he just watched, but he had a satisfied smile on his face, and when young Kipoft threw his portrait into the fire, Orschwir looked downright happy, believe me! And the whole thing happened so fast, you know. Before I had time to blink, everything on the walls was gone. The only person who looked a bit peeved was Schloss."

When Diodemus gave me this account, it was two days later and the rain hadn't stopped falling since that festive evening at Schloss's inn. It was as if the heavens needed to do a big wash, to launder men's dirty linen, since they weren't up to doing it themselves. The walls of our houses seemed to be weeping, and in the streets, rivulets of water turned brown by earth and stable dung streamed among the paving stones, ferrying along small pebbles, straw bits, sundry peelings, flecks of grime. What's more, it was an odd rain, a continuous deluge coming down from a sky we couldn't even see, so thick, dirty, and waterlogged was the blanket of clouds that kept it constantly hidden. We'd waited for that rain for weeks. For weeks, the village had baked in the heat, and with the village the bodies of the villagers, their nerves, their muscles, their desires, their hearts; and then the storm came, the great splashing havoc of the storm, which corresponded on a gigantic scale to the human havoc, the contained fury inside Schloss's inn, for precisely at the moment when that sort of minor rehearsal for the *Ereigniës* was going on, when effigies were being burned as a preliminary to killing the man, the overloaded sky split in half along its entire width, from east to west, and torrents of gray rain spilled out of it like guts, an immense downpour of water as greasy and heavy as dishwater.

Schloss put everyone out, including the mayor, and the whole jolly crew waded home through the storm, occasionally illuminated by lightning. Some of them lay down at full length in puddles and pretended to swim, shouting like unsupervised schoolboys, throwing handfuls of mud like snowballs at their companions' faces.

I like to think that the *Anderer* stood at his upstairs window and contemplated the spectacle. I imagine his little smile. The heavens were vindicating him, and everything that he saw below him—creatures soaked to the skin, vomiting and shouting insults at one another, heartily mingling their laughs, their slurred words, and their streams of piss—could but make his destroyed portraits seem even truer to life. It was, in a way, something of a triumph for him. The coronation of the master of the game.

But down here, it's best never to be right. That's one thing you always end up paying a very high price for.

he next day was hangover day, when the skull pounds away like a drum, all on its own, and one isn't sure whether what he remembers was dreamed or lived. I believe the majority of those who'd gone wild the previous night must have felt like great fools once they returned to the sober state; perhaps they'd obtained some relief, but they also knew they'd been damned stupid. Not that they were ashamed of their treatment of the *Anderer,* not at all; in that regard, their minds were set and nothing could change them; but when they thought about it, their furious attack on some scraps of paper could not have seemed the stuff of manly heroism.

The rain suited them fine. They didn't have to leave their houses or encounter one another or converse or see in others' eyes what they themselves had done. Only the mayor braved the storms that came sweeping over the village in rapid succession, as if it were April and not August. That evening, he left his house and went directly to the inn. When he arrived, he was soaked to the skin. Schloss was quite surprised to see his door open, since it had remained insistently shut all day long. Moreover, he hadn't exactly spent the day wishing for customers. It had taken him hours to clean up after the revelers and wash everything, including the floor, all the while maintaining a roaring blaze in the hearth to dry the tiles and consume the rancid air. He'd just finished the long job. Everything—the room, the tables, the walls—had at last regained its customary appearance, as if nothing had happened the previous evening. And at this point, Orschwir made his entrance. Schloss looked at him as if he were a monster, a monster that had taken on a great deal of water, but a monster all the same. The mayor removed the big shepherd's cloak he'd rigged himself out in and hung it on a nail near the fireplace. He took out a crumpled and rather dirty handkerchief, wiped his face with it, blew his nose in it, folded it up again, stuffed it in his pocket, and finally turned to Schloss, who was leaning on his broom, waiting.

"I have to talk to him. Go get him."

It was, obviously, an order. No need for Schloss to ask Orschwir to specify who "him" was; there were only two people in the inn, Schloss and the *Anderer*. As he did each morning, Schloss had placed a breakfast tray—round brioche, raw egg, pot of hot water—in front of his guest's door. A little later he'd heard, as he did each morning, footsteps on the stairs, followed by the sound of the little rear door opening and closing. That was the door his guest used when he went to visit his donkey and his horse in old Solzner's stable, which shared a wall with the inn. Shortly thereafter, Schloss had heard the little door open again and the stairs creak again, and then that was all.

In a village like ours, the mayor is somebody. No innkeeper is going to argue with him about what he's being told to do. So Schloss went upstairs and knocked on the door of his guest's room. Almost at once, he found himself face-to-face with the *Anderer*'s smile and presented Orschwir's request. The *Anderer* smiled a little more, made no reply, and closed the door. Schloss went back down and said, "I think he's coming."

Orschwir replied, "Very good, Schloss. Now, I suppose you have enough work to keep you busy in the kitchen, right?"

The innkeeper, no idiot, mumbled a yes. The mayor drew a complex, finely worked silver key from his pocket and opened the door to the smaller of the two public rooms in the inn, the one reserved for the *Erweckens'Bruderschaf.*

When Schloss told me all this, I asked him, "You don't have a key to that door?"

"Of course I don't! I've never even gone into that room! I have no fucking idea what it looks like. I don't know how many keys there are or who has them, apart from the mayor, and Knopf, and most probably Göbbler, but I'm not even sure about him."

Schloss came to our house not long ago. He waited until the night was black as pitch and scratched at the door like an animal. I suppose he'd crept along the walls of houses, careful to make no noise and especially trying to avoid being seen. It was the first time he'd ever stepped over our threshold; I wondered what in the world he could want. Fedorine looked at him as if he were rat droppings. She doesn't like him; as far as she's concerned, he's a thief who buys a few commodities cheap and then sells them at very high prices. She calls him *Schlocheikei,* which in her ancient language is an untranslatable pun combining the innkeeper's name with a word that means "profiteer." Soon after he arrived, she made an excuse about having to put Poupchette to bed and left us alone. When she said Poupchette's name, I saw a sad light glimmer in the innkeeper's eyes, and I thought about his dead infant son; then, very quickly, the light went out.

"I wanted to talk to you, Brodeck. I have to talk to you. I have to try again to make you see I'm not your enemy, I'm not a bad man. I know you didn't really believe me that other time. I'm going to tell you what I know. You can do what you want with it, but I warn you, don't say you got it from me, because if you do, I'll deny everything. I'll say you're lying. I'll say I never told you that. I'll even say I never entered your house. Understand?"

I didn't reply to Schloss. I hadn't asked him for anything. He'd come on his own. It was up to him to say his piece, without trying to obtain anything at all from me.

Eventually, he told me, the *Anderer* came downstairs, and the mayor showed him into the little room used by the brotherhood. Then he closed the door behind them.

"Me, I stayed in my kitchen the way Orschwir suggested. But here's the thing: the closet where I keep the brooms and buckets is built into the wall, and the back of the closet is nothing but planks of wood. I don't think they were nailed up straight in the first place, and over the years they've developed openings as big as eyes. Now, the back of the closet faces their little room. Gerthe knew it. I'm sure she listened to what was said and done in there on certain evenings, even if she never would admit it to me. She knew very well I'd be furious."

So on the evening in question, Schloss did what he had never before allowed himself to do. Why? Men's actions are very bizarre; you can cudgel your brains endlessly about human behavior without ever getting to the bottom of it. Did Schloss consider eavesdropping the way for him to become a man, to defy a prohibition and pass a test, to change camps definitively, to do what he thought was just, or to satisfy a curiosity too long suppressed? Whatever his motive, he wedged his big body in among brooms, shovels, buckets, and old dusting rags and glued his ear to the planks.

"Their conversation was weird, Brodeck, believe me! Very weird . . . In the beginning, you would have thought they understood each other very well; they didn't need a lot of words; they spoke the same language. The mayor started by declaring that he hadn't come to apologize. What had happened the previous evening was no doubt regrettable, but it was pretty understandable, he said. The *Anderer* didn't move.

" 'The people here are a little uncouth, you see,' the mayor went on. 'If they have a wound and you throw pepper in it, they're going to kick your butt hard and more than once. And your drawings were big handfuls of pepper, weren't they?'

" 'The drawings are of no importance, Mr. Mayor. Don't give them another thought,' the *Anderer* replied. 'Had your people not destroyed them, I would have done so myself . . .' "

At this moment in the recital of his tale, which he was declaiming as if he'd learned it by heart, Schloss paused: "One thing you have to know, Brodeck, is that their conversation was full of long silences. When one of them asked a question, it was a good while before the other replied, and vice versa. I'm sure they were sizing each other up, those two. They reminded me of chess players and the little games they play between moves. You understand what I'm trying to say?"

I made a noncommittal movement with my head. Schloss looked at his hands, which he was pressing together, and went on with his story. Orschwir's reply to the *Anderer* was a question: "May I ask you what it was, exactly, that you intended to do when you came to this village?"

"Your village appeared to me to be worthy of interest."

"But it's far away from everything."

"Perhaps that was the very reason. I wished to see what sort of people live far away from everything."

"The war brought its ravages here as it did elsewhere."

" 'War ravages and reveals—' "

"What do you mean?"

"Nothing, Mr. Mayor. It's a verse translated from a very ancient poem."

"There's nothing poetic about war."

"Of course not, of course not . . ."

"I think it would be best for you to leave the village. You stir up—whether intentionally or not—you wake up things that have gone to sleep. No good can come of that. Leave the village, please . . ."

Schloss didn't remember the rest word for word, because Orschwir abandoned his short phrases and lost himself in an interminable series of confused ramblings. But I know Orschwir's too crafty to rattle on at random. I'm sure he weighed his thoughts and his words, one by one. He was just feigning uncertainty and confusion.

"It was pretty sly," Schloss said. "In the end, everything he said was a veiled threat, but it could also be taken to mean just the opposite. And if the *Anderer* had ever objected to being threatened, Orschwir could always have claimed he'd been misunderstood. Their little encounter lasted for a while longer, but I was getting numb in the closet, and I needed air. My ears were buzzing. I felt as though bees were flying around me. I have too much blood in my head, and sometimes it knocks me for a loop. In any case, at some point I heard them get up and head for the door. And before he opened it, the mayor said a few more words, and then he asked his last question, the one that struck me the most, because his voice changed when he said it, and I know that not much gets to him, but I heard a little fear in his tone. But before that, he said, 'We don't even know your name.' "

" 'How important can it be now?' the *Anderer* replied. 'A name is nothing. I could be nobody or everybody.'

"Several long seconds passed before Orschwir went on: 'I wanted to ask you one more question. It's something that's preyed on my mind for a good while now.'

" 'I am at your service, Mr. Mayor.'

" 'Were you sent here by someone?'

"The *Anderer* laughed, you know, his little laugh, almost like a woman's. Then, after a long, long pause, he finally said, 'It all depends on your beliefs, Mr. Mayor, it all depends on your beliefs. I shall let you be the judge . . .'

"And then he laughed again. And that laugh—I tell you, Brodeck, it sent a chill up my spine."

Schloss was talked out. He looked exhausted but at the same time relieved to have let me in on his secret. I went and got two glasses and a bottle of brandy.

While I was filling the glasses, he asked, with a hint of anxiety, "Do you believe me, Brodeck?"

"Why wouldn't I believe you, Schloss?"

He bowed his head very low and sipped his brandy.

Whether Schloss told me the truth or not, whether the conversation he reported took place or not, in the exact terms that I've transcribed or in other more or less similar terms, the indubitable fact is that the *Anderer* did not leave the village. What's likewise indubitable is that, five days later, when the rain stopped and the sun appeared again and people started coming out of their houses and talking to one another, you could hear the last bit of the exchange between the mayor and the *Anderer* repeated everywhere. Those words were worse than the driest tinder, ready to burst into flames! If we'd had a priest with a functioning brain, he would have thrown buckets of holy water on that blaze; he would have put it out with some well-chosen words and a little common sense. But instead, Peiper poured a little more oil on the fire the following Sunday with his drunken raving during his sermon, babbling something—in what connection, I don't know—about the *Antichrist* and the *Last Judgment.* I don't know who spoke the word "Devil" first, either, whether it was the priest or someone else, but it suited most of the congregation, and everyone seized upon it. Since the *Anderer* didn't want to give his name, the village had found one for him. A name made to his measure. A name which has been put to much use over the centuries, but which never wears out. A name that's always striking. Effective. Definitive.

Stupidity is a sickness that goes very well with fear. They batten on each other, creating a gangrene that seeks only to propagate itself. Peiper's sermon and the things the *Anderer* was supposed to have said combined to make a fine mixture indeed!

He still suspected nothing. He continued to take his little walks until Tuesday, September 3. He didn't seem surprised when people no longer returned his greetings or crossed themselves in self-defense when they passed him. Not a single child followed him anymore. Having been sternly warned at home, the children all took to their heels as soon as they saw him coming a hundred meters away. Once the cheekiest of them even threw a few stones at him.

Every morning, as was his habit, he went to the stable to

visit his horse and his donkey. But in spite of his arrangements with Solzner and the sums he'd paid the stable owner in advance, the *Anderer* noticed that his animals had been left to themselves. Their drinking trough was empty, as were their mangers. He didn't complain; he performed the necessary chores himself, rubbed down his two beasts, groomed them, whispered in their ears, reassured them. Miss Julie displayed her yellow teeth, and Mister Socrates bobbed his head up and down while waggling his short tail. This happened Monday evening; I witnessed the scene myself on my way home from a day in the forests. Since I was behind the *Anderer*, he didn't see me. I was on the point of stepping into the stable or coughing or saying something, but I did nothing. I stood in the doorway, unmoving. Unlike their master, the animals saw me. Their big soft eyes rested on me. I remained for a moment, hoping one of them would react to my presence— with a little kicking, say, or a grunt or two—but they did nothing. Nothing at all. The *Anderer* kept on stroking them with his back to me. I continued on my way.

XXXVI

The following day, Diodemus arrived at my house panting, his shirt unbuttoned, his trousers askew, his hair disheveled. "Come! Come quick!"

I was busy carving some clogs for Poupchette out of cubes of black fir. It was eleven o'clock in the morning.

"Come on, I said! Come see what they've done!"

He looked so panic-stricken that there was no possibility of discussion. I put down my gouge, brushed off the wood shavings that had fallen on me like down from a plucked goose, and followed Diodemus.

Along the whole way, he spoke not a word. He hurried on as if the world's fate depended on his speed, and I had trouble matching strides with his long legs. I saw that we were heading toward the sharp bend in the Staubi, where it curves around the fields of vegetables belonging to Sebastian Uränheim, the biggest producer of cabbages, turnips, and leeks in our valley, but I didn't understand why. As soon as we got past the last house, I saw. I saw the big crowd on the riverbank, close to a hundred people, men, women, and children, all of them facing away from us and looking in the direction of the water. A surge of panic made my heart beat faster, and I thought, rather stupidly, of Poupchette and Amelia. I say "rather stupidly" because I knew they were at home.

A few minutes earlier, I thought, when Diodemus came to get me, they were there in the house. Therefore, they can't have been involved in whatever misfortune has just taken place out here. Thus making myself see reason, I joined the silent crowd.

Nobody spoke, nor was there any expression on anyone's face as I slowly pushed my way to the front. The scene was utterly strange: the expressionless features, the staring, unblinking eyes, the closed mouths, the bodies I jostled, standing aside to let me pass, and me going through them, as if they were insubstantial. After I passed, the crowd regained its shape and people popped back into their original positions, like rocking toys.

I was perhaps three or four meters from the water's edge when I heard the moaning, a sad, wordless, one-note song that got in your ears and froze your blood, though God knows it was hot that morning; after the great deluge and the carnival of waterspouts and lightning, the sun had reclaimed its rights. I had come almost all the way through the crowd. In front of me were only the eldest Dörfer boy and, at his side, his little brother Schmutti, who's simpleminded and carries on two rather feeble shoulders a disproportionately large head, as big as a pumpkin and as hollow as the trunk of a dead tree. I gently pushed them aside, and then I could see.

The crowd had gathered by the spot where the Staubi runs deepest. It can't be much less than three meters to the bottom, but it's a little difficult to gauge because the water is so clear and pure that the riverbed looks as though you could touch it with your finger.

In my life, I've seen many men weep. I've seen many tears flow. I've seen many people crushed like nuts between stones until nothing was left but debris. That was part of the daily routine in the camp. But despite all the sorrow and tragedy I've witnessed, if ever I had to choose one from among my memory's infinite gallery of suffering faces, of persons who suddenly realized that they'd lost everything, that everything had been taken from them, that they had nothing left, the person who would spring to mind would be the *Anderer,* and the face his face as it looked that morning, that morning in September, on the banks of the Staubi.

He wasn't weeping. He wasn't gesticulating. It was as though he'd been divided in two. One part was his voice, his unceasing lament, which resembled a song of mourning, something beyond words, beyond all language, rising from the depths of the body and soul: the voice of grief. And then there was the other part, his trembling, his shuddering, his round head, which turned from the crowd to the river and back again, and his body, wrapped in a luxurious dressing gown, all brocade, totally alien to the landscape; the dripping skirts of his robe, saturated with mud and water, swayed against his short legs.

I didn't understand right away why the *Anderer* was in such a state, why he looked like an automaton doomed perpetually to repeat gestures of stark madness. I stared at him so hard, hoping to discover something in his face, in his partially open mouth, in his plenipotentiary minister's bathrobe, that I didn't immediately notice his right hand, which was clutching something that looked like a hank of long, slightly faded blond hair.

It was the hair of his horse's tail, which emerged from the Staubi like a mooring line with one end still attached to the quay and the other to an irretrievably sunken vessel. I could see two large masses below the surface of the water, calm, ponderous bulks which the river currents were very gently stirring. The sight was unreal and almost peaceful: the big horse and the smaller donkey, both drowned, floating underwater with wide-open eyes. Because of some unknown phenomenon, the donkey's coat was decorated with thousands of minuscule air bubbles, as polished and shiny as pearls, and the horse's full, flowing mane mingled with the algae which in that place grew in thick scarves. It was like looking at two mythological creatures performing a fantastic dance. An eddy made them execute a circular movement, a slow waltz, without any music apart from the intrusive and suddenly obscene song of a blackbird, which soon resumed poking its brown beak into the soft soil of the bank and pulling out long red worms. At first, I thought that a last reflex had made both horse and donkey curve their bodies and gather their legs so that all four hooves were nearly touching, the way one might curl up and roll himself into a ball in order to present nothing but a rounded back to danger or cold. But then I saw the cords and realized that in fact the beasts' legs were hobbled and solidly bound together.

I didn't know what to do or say. And even if I had spoken, I'm not sure that the *Anderer,* shut up inside his lamentation, would have heard me. He was trying to drag the horse out of the water—without success, of course, because the animal's weight was so disproportionate to the *Anderer's* strength. Nobody helped him. Nobody made a move in his direction. The assembled multitude's sole movement was a backward surge. The crowd had seen enough. Here and there, people began to leave. Soon no one remained except the mayor, who had arrived after everyone else, accompanied by *Zungfrost,* driving a team of oxen. *Zungfrost* contemplated the spectacle without appearing in the least surprised, either because he'd already seen it, or because he'd been told about it, or because he was in on it. As for me, I hadn't moved. Orschwir looked at me suspiciously and addressed me without even acknowledging the presence of the *Anderer*.

"What do you think you're going to do, Brodeck?"

I didn't see why the mayor was asking me that question or how I could reply to it. I was on the verge of saying, "A horse and a donkey don't tie their legs together all by themselves," but I decided to keep silent.

"You'd best do like the others, Brodeck, and go home," Orschwir continued.

Basically, he was right, so I started to do what he said, but before I could go three meters, he called me back: "Brodeck! Please take him back to the inn."

Zungfrost had succeeded, I don't know how, in making the *Anderer* release his grip on Miss Julie. Now he stood on the riverbank, unmoving, his hands hanging down, and watched the stammerer tie the horse's tail to a heavy leather strap whose other end was attached to the oxen's yoke. I put my hand on the *Anderer*'s shoulder, but he didn't react. Then I slipped my arm under his, turned, and started walking away. He let himself be led like a child. His keening had stopped.

One man alone couldn't do away with two beasts like that. Nor could two men manage it. Such a job would require several men. And, besides, what an expedition! To enter the stable—at night, no doubt—wasn't much of a trick. Nor was getting the animals out, because they were docile, good-natured, anything but wild. But then, by the riverside (because it can have happened nowhere else), to make the two beasts lie on their sides, maybe by pushing them over, to seize their legs, put them together, and bind them solidly, and then to carry or drag the animals to the water and throw them in—that was quite a feat. After careful consideration, I believe there couldn't have been fewer than five or six of them, five or six beefy fellows who, on top of everything else, had to be unafraid of getting kicked or bitten.

The cruelty of the animals' death didn't seem to strike anyone. Some villagers declared that such beasts could be nothing less than demonic creatures. Some even murmured that they had heard the beasts talking. But most people said that what had happened was maybe the only way to get rid of the *Anderer,* the only way to compel him to get the hell out of our village and go back to where he came from, that is, to a far-off place nobody even wanted to think about. This imbecile savagery was, among other things, rather a paradox, since killing the *Anderer*'s mounts in order to make him understand that he must go away deprived him of the only quick means of leaving the village. But murderers, whether of animals or of men, rarely reflect on the deed they do.

've never killed any donkeys or horses.

I've done much worse.

Yes, much worse.

At night, I walk along the rim of the *Kazerskwir.*

I see the railway car again.

I see the six days I spent in the railway car.

I see the six nights again, too, and especially, like a never-fading nightmare, the fifth of those nights.

As I've already said, we were held for a week at the train station in S., and then we were separated into two columns and put on trains. We were all *Fremdër.* Some rich, some poor. Some from the city, others from the country. Such distinctions were quickly blurred. We were shoved into big, windowless freight cars. There was a bit of straw, already soiled, on the wooden floor. Under normal conditions, each car had room for about thirty persons to sit very close together. The guards pushed more than double that number into our car. There were cries, moans, protests, tears. An old man fell down. Some people near him tried to raise him up, but the guards thrust in still more prisoners, causing unpredictable, abrupt movements among those already there. The old man was trampled by the very people who had tried to save him.

He was the first to die in our car.

A few minutes later, having loaded the freight onto the cars, the guards slid the big iron doors shut and bolted them, plunging us into darkness. The only daylight that entered the car came through a few small cracks. The train started moving with a great lurch, which served to press us even more tightly together. The journey began.

It was in these circumstances that I made the acquaintance of the student Kelmar. Chance had placed us side by side. Kelmar was on my right, while on my left was a young woman with a child in her arms, a baby a few months old. She held the child close the whole time. We felt our companions' heat and smelled the odors of their skin, their hair, their perspiration, their clothes. You couldn't move without making your neighbor move. You couldn't get up or shift position. The occasional jolts of the train further compressed us. People spoke in low voices at first; later, they didn't speak at all. There was some weeping, but very little. Sometimes a child hummed a tune, but most of the time there was silence, nothing but silence, and the sound of the axles and the iron wheels pounding the rails. Sometimes the train rolled along for hours without stopping; sometimes it remained at a standstill, but we never knew where or why. Over the course of six days, the big door was opened only once, and that wasn't until the fifth day, nor was it done with any intention of letting us out; hands with no faces behind them doused us with several buckets of tepid water.

Unlike some of our more provident companions, neither Kelmar nor I had brought anything to eat or drink. But strangely enough—at least for the first few days—we didn't suffer much from hunger and thirst. We talked softly to each other. We evoked memories of the Capital. We discussed the books we'd read, the comrades we'd had at the University, and the cafés I used to pass with Ulli Rätte, the same cafés in which Kelmar, who came from a well-to-do family, used to meet his friends to drink burned brandy and beer and large cups of creamy chocolate. Kelmar told me about his family: about his father, who was a fur merchant; about his mother, who spent her days playing piano in their great house on the banks of the river; and about his six sisters, who ranged in age from ten to eighteen. He told me their names, but I can't remember them. I talked to him about Amelia and Fedorine, about our village and its surroundings, its landscapes, its springs, its forests, its flowers, and its animals.

Thus, for three days, our food and drink were words, and we nourished each other with them in the stinking heat of the railway car. Sometimes at night we managed to sleep a little, but when we couldn't, we continued our conversations. The child in the young woman's arms made no sound. He took her breast when she gave it to him, but he never demanded it. I watched him with the nipple in his little mouth, creasing his cheeks in his effort to draw out some milk, but his mother's breasts looked flaccid and empty, and the baby soon grew tired of sucking in vain. Then his mother produced a glass demijohn enclosed in wickerwork and poured a little water into his mouth. Others in the car had similar treasures—a bit of bread, a chunk of cheese, some cookies or sausage or water, which they guarded jealously and kept under their clothes, next to their skin.

In the beginning, I was very thirsty. My mouth burned. I felt as though my tongue was becoming enormous and dry, like an old stump, filling my mouth to the point of bursting. I had no more saliva. My teeth were like red-hot daggers, thrusting their little points into my gums. I believed they were bleeding, but then I passed my fingers over them and saw that it was only an illusion. Gradually, bizarrely, my thirst disappeared. I was feeling weaker and weaker, but I wasn't thirsty anymore. And barely hungry. The two of us, Kelmar and I, kept on talking.

The young woman paid no attention to us. She surely must have heard us, however, and I know she could feel me as I felt her, her hip against mine, her shoulder, sometimes even her head, striking my head or leaning on me in sleep. She never said a word to us. She held her baby close, and likewise her equally precious demijohn, rationing the water methodically and sparing only a little at a time for herself and her child.

We had lost all sense of time and place. I don't mean the immediate place we were in, bounded by the dimensions of the freight car, but the geography our train was slowly lumbering through. What direction were we traveling in? What was our destination? What regions, what countries were we crossing? Did they exist on any maps?

Today I know that they existed on no map and came into being as our train rolled over them. Our freight car and all the other cars like ours—carriages in which, as in ours, dozens of women, children, and men, gasping for air, consumed by thirst, fever, and hunger, were pressed against one another, sometimes the dead against the living—our car and the other cars were inventing, from one minute to the next, a country, the land of inhumanity, of the negation of all humanity, and the camp was going to be that country's heart. That was the journey we were making, the likes of which nobody had ever made before us—I mean not so methodical, so thorough, so efficient a journey as ours, which left no leeway for the unforeseen.

We'd stopped counting the hours, the nights, the appearances of the sun through the cracks. In the beginning, such calculations had helped us, as had our efforts to orient ourselves, to say that we were traveling east, or rather south, or now in a northerly direction. But then we gave up what was only a source of sorrow. We made no more estimates and had no idea where we were. I don't even think we hoped to arrive anywhere. The desire to do so had abandoned us.

Only much later, in thinking over that terrible journey, in trying to remember it, in trying to relive it, did I come to the conclusion that it lasted six days and six nights. And since reaching that conclusion, I've often thought that such a period of time was no accident. Our tormentors believed in God. They were well aware that, according to the Scriptures, it had taken Him six days to create the world. I'm sure they told one another they needed six days to start destroying it. Destroying it in us. And if the seventh day was the day of rest for Him, for us, when the guards opened the doors of the freight cars and drove us out with their truncheons, it was the end.

But for me and for Kelmar, there had also been the fifth day. That morning, the door of the freight car was opened a little and buckets of water thrown at us—warm, muddy water, which splashed over our filthy, jumbled, and in some cases dead bodies, and which, instead of refreshing and soothing us, did the opposite; it burned us and scalded us. That stale water recalled to our memories all the pure, clear, limpid water we'd drunk so avidly in days gone by.

The thirst came back. But this time, no doubt because our bodies were nearing extinction and our enfeebled minds were abandoning themselves to delirium, the thirst we felt made madmen of us. Let no one misunderstand me: I'm not seeking to excuse what we did.

The young woman beside me was still alive, and so was her baby. They were breathing rather feebly, but nonetheless they were breathing. It was their demijohn of water that had kept them alive, and in that demijohn, which seemed to Kelmar and me inexhaustible, there was still some water. We could hear it lapping against the inner sides of the bottle at every movement of the freight car, making a beautiful and unbearable music reminiscent of little streams, of flowing springs, of fountain melodies. The exhausted young woman more and more frequently closed her eyes and let herself drop into a sort of thick sleep out of which she would awaken abruptly, with a start, a few minutes later. Over the course of the past several days, her face had aged ten years, and so had her baby's face, which took on the strange features of a little old man reduced to the proportions of a newborn.

Kelmar and I had long since stopped talking. Each of us was coping as best he could with the shocks and aftershocks in his brain. We were both trying to reconcile, if possible, our past history and our present state. The car stank of enervated flesh, of excrement and sour humors, and when the train slowed down, it was assailed by countless flies, which abandoned the peaceful countryside, the green grass, and the rested soil to penetrate between the planks and fall upon us, rubbing their wings together as a commentary on our agony.

I believe we saw what we saw at the same instant. Then we turned our heads toward each other with the same movement, and that exchange of looks contained everything. The young woman had dozed off once again, but unlike the previous times, her weakened arms had loosened their grip on her child and her big glass bottle. The baby, who weighed very little, remained attached to his mother's body, but the demijohn had rolled onto the floor near my left leg. Kelmar and I understood each other without saying a word. I don't know if we gave the matter any thought. I don't know if there was anything to think about, and I especially don't know if we were still capable of thinking. I don't know what it was, deep down inside of us, that made the decision. Our hands grasped the demijohn at the same time. There was no hesitation. Kelmar and I exchanged one last look, and then we drank in turn, he and I, we drank the warm water from its glass container, we drank it to the last drop, closing our eyes, swallowing greedily, drinking as we'd never drunk water before, in the certainty that what was flowing down our throats was life, yes, life, and the taste of that life was putrid and sublime, bright and insipid, happy and sorrowful, a taste I believe I shall remember with horror until my dying day.

After screaming for a long time, the young woman died. Her child, the baby with the pale, wrinkled little body, the worried brow, and the swollen eyelids, survived her by a few hours. Before she died, she called the people around her thieves and murderers and struck out at everyone within her reach. Her fists were so small and weak that I felt her blows as caresses. I pretended to be asleep. So did Kelmar. The little water we'd drunk had given us back much of our strength and cleared our heads as well—cleared them enough for us to regret what we'd done, to find it abominable, and to keep our eyes shut, not daring to open them and look at her and look at ourselves. The young woman and her baby would doubtless have died in any case, but this thought, however logical it may have been, did not suffice to erase the ignominy of the crime we'd committed. That crime was our tormentors' great triumph, and we knew it. Kelmar even more than I, perhaps, at that moment, since shortly afterward he chose not to go on. He chose to die quickly. He chose to punish himself.

As for me, I chose to live, and my punishment is my life. That's the way I see things. My punishment is all the suffering I've endured since. It's Brodeck the Dog. It's Amelia's silence, which I sometimes interpret as the greatest of reproaches. It's my constantly recurring nightmares. And more than anything else, it's this perpetual feeling of inhabiting a body I stole in a freight car with the help of a few drops of water.

XXXVIII

When I left the shed yesterday evening, I was drenched with sweat in spite of the cold, the mist, and the *Graufrozt*—the light frost, not white but gray, that occurs only around here—covering the roofs of all the houses. I had only about ten meters or so to cover before I'd find Fedorine in her kitchen, Poupchette in her little bed, and Amelia in ours, but the distance seemed vast to me. There was a light burning in Göbbler's house. Was he by any chance watching me? Had he been outside the shed, listening to the sporadic clacking of my typewriter? I couldn't possibly have cared less. I'd traveled my road again. I'd returned to the freight car. I'd written it all down.

In our bedroom, I wrapped my pages in the linen pouch, as I do every evening, and then I slipped into the warm bed; and this morning, as I do every morning, I tied my linen-wrapped confession around Amelia's waist. That's been my procedure for weeks and weeks. Amelia never puts up any resistance or pays any attention to what I'm doing, but this morning, just as I was about to remove my hands from her stomach, I felt her put one of her hands on one of mine and squeeze it a little. Not for long, nor did I see it, because it was still dark in the room. But I wasn't dreaming. I'm sure it happened. Was it an involuntary movement, or could it have been something like a caress, like the beginning or the renewal of a caress?

It's now a little after twelve o'clock, in the middle of a colorless day. Night has yet to depart completely. The day's too lazy to hold on to its light, and the frost is still covering the roofs and the treetops. Poupchette's pulling the skin of Fedorine's face into grotesque shapes, and Fedorine smiles and lets her do it. Amelia's in her place at the window, looking out. She's humming.

I've just finished the Report. In a few hours, I'm going to submit it to Orschwir and the thing will be over and done with, or at least so I hope. I've kept it simple. I've tried to tell the story faithfully. I haven't made anything up. I haven't put anything right. I've followed the trail as closely as possible. The only gaps I've had to fill in occurred on the *Anderer*'s last day, the one that preceded the *Ereigniës*. Nobody wanted to talk to me about it. Nobody wanted to tell me anything.

In any case, on the notorious morning when the drowned carcasses of the donkey and the horse were found, I accompanied the *Anderer* back to the inn. Schloss opened the door for us. We looked at each other without exchanging a word, Schloss and I. The *Anderer* went up to his room and stayed there the entire day. He didn't touch anything on the tray Schloss brought up and placed outside his door.

People resumed their usual activities again. The diminished heat made it possible for the men to go back to the fields and the forests. The animals, too, raised their heads a little. A pyre was constructed on the riverbank, and there the carcasses of Mister Socrates and Miss Julie were burned. Some of the village kids watched the spectacle the entire day, occasionally casting branches into the fire, and returned home with their hair and clothing reeking of cooked flesh and burned wood. And then night fell.

The cries started about two hours after sunset. A slightly high-pitched voice, filled with distress but perfectly clear, was shouting before the door of every house, "Murderers! Murderers!" It was the *Anderer*'s voice. Like some strange night watchman, he was crying out in the street, reminding the villagers of what they had done or what they hadn't prevented. No one saw him, but everyone heard him. No one opened a door. No one opened a shutter. People stopped their ears. People burrowed into their beds.

The following day, in the shops, in the cafés, at the inn, on the street corners, and in the fields, the cries in the night were the subject of some conversation. Some, but not much; people quickly passed on to other subjects. The *Anderer* remained out of sight, shut up in his room. It was as though he'd vanished into thin air. But again that second evening, a couple of hours after sunset, the same mournful refrain echoed in every street, before every door: "Murderers! Murderers!"

I prayed he would stop. I knew how it was all going to end. The horse and donkey would be just the prelude. Killing his animals would suffice to cool the hotheads for a time, but if he got on their nerves again, they'd get some new ideas, and those ideas would be conclusive. I tried to tell him so. I went to the inn and knocked at the door of his room. There was no response. I applied my ear to the wood and heard nothing. I tried the handle, but the door was locked. Then Schloss found me.

"What are you up to, Brodeck? I didn't see you come in!"

"Where is he?"

"Where's who?"

"The *Anderer*!"

"Stop, Brodeck. Please stop . . ."

Those were the only words Schloss spoke to me that day. Then he turned around and left.

That evening, at the same time as the two previous evenings, the *Anderer* made his rounds again, crying out as before. And this time, shutters were banged open, and stones and insults flew through the air. But nothing discouraged the *Anderer* from continuing on his way or stopped him from shouting into the darkness, "Murderers! Murderers!" I had trouble falling asleep. On nights like that, I've learned that the dead never abandon the living. They find one another even if they're strangers. They gather. They come and sit on the edge of our bed, on the edge of our night. They gaze upon us and haunt us. Sometimes they caress our foreheads; sometimes they stroke our cheeks with their fleshless hands. They try to open our eyelids, but even when they succeed, we don't always see them.

I spent the following day brooding. I didn't move much. I thought about History, capitalized, and about my history, our history. Do those who write the first know anything about the second? Why do some people retain in their memory what others have forgotten or never seen? Which is right: he who can't reconcile himself to leaving the past in obscurity, or he who thrusts into darkness everything that doesn't suit him? To live, to go on living—can that be a matter of deciding that the real isn't completely so? A matter of choosing another reality when the one we've known becomes too heavy to bear? After all, isn't that what I did in the camp? Didn't I choose to live in my memory of

Amelia, to make her my present, to cast my daily existence into the unreality of nightmare? Could History be a greater truth made up of millions of individual lies, sewn together like the old quilts Fedorine used to make so she could buy food for us when I was a child? They looked new and splendid with their rainbow of colors, and yet they were sewn together from fabric scraps of differing shapes, uncertain quality, and unknown origins.

After the sun went down, I remained in my chair. And in the dark: Fedorine hadn't lit a candle. The four of us were there, surrounded by darkness and silence. I was waiting. I was waiting for the *Anderer*'s cries, his lugubrious recriminations, to ring out in the night again, but no sound came. The night was silent. And then I became afraid. I felt fear come upon me and pass into my stomach, under my skin, inside my whole being, in a way that hadn't happened in a long time. Poupchette was singing softly. She had a bit of fever. Fedorine's syrups and herbal teas weren't bringing it down, so she tried to calm the child by telling her stories. She'd just gotten started on "Bilissi and the Poor Tailor" when she interrupted herself and asked me to fetch her some butter from Schloss's inn so that she could make little shortbreads for Poupchette to dunk in her milk at breakfast. I didn't react for a few seconds. I had no desire to leave the house, but Fedorine insisted. In the end, I got up from my chair, grabbed my coat, and headed for the door as the old woman was starting the story again, and my Poupchette, all pink and glowing with fever, stretched out her little hands to me and said, "Daddy, come back! Daddy, come back!"

It's an odd tale, the tale of Bilissi. It's the one that fascinated me the most when I was little and Fedorine would tell me stories;

as I listened to it, I had the feeling that the earth was slipping away under my feet, that there was nothing for me to hold on to, and that maybe what I saw before my eyes didn't completely exist.

"Bilissi was a very poor tailor who lived with his mother, his wife, and his little daughter in a crumbling shack situated in the imaginary town of Pitopoï. One day, three knights paid him a visit. The first knight came forward and ordered a suit of red velvet from Bilissi for his master the King. Bilissi accepted the order and produced the most beautiful suit he had ever made. When the knight picked up the suit, he said to Bilissi, 'The King will be happy. In two days, you shall receive your reward.' Two days later, Bilissi saw his mother die before his eyes. 'Is this my reward?' Bilissi thought, and he was filled with sadness.

"The next week, the knights returned. The second knight came forward and knocked on Bilissi's door. He ordered a suit of blue silk from Bilissi for his master the King. Bilissi accepted the order and produced the most beautiful suit he had ever made, much more beautiful than the suit of red velvet. When the knight came to pick up the suit, he said to Bilissi, 'The King will be happy. In two days, you shall receive your reward.' Two days later, Bilissi saw his wife die before his eyes. 'Is this my reward?' Bilissi thought, and he was filled with sadness.

"The next week, the knights returned. The third knight came forward and knocked on Bilissi's door. He ordered a suit from Bilissi for his master the King, a suit of green brocade. Bilissi hesitated, tried to refuse, said that he had too much work, but the knight had already drawn his sword from its sheath. In the end, Bilissi accepted the order. He produced the most beautiful suit he had ever made, much more beautiful than the suit of red velvet, and much more beautiful even than the suit of blue silk. When the knight returned to pick up the suit, he said to Bilissi, 'The King will be happy. In two days, you shall receive your reward.' But Bilissi replied, 'Let the King keep the suit, but I want none of his reward. I'm very happy as I am.'

"The knight looked at Bilissi in surprise. 'You are wrong, Bilissi. The King has the powers of life and death. He wished to make you a father by giving you the little daughter you have always desired.'

" 'But I already have a little daughter,' Bilissi replied, 'and she's the joy of my life.'

"The knight looked at the tailor and said, 'My poor Bilissi, the King took from you what you had, your mother and your wife, and you did not grieve overmuch, but he wished to give you what you do not have, a daughter, for the little girl whose father you believe yourself to be is naught but an illusion, and you are all bereft. Do you really think that dreams are more precious than life?'

"The knight did not wait for Bilissi's reply, nor did the tailor make any. He told himself that the knight had sought to deceive him. He went back into his house, took his child in his arms, sang her a song, gave her some nourishment, and ended by kissing her, without realizing that his lips touched only air and that he had never, ever, had a child."

I won't go back over events I've already described in the beginning of this long account: my arrival at Schloss's inn, the mute gathering of all the men in the village, their faces, my fright, my terror when I understood what they'd done, and then, the ring of their bodies closing in upon me, their request, and my promise to write the Report on my old typewriter.

The Report is finished, as I've said. I have therefore performed the task they assigned to me. Nothing remains to be done, apart from delivering the Report to the mayor. Let him do with it what he will; it's no longer my problem.

XXXIX

Yesterday—but was it really yesterday?—I delivered
the Report to Orschwir. I tucked the pages under my arm and
went to his house without letting him know I was coming. I
walked across the village. It was very early, and I saw nobody except for *Zungfrost*: "Not too huh . . . huh . . . hot, Brodeck!"

I gave him a little greeting and continued on my way.

I entered Orschwir's farm. I passed his farmhands and I
passed his pigs. Nobody paid any attention to me. Neither the
men nor the animals looked at me.

I found Orschwir seated at his big table, where he'd been sitting when I came to see him the morning after the *Ereigniës*. But
yesterday morning, he wasn't busy with his breakfast. He was simply sitting there. His hands were joined on the table in front of
him, and he seemed to be lost in thought. When he heard me,
he raised his head, looked at me, and smiled a little. "Well, here
you are, Brodeck," he said. "How are you doing? You may not believe it, but I've been waiting for you. I knew you'd come this
morning."

On another occasion, maybe I would have asked him how
he could possibly have known such a thing, but oddly enough, I
found that I was indifferent to or, rather, detached from a great

many questions and their answers. Orschwir and the others had played with me enough. The mouse had learned to pay no more attention to the cats, so to speak, and if they needed entertainment, they had only to scratch one another with their sharp claws. They could stop counting on me to amuse them. They'd given me a mission, and I had accomplished it. I'd told the story.

I placed before the mayor all the pages containing my presentation of the events in question. "Here's the Report you and the others asked for."

Orschwir picked up the sheets absentmindedly. I'd never seen him so distant, so thoughtful. Even his face was missing the brutal features it ordinarily presented to the world. A kind of sadness had erased a little of his ugliness.

"The Report . . . ," he said, scattering the pages.

"I want you to read it right away, right here in front of me, and tell me what you think. I've got time. I'll wait."

Orschwir smiled at me and said simply, "If you wish, Brodeck, if you wish . . . I've got time, too . . ."

Then the mayor started reading from the beginning, from the first word. My chair was comfortable, and I settled myself in it, prepared to wait a long time. I tried to tell what Orschwir might be feeling by scrutinizing his facial expressions, but he read without betraying the smallest reaction. Nevertheless, from time to time he passed one big hand over his forehead, rubbed his eyes, or pinched his lips, harder than he seemed to realize.

From outside came the sounds of the big farm waking up. Footsteps, cries, squeals, bucketfuls of water striking the ground, voices, the shriek of axles—all the noises of a way of life resuming its course, beginning a day which would be, all in all, like the other days, during which some people would be born and others would die, everywhere in the world, in a kind of perpetual motion.

The reading took a few hours—I couldn't say exactly how many. My mind seemed to be at rest. I let it roam as after a great effort, free to relax a little, to loaf, to go where it would.

The clock struck. Orschwir had finished his reading. He cleared his throat—three times—gathered up the pages, jogged them into an orderly stack, and brought his big, heavy eyes to bear on me.

"Well?" I asked.

He waited awhile before answering me. He rose to his feet without a word and started walking slowly around the big table, rolling up the papers until they formed a kind of little scepter. Then he spoke: "Brodeck, I'm the mayor, as you know. But I don't think you know what that fact means to me. You write well, Brodeck—we were right to choose you—and you love images, maybe a little too much, but still . . . I'm going to talk to you in images. You know our shepherds well—you've often observed them in the stubble fields and the meadows. Whether or not they love the animals entrusted to them, I have no idea. Besides, how they feel about them is none of my business, and I don't think it's any of theirs, either. The animals are placed in the shepherd's care. He must find them grass in abundance, pure water, and sheepfolds sheltered from the wind. He must protect his flock from all danger and keep it away from excessively steep slopes, from rocks where the animals could slip and break their backs, from certain plants which would cause them to swell up and die, from various pests and predators which might attack the weakest of them, and of course from the wolves that come prowling near the flock. A good shepherd knows and does all that, whether he loves his animals or not. And what about the animals, you may ask. Do they love their shepherd? I put the question to you."

As a matter of fact, Orschwir wasn't putting any question to me. He continued walking around the big table, keeping his head down, tapping his left hand with the rolled-up Report, which he held in his right, and talking all the while. "Furthermore, do the animals know they have a shepherd who does all that for them? Do they know? I don't believe so. I believe they're interested only in what they can see at their feet and right in front of their eyes: grass, water, straw to sleep on. That's all. A village is a small thing, and a fragile one, too. You know that. You know it well. Ours nearly didn't survive. The war rolled over it like an enormous millstone, not to extract flour from it but to smother and flatten it. All the same, we managed to deflect the stone a little. It didn't crush everything. Not everything. The village had to take what was left and use it to recover."

Orschwir came to a stop near the big blue-and-green tiled stove that occupied a whole corner of the room. A small, carefully laid stack of firewood stood against the wall. Orschwir stooped, picked up a log, opened the door to the firebox, and thrust in the log. Lovely flames, short and agile, danced around it. The mayor didn't close the door right away. He gazed at the flames for a long time. They made a joyful music, like the sounds a hot wind sometimes draws from the branches of certain oaks covered with dry leaves in the middle of autumn.

"The shepherd always has to think about tomorrow. Everything that belongs to yesterday belongs to death, and the important thing is to live. You're well aware of that, Brodeck—you came back from a place people don't come back from. My job is to act so that the others can live, so that they can see tomorrow and the day after that . . ."

That was the moment when I understood. "You can't do that," I said.

"Why not, Brodeck? I'm the shepherd. The flock counts on me to protect it from every danger, and of all dangers, memory's one of the most terrible. I'm not telling you anything you don't know, am I? You who remembers everything, who remembers too much?"

Orschwir gave me two little taps on the chest with the Report, either to keep me at a distance or to drive an idea into me, like a nail into a board. "It's time to forget, Brodeck. People need to forget."

After those last words, Orschwir very gently slipped the Report into the stove. In a second, the pages, which had been tightly wrapped around one another, opened up like the petals of a strange, enormous, tormented flower, writhed, became incandescent, then black, then gray, and collapsed upon themselves, mingling their fragments in a red-hot dust that was quickly sucked into the flames. "Look," Orschwir whispered in my ear. "There's nothing left, nothing at all. Are you any unhappier?"

"You burned a stack of paper. You didn't burn what's in my head!"

"You're right, it was only paper, but that paper contained everything the village wants to forget—and will forget. Everyone's not like you, Brodeck."

When I got back home, I told Fedorine the whole thing. She was holding Poupchette, who was taking a nap on her lap. The child's cheeks were as soft as peach-flower petals. Our peach orchards are blossoming now, the first to gladden our early spring with their very pale pink bloom. People here call them *Blum-paradz,* "flowers of Paradise." It's a funny name when you think about it; as if Paradise could exist on this land, as if it could exist anywhere at all. Amelia was sitting by the window.

When I finished my account, I asked Fedorine, "What do you think?"

She didn't reply, apart from a few disconnected words that made no sense. Then, after a few minutes, she finally did say something: "It's up to you to decide, Brodeck. You alone. We'll do what you decide."

I looked at the three of them, the little girl, the young woman, and the old grandmother. The first was sleeping as if she hadn't been born yet, the second was singing as if she were somewhere else, and the third was talking as if she were already gone for good.

Then I said in an odd voice that didn't sound much like mine, "We'll leave tomorrow."

got out the old cart, the one we arrived with, Fedorine and I, a long time ago. I never thought we were going to need it again one day. I never thought there would be another departure. But maybe there can only be departures, eternally, for those like us, for those made in our image.

Now I'm far away.

Far away from everything.

Far away from the others.

I've left the village.

Then again, maybe I'm nowhere anymore. Maybe I've left the story. Maybe I'm like the traveler in the fable, in the unlikely event that the hour of fables has come.

I left the typewriter in the house. I don't need it anymore. Now I write in my brain. There's no more intimate book. No one will be able to read it. I won't have to hide it. It's nowhere to be found, forever.

When I got up this morning, very early, I felt Amelia lying against me and saw Poupchette asleep in her little bed with her thumb in her mouth. I took both of them in my arms. In the kitchen, Fedorine was ready and waiting for us. The bundles were already made up. We left without making any noise. I took Fedorine in my arms, too; she weighs nothing, she's so old and frail.

Life has worn her thin, like a cloth that's been washed a thousand times. I started walking, carrying my three treasures like that and pulling the cart. There's an old story, I think, about a traveler who left this way, fleeing his burning city and carrying his old father and his young son on his shoulders. I must have read that tale somewhere. Yes, I must have read it. I've read so many books. Could it be something Nösel told us about? Or maybe I heard it from Kelmar or Diodemus.

The streets were quiet and the houses asleep, and so were the people inside those houses. Our village was like unto itself, like a flock, as Orschwir had said, yes, a flock of houses pressed against one another, tranquil under the still-black but already starless sky, and as inert and blank as every stone in their walls. I passed Schloss's inn. A little light was shining in his kitchen. I passed Mother Pitz's café, Gott's forge, and Wirfrau's bakery, and I heard the baker kneading his dough. I passed close to the covered market and the church and in front of Röppel's hardware store and Brochiert's butcher's shop. I passed all the fountains and drank a little water as a sign of farewell. All those places were alive, intact, preserved. I stopped a moment in front of the monument to the dead and read there what I'd always read: the names of Orschwir's two sons; the name of Jenkins, our policeman who died in the war; Cathor's name, Frippman's name, and mine, half effaced. I didn't linger, as I felt Amelia's hand on my neck. I'm sure she was trying to tell me to go on; she'd never liked it when we passed the monument and I stopped to read the names aloud.

It was a beautiful night, clear and cold, a night that seemed to have no desire to end, wallowing in its own darkness, turning round and round in it, as one sometimes likes to remain between warm sheets on a cold morning. I skirted the mayor's farm and heard the pigs moving about in their pens. I also saw Lise, *Die Keinauge,* cross the farmyard, holding a bucket that seemed to be full of milk and overflowed at every step, leaving a little white trail behind her.

I went on. I crossed the Staubi on the old stone bridge. I stopped a moment to listen to the murmur of the water one last time. A river tells many stories, if you know how to listen to it. But people never listen to what rivers tell them, or forests, or animals, or trees, or the sky, or the rocks on the mountainsides, or other people. Nevertheless, there must be a time for listening as well as a time for speaking.

Poupchette hadn't woken up yet, and Fedorine was dozing. Only Amelia had her eyes wide open. I carried the three of them along without any trouble. I felt no fatigue. Shortly after we crossed the bridge, I saw *Ohnmeist* about fifty meters away. He seemed to be waiting for me, as if he wanted to show me the way. He started trotting as I approached, and he went ahead of me like that for more than an hour. We climbed the path in the direction of the Haneck plateau. We passed through the great conifer woods, with their pleasant aromas of moss and needles. Snow formed gleaming corollas at the feet of the tall firs, and the wind swayed the tops of the trees and made their trunks pop and creak. When we reached the upper limit of the forest and started to cross Bourenkopf's stubble fields, *Ohnmeist* broke into a run and climbed atop a boulder. The first rays of the dawning sun shone on him then, and I perceived that he was no longer a masterless dog, no longer the *Ohnmeist* that walked down our streets and through our houses as though everything were part of his realm, but a fox, a very handsome and very old fox as far as I could judge. He struck a pose, turned his head in my direction, gazed at me for a long time, and then, with one agile, graceful bound, disappeared among the broom.

I walk tirelessly. I'm happy. Yes, happy.

The summits around me are my accomplices. They're going to hide us. I turned around a few moments ago, near the wayside cross with the strange and beautiful Christ, to take a last look at our village. There's usually such a fine view from that spot—the village looks small, the houses like tiny boxes. If you stretched out your arm, you could almost scoop them up in the palm of your hand. But this morning, I saw none of that. It was no use looking; I didn't see anything. Although there was no fog, no clouds, no mist, there was also no village there below me. There was no village anymore. The village, my village, had completely disappeared. And with it, all the rest: the faces, the river, the living beings, the sorrows, the springs, the paths I'd just taken, the forests, the rocks. It was as though the landscape and everything it contained had receded as I passed. As if, at every step, the set were being dismantled behind me, the painted backdrop rolled up, the lights extinguished. But I, Brodeck, am not responsible for any of that. I am not guilty of that disappearance. I have neither provoked nor desired it, I swear.

I'm Brodeck, and I had nothing to do with it.

Brodeck is my name.

Brodeck.

For pity's sake, don't forget it.

Brodeck.

AUTHOR'S NOTE

Here and there in these pages, the reader will find phrases which I have consciously borrowed from other authors without asking their permission. May they pardon me and accept my thanks.

Alle verwunden, eine tödtet ("They all wound; one kills") is a motto inscribed on an eighteenth-century German carriage clock made by Benedik Fürstenfelder, a watchmaker in Freidberg, and put up for auction in a French salesroom a few years ago.

Talking is the best medicine is a sentence drawn from Primo Levi's story "The Molecule's Defiance."

Hasn't the hour of fables come? is a question asked in André Dhôtel's *La chronique fabuleuse*.

I've learned that the dead never abandon the living is a slightly altered version of a line I found in Fady Stephan's lovely book *Le berceau du monde*.

I write in my brain is, if I remember correctly, a remark made by Jean-Jacques Rousseau in his *Confessions*.

ACKNOWLEDGMENTS

I want to extend my heartfelt thanks to Marie-Charlotte d'Espouy, Laurence Tardieu, and Yves Léon, who through their joint efforts managed to save *Brodeck* from the irretrievable digital depths of my computer.

I would also like to mention, in connection with this book, several persons who have been important to me at different moments in my life and who, having passed away during the two years I worked on my novel, accompanied my thoughts as it unfolded: Marie-Claude de Brunhoff, Laurent Bonelli, Marc Vilrouge, René Laubiès, Jean-Christophe Lafaille, Patrick Berhault, Jacques Villeret.

And finally, my thanks go to the entire team at Éditions Stock, my French publisher, who, under the leadership of Jean-Marc Roberts, have honored me with their trust and their friendship, and also to Michaela Heinz, faithful reader and dispenser of precious advice from the other side of the Rhine.

Philippe Claudel is the author of many novels, among them *By a Slow River*, which has been translated into thirty languages and was awarded the Prix Renaudot in 2003 and the *Elle* Readers' Literary Prize in 2004. His novel *La Petite Fille de Monsieur Linh* was published in 2005, and *Brodeck* won the Prix Goncourt des Lycéens in 2007. Claudel also wrote and directed the film *I've Loved You So Long*, starring Kristin Scott Thomas and Elsa Zylberstein, which opened in movie theaters in the United States in the fall of 2008 and in thirty other countries around the world.

A NOTE ABOUT THE TYPE

This book has been typeset in Adobe Garamond, a version of Garamond designed by Robert Slimbach in 1989. The original Garamond was first introduced in 1541. This beautiful, classic font has been a standard among book designers and printers for more than four hundred years. While opinion varies as to the role that typecutter Claude Garamond played in the development of the typeface that bears his name, there is no doubt that this font had great influence on the evolution of other typefaces from the sixteenth century to the present.